PRAISE FOR &

"Robin Lee Hatcher never disappoints! I loved both eras of this dual timeline story, each with characters you will grow to genuinely care for. The beautiful overarching umbrella for both generations' stories is redemption from the pain of past betrayals. Another keeper from one of my favorite authors!"
—Deborah Raney, author of *Bridges* and the Chandler Sisters Novels series, on *Make You Feel My Love*

"What a delight to step back in time with the charming community of Chickadee Creek! Robin Lee Hatcher is one of my favorite storytellers, and I loved both the past and present threads in her latest novel as the main characters partnered together to overcome their difficult pasts and find genuine hope in God. With endearing characters and elements of suspense, this heartwarming romance was pure joy to read."
—Melanie Dobson, award-winning author of *The Curator's Daughter* and *Catching the Wind*, on *Make You Feel My Love*

"Robin Lee Hatcher tells the story of two people dealing with addiction in their lives in *Cross My Heart* . . . This is a good romance that deals with some very tough issues that happen all the time now." —Parkersburg News & Sentinel

"As usual, Hatcher is an auto-buy for all library collections."
—Library Journal on *Cross My Heart*

"Hatcher (*Who I Am with You*) continues her chronicle of the Henning family in the powerful second installment of her Legacy of Faith series."
—Publishers Weekly on *Cross My Heart*

EVEN FOREVER

BOULDER CREEK ROMANCE
BOOK 1

ROBIN LEE HATCHER

Published by RobinSong, Inc.
Meridian, Idaho

Paperback ISBN: 978-0-9990912-5-8
Kindle ASIN: B093Y1TWKL

1

Boulder Creek, Idaho Territory
May 1890

Your pa's coming home."

The soup ladle dropped from Rosalie Tomkin's hand into the kettle, splashing an ugly stain onto her apron. She closed her eyes and drew in a deep breath, hoping against hope that when she opened them she would find she'd only imagined her mother's words. But when she looked, she still stood before the stove in the kitchen of the Crescent Valley Room and Board.

Rosalie turned around. Her heart raced and an odd buzzing sounded in her ears. She felt choked by the icy panic swelling inside of her. "He's coming *here*?" Her voice was little more than a whisper.

Her ma, Virginia Tomkin, nodded as she lifted the letter in one hand.

It can't be true. It can't be true. "When?"

"Couple weeks, according to his letter. Doesn't say

exactly when they let him out, just when he should get to Boulder Creek."

Rosalie shook her head, trying to clear her thoughts. "But why's he coming *here*?"

"Where else is he to go? He lost the saloon while he was in prison. Besides, for all he's done, this *is* still his home ... and I'm still his wife."

Rosalie's voice sharpened. "This was *never* a home, not as long as he was in it. Ma, you can't let him come back. You *can't*."

Ma lifted her shoulders in a helpless gesture. "For better or worse, I'm his wife. That's the vow I took when I married him. He's got a right to come back, if that's what he wants. I can't rightly stop him."

Rosalie opened her mouth to protest again, then turned toward the stove. If her ma had wanted to change her life, she would have done it long before now. She would have done it the first time her husband hit her. Or she would have done it the first time he struck one of their children.

No, there was nothing Rosalie could do to keep her pa from coming back to Boulder Creek and resuming his life in the boarding house. And once he was there, there would be nothing she could do to keep him from hurting Ma—or from hurting *her*.

She closed her eyes as her hands clenched against her stomach. Pa was coming back. Pa was going to move into the boarding house and stay in the room next to her own. And then he would drink, and when he got drunk, he would strike out at them in the black rages Rosalie remembered all too well. Mostly he would hit Ma. He would hit her until she had to hide in the house so nobody would see her black eyes or her swollen lips. There wouldn't be anything Rosalie could do about it. Everything would be the way it used to be, before he went away. Everything would be the same.

Rosalie stiffened her spine and opened her eyes. No, it wouldn't be the same. She was older now. She wouldn't let him hurt Ma, and she wasn't going to let him hurt her either. Never again. Not ever again.

She turned to face Ma a second time. "I've got almost forty-five dollars saved from working at the restaurant. We could leave Boulder Creek. We could go to San Francisco … or as far as it'll take us. I could find work. I'd take care of you, Ma."

Ma's smile was bittersweet. "You shouldn't ought to have to take care of your ma. You're too young to have such worries."

"I'm not a child anymore. I'm going on nineteen. Say you'll come with me."

"I can't go, Rosalie."

"Then I'll go alone."

"Rosalie—"

"I can't stay, Ma. I hate what he did to you and to me and to…" She felt the old sickness churning in her stomach as a vision of the burning sawmill sprang into her mind. But Rosalie had never told anyone what she suspected her pa had done the day he left Boulder Creek nearly a decade ago, and so she stopped herself before she could speak those suspicions aloud.

Ma's shoulders sagged. "If you feel you have to go, I'll give you what money I can spare."

"You haven't anything to spare." Rosalie knew that whatever profit the boarding house made, her brother, Mark, drank up at the Pony Saloon. "We don't have any boarders now. You'll need anything you have to see you through." She untied her apron as she spoke, hanging it on a peg near the stove. "I'd better get ready for work." She headed toward the hall.

"Rosalie?"

She stopped and glanced over her shoulder.

"When will you leave?"

"Before he gets here. On the next stage."

"So soon?"

"I've got to, Ma."

Ma nodded in resignation. "I'll miss you, Rosalie."

"I'll miss you, too."

Michael Randolph stopped his horse and stared down the lone street of Boulder Creek. He'd known it wasn't a city like Denver or San Francisco, but he'd hoped it would be bigger than the small town that lay before him.

He nudged the roan gelding with his boot heels and started down the street, his eyes perusing each building, making note of things most folks wouldn't see. For instance, though it had a fresh coat of paint, the Barber Mercantile had been around longer than the other buildings in town, probably twelve to fifteen years longer. The First Bank of Boulder Creek, in contrast, hadn't been built more than two years ago, judging by the appearance of the red brick walls.

Besides the bank and general store, there were the usual businesses that made up small towns across the West—a church, a school, a livery and blacksmith shop, restaurant, saloon, barber shop and bath house, post office, and a jail. Michael had seen the like in a hundred different places. What was missing, of course, was a hotel.

And that was why Michael Randolph had come to Boulder Creek.

John Thomas must be getting senile to send me to a town like this.

John Thomas Randolph had never operated a hotel in any but the biggest cities in America. Michael's father had taught him everything about building and running a hotel in cities like San Francisco, Denver, Chicago, and New York. How was he supposed to run a profitable hotel in a backwater burg like this?

His mouth thinned.

Of course, that was no doubt *why* John Thomas had chosen Boulder Creek. Because Michael would have to prove himself in unfamiliar territory.

"Since you and Dillon don't seem inclined to agree on anything," his father had announced several months ago, "there's only one thing for me to do. I'll leave Palace Hotels to one of you when I'm gone. It'll be up to you to prove who that one will be."

The surprise and betrayal Michael had felt then was just as strong today. He shouldn't have to prove himself. He'd known since the time he was a small boy that the business would be his. It should be his without question. He was the oldest Randolph son as well as the legitimate heir. Dillon, while indisputably John Thomas's son, had no right to any part of Palace Hotels.

Michael shoved those thoughts from his mind. He had no time to examine old wounds that continued to fester. He was in Boulder Creek to win what was rightfully his, and unless he wanted to lose the management and eventual ownership of Palace Hotels to his half-brother, he'd better set his plans in motion. He would need a place to stay, but before that he wanted something to eat. He stopped his horse in front of a wooden building with a sign that identified it as Zoe's Restaurant.

Dismounting, he brushed the trail dust from his trousers and the sleeves of his shirt, then stepped onto the boardwalk and entered the establishment. Delicious odors greeted him, and his stomach growled in response. The place was empty of customers. If it weren't for the sounds and smells coming from the kitchen, he would wonder if the restaurant was open for business. Certainly no one bothered to answer the bells that jingled when he opened the door.

He selected a table against a wall, with a view of both the front door and the entrance to the kitchen, and sat down, placing his hat on one of the other chairs. He was untroubled by the wait. His stepmother said that Michael had the patience of Job. She also said he had the stubbornness of a mule. He was willing to act or wait, whichever was most beneficial. He was hungry now, so he waited.

About five minutes later, the bells jingled again as the front door of the restaurant swung inward, and a young woman hurried through the opening. Michael had a quick impression of shiny, chestnut colored hair swept smoothly up from her neck, gathered in a bun atop her head, and of a pleasingly female figure compacted into a body barely five feet tall.

She stopped short when she saw him.

"Rosalie, is that you?" a voice called from the kitchen.

She looked away from him. "Yes, it's me, Mrs. Paddock."

A middle-aged woman came out of the kitchen. Michael supposed she could be the Zoe of Zoe's Restaurant as well as the young woman's Mrs. Paddock. "I was just—" Her words broke off when she noticed Michael. "Oh, dear. I didn't know we had a customer."

"No trouble, ma'am." He nodded in her direction. "I didn't mind the wait."

"Rosalie, will you take the gentleman's order?" Mrs. Paddock turned away. "I've got chickens roasting."

Michael watched as Rosalie followed the woman through the swinging door, reappearing a moment later wearing a crisp white apron over her simple blue blouse and skirt. A white cap now covered much of her dark hair. She carried a small paper tablet in her left hand and a pencil in her right.

She crossed the room, stopping on the opposite side of the table from him. "What would you like, sir?" She pointed toward the wall near the entrance.

Her eyes weren't brown, he realized. They were hazel, the dark centers flecked with gold. She was young, but something about her eyes made her seem older, wiser, a little sad. He wondered why.

"Sir?"

"Sorry." He turned his gaze in the direction she'd pointed. Written on a blackboard in precise letters was the menu for the day. He considered his choices. "I'll have the corn-dodgers, chicken-fixins, and coffee."

Rosalie slipped the pencil into the pocket of her apron. "I'll bring your coffee right out." With that, she disappeared into the kitchen.

Two men entered the restaurant soon after. One was dressed in a business suit and bow tie, the other in denim trousers and a vest with a badge pinned to it. There was a look about the first man that almost shouted "Banker." Michael knew it was wise to get on good terms with the town financier as soon as possible. Such men tended to wield a strong voice in any community. Folks listened to their advice as if it were gospel. The second man was obviously the sheriff. He had steel gray hair and eyes to match and was built like a grizzly bear. When the sheriff looked his way, Michael nodded, silently admitting he was a stranger in town.

By the time the men were settled at a table, two more customers arrived, an older couple who reminded Michael of the nursery rhyme about Jack Sprat and his wife. The man was bean pole thin with a shiny bald head, the woman merrily plump with thick gray hair. They, too, glanced his way. The woman's eyes sparkled with curiosity, as if to say, *We don't get many strangers in Boulder Creek.* As with the sheriff, Michael acknowledged her frank appraisal with a slight nod.

Just then, the waitress entered the dining room, carrying Michael's cup of coffee.

"Afternoon, Rosalie," the other woman called.

Rosalie smiled. "Afternoon, Mrs. Barber, Mr. Barber." She set Michael's coffee on the table, then headed toward her other customers. "Sheriff, Mr. Stanley." She pulled her small tablet and pencil from the pocket of her apron. "What can I get for you today? Mrs. Paddock's got some mighty good chicken-fixins ready, and there's beef steak available. She's also baked up some cider cakes and cherry pies."

Michael sipped his coffee, observing the waitress as she took each of their orders. Now that he wasn't distracted by the sorrow he'd read in her eyes, he could study the rest of her appearance. He found it much to his liking. She was sweetly pretty with a heart-shaped face and dimples that appeared whenever she smiled. Her mouth was small and pink, her nose dainty. Long lashes—the same dark chestnut color as her hair—framed her expressive eyes.

He lowered his gaze. He didn't feel guilty for noticing the pretty waitress, but he wondered if he should. He'd kept company with Louise Overhart for more than a year, and all of their friends and acquaintances expected them to marry. Coming from one of San Francisco's most distinguished families, Louise was beautiful, sophisticated, and intelligent. There was no reason why he shouldn't marry her, yet he felt no urgency to do so.

He looked up again, gazing across the restaurant at the waitress called Rosalie. What would it be like to be married to someone like her instead? The question made him think of home cooked suppers and bedroom slippers and long nights spent nestled in a featherbed in a house in a small town like Boulder Creek.

But those things weren't for Michael Randolph. He thrived on the bustle of the big city. He loved the challenge of business. He enjoyed nothing more than a night at the theater or a brutal game of cards with the men at his club.

He wasn't interested in a small town waitress with sad eyes. And he never would be.

"Who's the stranger?" Zoe asked when Rosalie entered the kitchen, bringing more orders with her.

"I didn't ask. He didn't say." Rosalie glanced down at her tablet. "I need one beef stew, an order of chicken-fixins, corn-dodgers, and a slice of cherry pie, and two orders of ham, mashed potatoes, and slaw." She dropped the tablet into her pocket. "I'll serve the coffee."

Rosalie wasn't as disinterested in the stranger's identity as she pretended. Outsiders passed through Boulder Creek on their way to the mining areas or the logging camps. Others came looking for land with intentions of settling in this valley or the next one over. But few of them were as handsome or as well-dressed as this particular traveler, and she couldn't help wondering what had brought him to there.

As she carried a tray into the dining room, Rosalie cast a surreptitious glance in the stranger's direction. She wasn't mistaken about his good looks. He had hair the color of spun gold, and his eyes were the blue of a summer sky. His masculine features seemed nothing short of perfect, from his straight nose, to his firm mouth, to his beardless jaw. His profile spoke of power and confidence, yet she sensed a measure of gentleness beneath the surface.

Looking at him, she was reminded of the books she'd read in school, her studies of Greek gods of mythology or romantic medieval knights from ancient poetry. But she'd never thought they could be real until she saw this man.

He looked up and their gazes met. Rosalie glanced away, but not before she felt heat rise in her cheeks.

"You seem to have an admirer," Emma Barber said softly as Rosalie set two cups of coffee on the table. "Who is he?"

"I don't know. I never saw him before."

"Sam, you know who he is?" Emma asked.

Her husband looked across the room, then back at Emma. "Nope." He picked up his coffee and blew on the steamy hot liquid.

"New in town," Emma continued, undeterred by her husband's lack of interest. "I wonder if he's come to stay."

Rosalie had wondered the same thing but wasn't about to admit it. Besides, it didn't matter. She wouldn't be around more than a few days. What did she care if this stranger stayed? She was leaving Boulder Creek.

She felt a tiny flutter in her stomach, a niggle of fear along her spine. She couldn't remember living anywhere but here. What would it be like, out there on her own?

Silently, she set the other two cups of coffee in front of the sheriff and Vince Stanley, then returned to the kitchen to help Zoe, trying not to think about how frightening it might be to leave Boulder Creek.

Still, she knew it would be worse to stay, now that Pa was coming back.

∼

Not a scrap of food remained on Michael's dinner plate when the woman at the next table—Mrs. Barber, he remembered Rosalie calling her—caught his eye.

She smiled and said, "You're new to Boulder Creek."

He nodded as he rose from his chair and picked up his hat. "Yes, ma'am." He pulled some coins from his pocket and left the payment for his meal beside his empty plate.

"Are you settling in the area?"

"I'm here on business." He walked toward her table. Turning his eyes on her husband, he held out his hand and said, "I'm Michael Randolph."

"Sam Barber." The men shook hands. "This here is my wife, Emma."

"I'm pleased to meet you both." He offered a polite bow. "Perhaps you can help me. I need a place to stay. Are there any rooms for rent in Boulder Creek?"

"There's the boarding house down near the church. Crescent Valley Room and Board. Mrs. Tomkin's rates are reasonable, and she's a good cook. You'll be comfortable there."

"Tomkin, did you say?"

"Yes, Virginia Tomkin. She's run the place for more than ten years now. Used to be called Tomkin's Rooming House, but when we started getting so many newcomers to the valley, Virginia did some fixing up and adding on and changed the name. You can't miss it." She pointed down the street toward the west end of town. "Big, two-story place. There's a sign on the porch."

"Much obliged." Michael placed his black Stetson over his hair, then touched the brim and nodded before turning and leaving the restaurant.

2

Yale James hadn't figured on ever falling in love, but then he hadn't reckoned he would meet a gal like Skylark Danson either. Sometimes he thought he could spend the rest of his life just looking at her and be plumb satisfied.

He especially liked the way she looked now, standing beside her bay gelding, her hand on the horse's neck. Behind her, tall mountains loomed, white snow icing their craggy peaks, their sides thick with green pines. The look in Skylark's eyes—eyes as soft as blackstrap poured on a tin plate—was one of pure serenity. Her soft mouth curved up in a sweet expression. Her skin was the color of shelled almonds, revealing the perfect angles of her face. Her straight black hair was pulled into a braid, and a fringe of bangs skirted her forehead. She'd pushed off her hat, letting it hang from its string against her back.

"Yale James, what are you staring at?"

The truth popped out of him before he could stop it. "Just lookin' at you, Miss Skylark."

She turned toward him, and her eyes sparkled with mischief. "You're supposed to be watching the cattle."

As if he didn't know what he'd been hired to do.

There'd be trouble for certain if Yale's boss ever learned how he felt about Skylark. He would deserve the trouble, he reckoned. After all, the girl was near half his age, her a mere eighteen and him close to thirty. Besides, he was a cowpoke. He owned his saddle and horse, the clothes on his back, and not much else. He had nothing to offer any woman, let alone someone like Skylark Danson who'd grown up in that fine house and was used to having most everything her heart desired.

Skylark was full of life and a fair bit of sass. He supposed she was even a bit spoiled, but it didn't matter to him. She was pretty and smart, funny and educated. She'd been raised to live the life of a real lady, yet she didn't lord it over anyone. Skylark was special.

Yale, on the other hand, was a saddle bum, and any fool knew you couldn't hitch a horse with a coyote. Yale would have to be satisfied with looking.

But, mercy, he couldn't help wanting more. From the moment he first laid eyes on Skylark, nine months ago, she'd had him cinched to the last hole, and there hadn't been a blamed thing he could do about it.

"I love spring, don't you, Yale?" she asked, her melodic voice breaking into his reverie.

"Sure do."

"All the new calves and foals. Birds singing. Trees and flowers blooming." She motioned to him. "Come over here. There's something I want you to see." She started walking along the bank of Pony Creek, leading Dark Feather behind her.

Yale hesitated a moment. He really should get back to the herd. Will Danson didn't pay him to stand around, talking with Skylark. But what else could he do but obey her request? He would try to move mountains if that's what she wanted.

He stepped down from his saddle and followed her into a cluster of cottonwoods and aspens that lined the creek. She was staring up into the high branches where tiny buds were beginning to unfurl into leaves.

She pointed as he stepped to her side. "Look."

He followed the direction of her arm but couldn't see anything unusual. "What?"

"Yale James." Her voice had turned low and throaty.

He glanced down and found she'd moved closer, her eyes now centered on him.

"Don't you want to kiss me, Yale?"

His mouth went dry. "I don't think Mr. Danson would think much of me kissin' you, Miss Skylark."

"My father likes you, and since I like you, too, I think kissing would be a very good idea." She leaned a little closer. The tip of her pink tongue darted out to moisten her lips, and her eyes seemed filled with expectation.

If she kept looking at him like that, his resistance wouldn't last as long as a boiled shirt in a bear fight.

Her voice dropped even lower as she looked up at him through a curtain of long lashes. "Yale James, I'm not a little girl. I'm a woman, and I know my mind. My mother—my real mother—was married when she was younger than me."

"Skylark ..." His resolve was slipping fast.

She curled her arms around his neck and stood on tiptoe. "Don't you have sense enough to know I love you, Yale James?" She pressed her mouth to his.

"Ah, caterpillars," he murmured against her lips before wrapping her in his arms and savoring her as he'd longed to do from the start.

Rosalie had hoped to speak to Zoe Paddock about leaving Boulder Creek when they were alone, but that wasn't going to happen. The restaurant stayed busy late into the afternoon, and when Rosalie finally saw the last customer leave, she went to the kitchen, only to find Doris McNeal and her twelve-year-old granddaughter, Sarah, sitting at the table in the center of the room.

"Hello, Rosalie," Doris said.

"Afternoon, Mrs. McNeal. Hello, Sarah." She carried the tray of dirty dishes to the counter and set it down.

"How's your mother?"

"She's fine, thanks."

Rosalie glanced at Zoe. Would it be rude to ask to speak to her alone? Yes, and it wasn't as if she needed privacy. Zoe and Doris were close friends and shared every scrap of news and gossip anyway. "Mrs. Paddock?" She held her head high. "There's something I need to tell you."

The three other people in the kitchen turned their eyes upon Rosalie.

She drew in a deep breath. "I'm leaving Boulder Creek. So you'll need to hire yourself another waitress."

"Leaving?"

"Yes, ma'am. I'm going to San Francisco to find work there. I'll work for you right up through Tuesday, but I'm taking the Wednesday stage to Boise."

"But, Rosalie, why on earth would you—"

"I've got to, Mrs. Paddock. That's all."

Zoe stepped forward and placed a gentle hand on Rosalie's shoulder. "I'll be sorry to lose you. If you change your mind, you'll always have a job here. I want you to know that."

She didn't reply. She couldn't. Her throat was tight with emotion. With a nod, she crossed the room and hung up her apron, then she left the kitchen and walked toward the front door.

"Rosalie!"

She turned around.

Sarah hurried toward her. The girl's face was flushed with excitement. "Would you do me a favor when you get to San Francisco?"

"What's that, Sarah?"

"Would you write to me? Would you tell me what it's like there? You're so lucky to be going." Her eyes turned soft and dreamy. "It must be wonderful to go somewhere exciting like San Francisco. When I'm old enough, I'm going away, too. I'm going to go to Chicago and New York and London and Paris. Maybe I'll come see you in San Francisco."

What was it like to have a childhood like Sarah McNeal's? The girl had lost her parents at a tender age, but she'd been loved and pampered by her doting grandparents. Sarah wanted to see other cities simply for the adventure, simply to experience something new. Rosalie was leaving Boulder Creek because she was desperate to escape the pain that would return with her pa. Would she go away if not forced to? No.

"Sure, I'll write to you," she said softly. "I'll write and tell you how wonderful it is." She hoped she would be telling the truth.

Rosalie turned, opened the door, and stepped out on the boardwalk. She stood there for a moment, staring at the small town, wanting to memorize everything about it.

Mrs. Paddock's words replayed in her head. *"If you change your mind, you've always got a job here."*

Of course, she wouldn't—couldn't—change her mind. She couldn't stay. She couldn't go back to living the way they used to, seeing Ma hurt, hiding from Pa when he got drunk, pretending things were okay when they weren't. She couldn't live like that again.

Rosalie remembered the moment she'd heard that Pa had been sent to prison for bank robbery. She remembered what she'd felt. Relief. A relief so great she could scarcely contain it. Maybe it should shame her to have felt that way, but it didn't. From the day Glen Tomkin left Boulder Creek, nigh on ten years ago, Rosalie had dreaded the day he would return. After he was sentenced to prison, she'd started to hope he might not come back after all.

Once again, she'd been wrong.

With a shake of her head, Rosalie started toward the boarding house. There wasn't time for wishing things were different. There was too much she needed to get done before she left. She wanted to give the whole place a thorough cleaning so her ma wouldn't have to do it on her own later. At least not right away. Heaven knew, Ma would get no help from her husband or from Mark.

Rosalie wrinkled her nose at the thought of her brother. If ever a son took after his father, it was Mark Tomkin. Not only in his thick build, but in the way he bullied others. She was thankful he spent so little time at the boarding house. It made it easier to avoid his bad temper—and his fists.

"Rosalie! Rosalie!"

She stopped at the sound of the familiar voice and watched as Skylark trotted her bay down the center of the street. Her friend grinned from ear to ear.

Rosalie felt a wave of nostalgia wash over her as she remembered the first time she'd seen Skylark, nearly ten years ago. How had that sad, shy orphan ever grown into this energetic, self-confident beauty? It was some sort of miracle. Almost at once, the two girls had been like sisters. There wasn't a time through all the years since Skylark came to Boulder Creek that she hadn't played an important part in Rosalie's life.

How will I manage without you, my friend?

"You'll never guess what's happened!" Skylark exclaimed, pulling Rosalie's thoughts to the present. "Wait until I tell you."

She had something to tell as well, but she didn't want to spoil her friend's announcement, whatever it was.

Skylark hopped down from Dark Feather's back and grabbed hold of Rosalie's arms. "Yale kissed me."

"What?"

Skylark nodded. "It's true. He kissed me right on the lips. Not more than an hour ago."

"He didn't!"

"He did!" Skylark threw her arms around Rosalie and hugged her. "He did, and it was as wonderful as I hoped it would be. He's going to ask me to marry him. I know he is." She stepped back, her dark eyes sparkling with joy. "Isn't it wonderful? Oh, Rosalie, I'm so happy I could burst."

Rosalie felt a twinge of envy. Everything always seemed to go right for Skylark. She had the perfect family. Will and Addie Danson loved their adopted daughter every bit as much as they loved their own two children, and eight-year-old Preston and five-year-old Naomi adored their adopted older sister. Skylark had a lovely home and beautiful clothes and ...

She brought her thoughts up short. It wasn't Skylark's fault Rosalie had a mean-tempered jailbird for a father and a shiftless drunk for a brother.

"Then I'm happy for you, too," she said. "But are you sure your pa's going to let you marry Mr. James?"

"Of course he will, just as soon as I tell him how much I love Yale." Skylark turned on the boardwalk, threaded her arm through Rosalie's, and they started walking toward the boarding house. Her well-trained bay followed along behind. "Have you ever been kissed? Really kissed."

Rosalie wrinkled her nose. "Me? Why would I want to do that?"

"Well, one day you'll have to. You can't get married and not let your husband kiss you."

"I've told you before. I'm not getting married. I mean to have a say in my life. A woman loses that once she marries."

"You'd change your mind quick enough if you felt what I felt." Skylark laughed, the sound husky and mysterious. "His kiss sent tingles clear down to my toes. Made me feel all strange inside."

Rosalie stopped walking, pulling her friend to a halt beside her. "Skylark, there's something I've got to tell you."

Skylark must have heard a note of warning in Rosalie's tone, for the look of excited pleasure faded from her face. "What is it? What's wrong?"

"My pa's coming back."

"Oh, Rosalie ... No."

"I'm leaving town. I'm taking next Wednesday's stage."

"But, Rosalie, you—"

"I have to go. I can't stay and watch it happen all over again. I'm helpless to stop what he does. I've begged Ma to come with me, but she won't do it. She refuses to leave. It's been bad enough with Mark, but at least he never ..." She stopped. Even though Skylark knew the truth about her pa and the way he'd treated her and her mother, Rosalie still hated to say it aloud. It was too embarrassing. It made her feel as if the cruelty was her fault. If she was different somehow, better somehow, maybe her pa wouldn't behave that way. Perhaps, if she'd been more like Skylark, her pa would have loved her.

"You could come live at the Rocking D. You know my parents would let you. They care for you as much as I do. They'd be glad to have you come stay."

Rosalie shook her head. "I can't. I can't stay in Boulder Creek once Pa's here."

"Maybe he'll be different. Maybe prison's changed him."

"He hasn't changed. Unless he's worse."

"You can't be sure. Look how different we are from when he left."

Nonplussed, Rosalie stared at her friend.

"Well, it's true," Skylark persisted.

"We were children."

"Right. And now we're not."

Rosalie smiled despite herself. "Must you always be so optimistic?"

"You're not a child anymore, Rosalie. Your pa can't hurt you the way he used to."

"Even if he doesn't hurt me again, I know he'll hurt Ma. If being here would stop him, if it would protect Ma, I'd stay." She drew in a breath. "But it won't, and I can't watch it happen all over again, the way it used to. So what else can I do? Ma refuses to see reason and come with me."

Skylark was quiet for a long time, then asked, "How will I bear it if you go?" As soon as the words were out of her mouth, a horrified expression crossed her face. "Oh, Rosalie, I'm sorry. Everything's so terrible for you right now, and all I can think about is myself. I didn't mean to be selfish. Really I didn't. Forgive me."

"It's okay." Rosalie's voice quivered. "I wondered the same thing a while ago. I don't know how I'll manage without you."

They hugged again, Skylark unsuccessfully fighting tears. Rosalie felt the hot burn behind her eyes and in her throat, but she didn't let tears fall. Rosalie Tomkin never cried. She wouldn't let herself. But that didn't mean she didn't want to.

She released Skylark and stepped backward. "Listen, I have to get home and help Ma." She took a deep breath. "There's a lot I have to do before I leave."

"Do you ... do you need money? I'm sure I—"

"No, Skylark. I've got to do this on my own. I'm going to be taking care of myself from now on. I might as well start out that way."

"You've always been a fighter, Rosalie. I remember the day you butted Mark with your head and knocked the air clean out of him."

"Which time?" Rosalie asked, trying to make them both laugh.

It didn't work.

"Ah, Rosalie ..."

She leaned forward and kissed Skylark's cheek. "I'll see you in church Sunday. Maybe we can have a picnic or something. We'll spend the day together, just like we used to. Okay?"

"Okay."

"See you Sunday." She hurried toward the boarding house, the lump in her throat truly painful.

From the window of his room, Michael stared down at the street, watching as the petite waitress from Zoe's Restaurant hurried along the walk. He was surprised when she turned onto the path leading to the boarding house. He'd had the impression he was Mrs. Tomkin's only boarder.

He let the curtain fall back into place, then crossed the room and lay on the bed. Bracing the back of his head on his hands, he stared at the ceiling and listened to the silence. What on earth would a year in this place be like? He might die of boredom. In the few hours since arriving in Boulder Creek, he'd decided on the location of his new hotel. Tomorrow he would call on the banker and find out who owned the land, then arrange to buy it. Next week, he would order the lumber and begin construction. In no time at all, the hotel would be open for business. And then what?

"You're insane, all of you." He heard his stepmother's voice as clearly as if she were standing beside him now. *"John Thomas, have you taken complete leave of your senses? Do you mean to make war between your sons? There must be a better way."* Kathleen Randolph had never been one to mince words. *"And you, Michael. Isn't it time you quit punishing your brother for how he was born? Have you completely forgotten the friend he's been to you?"* There'd been no escaping her Irish temper. *"And you, Dillon. Will you never stop trying to prove to*

the world that you're as good as Michael? Be yourself instead." She'd glared at them all, her hands on her hips, her green eyes snapping with fury. *"You're all daft is what you are."*

She was right, of course. About everything. But there wasn't a thing Michael could do about it. He had to play his father's game and play it to win. John Thomas had left him no choice.

3
_____

As soon as Rosalie entered the house, her ma was there with the news.

"We've got us a boarder."

Her gaze flew to the stairway.

"Mr. Randolph from San Francisco. He came in by horseback this afternoon. I put him in the green room."

The stranger from the restaurant. It had to be.

Moments before, Skylark had asked Rosalie if she'd ever been kissed. Remembering the question, the image of the handsome stranger with his golden hair and blue eyes filled her mind. An unwelcome image, to be sure. She shook her head. She didn't believe in Greek gods or medieval knights who rescued fair damsels, and she definitely didn't believe in kissing one if he did exist.

Ma started toward the back of the house. "I've got a pork shoulder roasting. We'll need potatoes boiled, and there's some green beans we put up last summer, which will do nicely. Will you set the table?" She glanced over her shoulder. "Set it for four. I'm expecting Mark for supper."

Rosalie followed her mother into the kitchen, her mood darkening. It hadn't taken long for her brother to learn they had a boarder. He would come to demand whatever money had been paid in advance. It was always the same.

Ma stopped. "Try not to pick a fight with him. We rarely see him these days. Maybe if we made him feel more welcome—"

"Ma!" Rosalie balled her hands into fists at her sides. "Do you hear yourself?"

"He's my son. I can't turn my back on him."

Rosalie's fury nearly strangled her, but she couldn't fight with her mother over this. It had all been said before.

Every time Mark came looking for money to pay off his drinking debt at the saloon, Rosalie objected, to no avail. Her ma paid no heed to Rosalie's argument that it was Mark who'd turned his back on them. He did nothing to help them in any way. Even though he lived within a stone's throw of the boarding house, in a room above the Pony Saloon, he didn't come to see his mother or sister unless he was looking for a free meal or wanted to dip his hand into the till. And he always needed money. His own earnings from tending bar at the saloon went for his room and to pay for his constant supply of liquor.

With a sigh of frustration, Rosalie forced her anger to cool. It was an old debate, and she would change nothing by railing at her mother. "I'll put the potatoes on to boil, then set the table." She reached for her apron.

"Thank you, dear."

The two women worked in silence as they moved around the spacious kitchen. The routine tasks, performed countless times before, allowed Rosalie's mind to wander. At first, she thought about her brother, which only made her angry again. Then she thought about her father coming back to Boulder Creek, which was even more distressing. Finally, she forced herself to think about San Francisco.

There must be a world of golden opportunities waiting for a person there, even a woman alone. Maybe she would open her own business in good time. She could run a boarding house or she could operate a restaurant. She certainly had plenty of experience doing both. All she needed now was the money to see her through until she found the right opportunity.

Rosalie stared at the potatoes, the water in the pan boiling gently. There'd been times, after her pa left town, when she'd counted herself lucky to have a potato to eat. She had more than a nodding acquaintance with hardship, and it hadn't done her any lasting harm. She could survive whatever difficulties were ahead of her, as long as she didn't have to stay in Boulder Creek with Pa.

She turned away from the stove and went to the dining room where she put a fresh tablecloth over the scarred table, then got the plates out of the cupboard, her thoughts still churning.

She wondered how long it would take to reach San Francisco by train. Perhaps two days, maybe three? She wasn't certain how far it actually was. Chad Turner, the blacksmith, would know. He'd made a number of trips there to visit family. She could ask him. Maybe she could stay with his sister for a while, until she got on her feet.

She straightened, her gaze turning up in the general direction of the green room. Mr. Randolph, their boarder, was from San Francisco. That's what Ma had said. Maybe he could help her. He would know how long a train trip it was, what to expect when she first got there, perhaps even recommend an inexpensive place for her to stay when she arrived. Feeling her spirits growing lighter, more confident, she returned to the sideboard and selected the silverware from the drawer.

"So, you do live here."

She whirled to face the doorway.

Their boarder offered a smile. "I wondered if you did when I saw you coming up the walk earlier." He stepped into the dining room. "I'm Michael Randolph."

"Have you ever been kissed?" Skylark's voice whispered in her head.

No, she hadn't. She'd never wanted to be kissed. But there was something about his mouth that made her wonder if he could change her mind. It looked as if a grin must always lurk in the corners, ready to spring to life.

Rosalie forced her gaze away from Michael's mouth, but she found his eyes even more disconcerting. Had he guessed her thoughts? "I ... I'm Rosalie Tomkin." She moved to the table and started placing the silverware beside the plates. "You're a bit early for supper."

"May I help?"

"Oh, no," she answered quickly, looking up to find him standing near. Her stomach tumbled.

He grinned, the look warm and friendly. "You think I can't set a table?" He reached for the silverware in her hand.

A shock ran up her spine the moment their fingers met, and her skin felt prickly, even after he'd moved away.

"I come from a family of five brothers and one sister. My stepmother never let a one of us boys slack off in our work, just because we were born male." As he spoke, he finished placing the silver around the table, each utensil in just the right place.

His family ... San Francisco ...

"My mother says you're from San Francisco. Does your family still live there?"

"Yes."

"It's always been your home?"

"The only one I remember. And has Boulder Creek always been your home?"

"The only one I remember," she echoed him softly.

There was something about his eyes—the unwavering way he watched her—that left her feeling strange inside. It wasn't an unpleasant sensation.

Skylark's comments about kissing and tingling toes returned to taunt her. She found herself looking at his mouth again. Her thoughts became all jumbled and muddled. Her questions about San Francisco seemed to vanish like a whiff of vapor.

"And what about you, Miss Tomkin? Do you have family besides your mother?"

"A brother." She couldn't stop the frown from wrinkling the bridge of her nose. "He doesn't live with us. He tends bar at the Pony Saloon."

When she didn't volunteer anything more, he asked, "And your father?"

"He's not here either." The specters of her brother and father spoiled the special feeling of moments before. "I'd better help Ma with supper. You can wait in the parlor if you'd like."

With that, she hurried from the dining room.

She was a mercurial creature, Michael thought as Rosalie disappeared into the kitchen. One moment she was all friendly smiles, the next she resembled a trapped doe, desperate to escape. He wondered why.

He went into the parlor, his eyes making a quick assessment of the room. Simple, clean, attractive. It wasn't anything like his own home or the luxurious suites he normally stayed in when on business, but it had a pleasant appeal that surprised him.

Michael moved to the large, open window at the front of the parlor. Brushing aside the lace curtain, he stared out at the main street.

A couple of horsemen passed in front of the boarding house, their faces shaded by wide-brimmed hats, their postures relaxed, almost lazy. Across the street, the sheriff, whom he'd seen at the restaurant earlier in the day, nodded and spoke to the two men as they rode past. Michael heard a tune being hammered out on the rinky-tink piano in the saloon a few doors down the street.

All in all, a quiet day in Boulder Creek. He supposed most days were like this. Heaven help him, it was going to be a long, long year.

He wondered how Dillon was getting along in the hamlet of Newton, Oregon. It helped a little to know his brother was as miserable as he was, perhaps more so. Maybe the two of them should have found a way to compromise. Dillon didn't really want the company. It wasn't in his blood like it was in Michael's. Dillon only wanted Palace Hotels because Michael did.

He should contact his brother and see if the two of them could find a compromise.

He shook his head. Dillon wouldn't call things off. He

wouldn't concede the competition. He had as much to prove, as much to gain, as Michael did. No, like it or not, he was stuck in Boulder Creek for the next twelve months.

He was about to step away from the window when he saw a man stride up the street and turn onto the walkway leading to the boarding house. He was a hard-looking fellow, close to Michael's own age, maybe a year or two younger.

A moment later, the man appeared in the parlor doorway. He stopped and glared at Michael, his expression surly, his eyes blurry and his nose red. "You must be Ma's boarder."

Could this be Rosalie Tomkin's brother? Unbelievable. Michael smelled whiskey from across the room. It was obvious he did more than tend bar at the saloon. He did his share of consuming the liquor as well.

"Name's Randolph. Michael Randolph."

"Mark Tomkin. You plan on stayin' in town long?"

"Until my business is finished."

"What sorta business you in?"

"I'm in the hotel business."

"Hotel?" Mark snorted. "And you got business *here*?"

Michael shrugged.

"I sure hope you paid in advance. Ma's not good about demanding the money up front, and she's had some who's left without payin' their bill."

Michael smiled without warmth. "I assure you, sir, I always pay my debts."

At that moment, Virginia Tomkin came out of the kitchen, saw her son, and hurried toward him. "Mark, I'm glad you could join us for supper."

He brushed her aside before she could embrace him. "Is it ready? I'm hungry." Mark headed for the dining room.

Virginia's shoulders slumped and a look of resignation

settled over her face. Without looking at Michael, she said, "Please be seated at the table, Mr. Randolph. Supper will be served in a moment."

Michael thought of his stepmother—the way Kathleen was loved by all the Randolph children, whether hers by birth or by marriage—and felt a wave of pity for this woman. Wordlessly, he entered the dining room.

4

————

S kylark, what *is* the matter with you?"
Skylark didn't answer her mother. Instead she went
to the window to stare out at the waning daylight.

"That's the fourth time you've checked outside to see if
your father's arrived. He might not even get home today, and
if he does, it'll likely be late."

Instead of replying, Skylark released a deep sigh.

"Please tell me what's troubling you."

Without turning around, Skylark asked, "How did you
know you were in love with Papa?" She knew by the silence
that the question had surprised her mother. She turned to
meet her concerned gaze. "How did you know?"

Mother took up her sewing again. "That isn't an easy
question to answer."

"Was it when he kissed you?"

She set aside her sewing a second time, her eyes darting
back to her daughter.

Skylark nodded. "Mother, I'm in love." She hurried
across the parlor and knelt on the floor beside her mother's

chair. "I'm in love, and it's the most wonderful feeling. I can't wait to tell Papa."

Mother leaned forward. "Just who is this young man who's captured your devotion?"

"Yale James," she whispered.

"Yale James? What has that man done to encourage your affections?"

"Absolutely nothing." Skylark laughed. "He has ignored me, time after time. But I was having none of that today. Not once I knew I was in love with him." She grinned. "So today I told him so."

"Oh, Skylark ..." Her mother spoke in a near whisper. "What happened?"

"He kissed me." She closed her eyes, remembering every tingle all over again. "It was the most wonderful thing that's ever happened to me. No wonder you and Papa kiss so often."

"We're married."

"You kissed before you were married. I remember. I saw you."

It was true. She remembered her adoptive parents when they were courting. She'd only been a young girl of eight when Mother and Papa married, but she remembered the whispered exchanges, the gentle touches, and the times when Papa leaned down to claim Mother's lips with his own, both before and after the wedding.

"Skylark Danson, you're barely eighteen. Mr. James is thirty if he's a day—"

"He's twenty-nine," she interrupted.

"Twenty-nine then. It makes no difference. He's still too old to be kissing an innocent, unsuspecting young girl. I shudder to think what your father will do when he finds out.

There's a good chance Mr. James will be looking for another job."

Skylark jumped to her feet. "That's not fair! I love him! I mean to marry him! Besides, it was *my* fault he kissed me."

"I don't doubt it for a moment." Mother sighed, then continued, "But he shouldn't have taken advantage of your infatuation."

Tears flooded Skylark's eyes. "It's *not* an infatuation. I love him. Don't you understand? I've been in love with him for months. If you send him away, I'll die. So help me, I'll die." She ran from the parlor and up the stairs.

Rosalie carried the last of the supper dishes into the kitchen, giving a wide berth to Mark who leaned against the cabinet beside the sink. Their mother already had her arms deep in soapy dishwater.

"Go away, Rosalie. I need to talk to Ma."

She tossed him a belligerent look. "Why don't you help with the dishes then?"

He straightened. "I said go."

"I won't. I know what you're after. You're going to ask Ma to give you the money Mr. Randolph paid. Well, you can't have it. Ma needs it."

"This ain't any of your concern, runt."

She hated it when he called her that. Her hands doubled into fists at her sides. "Leave Ma be."

"Rosalie ..." Ma twisted to glance behind her, her hands still in the sink. "Go on and talk to Mr. Randolph. I don't need your help with the dishes. Mark'll keep me company."

"Keep you company? Ma, he's just looking for money.

You can't spare any. You'll need everything you've got—" She broke off her words. Last thing she needed was for her brother to know she planned to leave Boulder Creek. Besides, it wouldn't change her mother's mind, and she knew it.

"What're you worried about, runt? You've got your job at the restaurant. You won't go hungry if Ma loans me a few bucks."

"Loan?" She made an unladylike sound in her throat. "I'd like to see the day you repay anything you've taken from us."

Mark drew back his hand, but Ma stepped between them before he could swing. Her hands dripping water onto the floor, she turned pleading eyes on her daughter. "Please, Rosalie. Go on and let us talk."

Tears burned behind Rosalie's eyes, but she didn't let them fall. Not when her brother might see.

She left the kitchen through the hall doorway, stopping as soon as she was in the dim passage. Why couldn't Ma stand up to Mark, just once in her life? And why couldn't she take Rosalie's side in an argument? Just once. That's all Rosalie wanted. But wanting it was a waste of time.

Drawing in a deep breath, she walked toward the parlor. Michael Randolph was there, sitting in a chair near the window, an open book in his lap. But he wasn't reading. He was staring out the window, obviously deep in thought, his eyes unfocused.

Rosalie hesitated, undecided whether to enter the parlor or go upstairs to her room.

He glanced up then, as if he'd sensed her presence. He stared at her like she was some sort of puzzle he was trying to solve.

"Am I disturbing you?" she asked.

"No." He closed the book. "I don't feel much like reading."

The last rays of sunshine cut through the window, spilling over his head and shoulders. The effect was rather like a halo, and for the third time that day, she thought of the Greek gods in Mrs. Danson's old school books.

"Was there something you wanted to say to me?" Michael asked.

The sun settled behind the mountains. The halo effect faded, and she felt embarrassed by her fanciful thoughts.

"Miss Tomkin?" He frowned and leaned forward.

"Yes, as a matter of fact, there was something I wanted to say. To ask, really." She entered the parlor and sat in the companion chair to the one he occupied. "I would like you to tell me about San Francisco."

He leaned back, his expression relaxing. "Ah, San Francisco. Great city. Good weather. Fine society. Terrific theaters with entertainers coming from all over the world. And one of the finest hotels to be found anywhere. What else would you like to know?"

"Well, you see, I'm going there next week."

"What takes you there? Family?"

Rosalie thought of her father. "I guess you could say so."

"And where do they live?"

She shook her head. There was no point in pretending. "No, I haven't any family living there. I'm going there alone. I want to find work and—"

"Alone? Miss Tomkin, San Francisco is no place for a young woman alone."

"If you could suggest a place I might stay. Some place respectable and reasonably priced. I haven't much money, but as soon as I get a job—"

The touch of his fingers on the back of her hand caused the rest of her words to catch in her throat. She looked at his fingers—long, tanned, well-manicured fingers—lying against her small hand, her skin red and rough in comparison. The sight made her stomach feel peculiar.

He drew back his hand. "Miss Tomkin, I hate to disappoint you, but I could never encourage a beautiful young woman such as yourself to go to San Francisco unescorted."

Beautiful?

"While there are parts of my city that are wonderful, we have many undesirable elements living there, too. They would take one look at you and know you were an innocent from the country and unable to take care of yourself. Why, you wouldn't be safe for even one day before—"

"What?" She scrambled to catch up. "Unable to take care of myself? You're wrong about that, Mr. Randolph. I've taken care of myself for years."

He stared at her for a few moments, then said, "Not in San Francisco." There seemed to be a hint of mockery in his voice.

She felt her temper start to boil. "You're certainly not under any obligation to give me the information I want." She got to her feet. "However, I assure you, I *am* going. I'm leaving on Wednesday's stage."

Michael Randolph looked at her with something akin to sympathy in his eyes. "Then I wish you well, Miss Tomkin."

Yale James was leaning against the side of the bunkhouse, smoking a cigarette, when his boss came to find him. The night was dark and the air cool. Yale wasn't surprised when he saw Will Danson's approach, although he'd thought the confrontation might have waited until morning. After two weeks in Oregon on a cattle buying trip, Will had to be plenty tired.

Yale dropped his cigarette and stepped on it, then moved away from the bunkhouse. "I reckon you're looking for me." Will's fist connected with Yale's jaw and knocked him to the ground. *That* he hadn't expected.

"I reckon I had that coming." He struggled to catch his breath and rubbed his jaw.

"You sure did."

"If I had a daughter, I'd do the same. Truth is, I'd kick the scoundrel so far it would take a hound dog six weeks to find his smell." Slowly, he got to his feet, hoping Will wouldn't knock him down again. "I don't suppose you'll believe me if I said I didn't do anything to encourage her feelings for me."

"I don't care what you say or do, as long as you do it some place other than the Rocking D. You're fired. Get your gear and get out of here."

"Before I go, I reckon I should tell you how I feel about Skylark."

"Don't bother."

"Truth is, I love her."

Will hit him again.

This time, Yale took the punch without falling. He made no move to retaliate. He didn't want to. "I had that one coming, too." Tasting blood, he touched the corner of his mouth. "I told Skylark you'd be madder than a peeled rattler when you found out. I know you don't think I'm any prize. I've been telling myself that ever since I first seen her."

"None of that matters to me."

"Skylark's a thoroughbred, and that's a fact. I don't know

what she sees in the likes of me. My family tree ain't no better than a shrub." He leaned down and picked up his hat where it had fallen in the dirt. "But I'd sure like to prove I can be something better."

"You're not proving it with my daughter." Will spun on his heel and started back toward the house.

"Mr. Danson!"

Will stopped and turned.

"I figure if a gal like Skylark can see something worth loving in me, then maybe I oughta try to live up to it. I know you think I'm nothing but a saddle bum. I reckon you'd feel that way about any man who was making eyes at your girl, no matter who he was. But I aim to prove her right and you wrong. And if she'll have me, when the time's right, I mean to ask her to be my wife."

Good thing Will didn't have a gun on him or Yale reckoned he'd be dead already.

"I'll get my gear and be gone by morning, sir."

"See that you are."

Softly, Yale added, "But this ain't over. She's gonna be my wife one day. You'll see."

5

Rosalie waited anxiously for Skylark to arrive at church. She had so much to share with her friend. She'd had a long talk with Mr. Turner the day before about San Francisco. Of course, she hadn't told him she planned to go there alone. She'd learned her lesson with Michael Randolph. The blacksmith would have reacted the same way if she'd told him the reason for her questions.

Seated in the church pew beside her mother, she glanced over her shoulder. The row the Danson family usually occupied remained empty. Was something wrong? The Dansons rarely missed services.

Before she turned toward the front again, she noticed Michael sitting at the back of the church. He looked even more handsome today, dressed in his black Sunday-go-to-meeting clothes. Most men in Boulder Creek looked uncomfortable in a tie and fancy suit. Not Michael Randolph. He looked as confident as ever.

He glanced her way, and their gazes met. His nod was

infinitesimal and for her alone. A private greeting. Somehow disturbing. She straightened, turning her eyes toward the pulpit, that odd feeling starting up in her stomach again.

She hadn't seen their boarder at all yesterday. Her mother had told her the only meal Michael had eaten at the boarding house was at noon. Rosalie wondered what had occupied his time.

Not that it mattered to her whether she saw him or not.

Reverend Jacobs stepped behind the pulpit. "Let us all stand and sing." He nodded to his wife, Priscilla, who sat at the pump organ. "A mighty fortress is our God," he began. His singing was strong and hale—and not quite in key.

From the corner of her eye, Rosalie caught sight of the Dansons slipping into the empty pew. She turned to look at them. Will Danson led the way, followed by his son, Preston, then his daughters, Skylark and Naomi, and finally by his wife. As soon as Rosalie looked at Skylark, she knew something was wrong. She didn't think she'd ever seen her friend look so sorrowful, not even when she'd first come to Boulder Creek as a frightened orphan.

Skylark kept her eyes cast downward. Her hands were folded in front of her, and her shoulders drooped. Her face looked puffy, and Rosalie guessed she'd been crying, though her cheeks were dry at the moment.

Will Danson stood with rigid shoulders, his chin up, his eyes straight forward. He didn't even pretend to sing. Anger seemed to emanate from him. At the end of the pew, Addie looked almost as sad and miserable as Skylark. She, too, stared toward the pulpit without singing.

Skylark told them about Yale.

Rosalie ached for her friend. She could imagine what must have happened when Will and Addie learned about their beloved daughter's feelings for one of the hired hands.

Michael made it a practice to attend church services, no matter what city or town he was in. His father had taught him that it was a sound business practice, and he knew it to be true. People were more apt to trust a man if he was seen in church on Sundays. Not that Michael wasn't a believer. He was. But he was also a man with plenty of common sense and an understanding of human nature. He had to be. Especially now when so much was at stake.

His stepmother liked to tell him that Palace Hotels was only a business, and that Michael should have more in his life than that. Find a wife and settle down. That was her constant advice. *"You have a right to your own life, Michael. Remember, your father isn't a saint. No one knows that better than we do."*

Michael felt an old knot of pain in his gut. John Thomas Randolph a saint? No, that he wasn't. Far from it.

He remembered Dillon the first time they'd met. Almost like looking into a mirror, except Dillon's hair was dark while Michael's was fair. He should have known the truth then, but he'd been ten years old. He'd been too excited at the thought of having a new friend living in the same house with him. His father's attention had been wrapped up in Kathleen, his new wife of only a few months, and Michael had grown lonely. But then Dillon had joined the Randolph household. The two boys had become inseparable, getting into mischief together, pulling pranks on the household servants, driving the hotel staff to distraction when the family traveled. The boys had been like shadows of each other, their thoughts somehow intertwined.

Until their sixteenth birthdays, celebrated only three days apart. That had been when John Thomas told them the truth.

Michael still struggled with resentment. From the moment Michael learned Dillon was his father's illegitimate son, his life had changed and his bond with Dillon had been severed. It seemed that John Thomas Randolph took pleasure in pitting Michael and Dillon against each other.

He closed his eyes against the memories. He wouldn't allow himself to get caught up in sentimentality or wishing for what could never be. Things were as they were.

Rosalie caught up with Skylark at the bottom of the church steps. "Skylark, wait."

Her friend lifted downcast eyes, then glanced at her father. "May I speak with Rosalie privately?"

"For a moment. We have a long trip ahead of us."

Skylark nodded as she took hold of Rosalie's elbow. Side by side, they walked toward the grove of trees that bordered the church property. When they were schoolgirls, this was where they'd come during lunch breaks and recesses to share their secrets and plan their futures.

"What did your pa mean about a long trip?" Rosalie asked the moment they stopped.

"He's taking the family to Boise City."

Rosalie felt a rush of relief, forgetting for a moment that she planned to go farther away than Boise.

Skylark turned to face her friend. "Papa thinks I'll forget

Yale if I don't see him for a while." Tears flooded her dark eyes. "He thinks I don't know what love is. He thinks I'm too young." She pulled a handkerchief from her reticule and pressed it to her nose. "He's wrong. I won't ever stop loving Yale."

"Oh, Skylark." She didn't know what else to say. She knew nothing about falling in love. She'd never wanted to know.

"He fired Yale and ordered him off the Rocking D. All because of me. It's unfair. Yale didn't do anything wrong. Papa just thinks he's wrong for me. He treats me like a child."

Rosalie placed her hand on Skylark's arm. "I'm sure it'll all work out." She hated platitudes, but they were the only words she had. "You'll see. It'll be okay."

"Rosalie, will you do me a favor?"

"Of course."

Skylark pulled a piece of paper from the pocket of her gown. "Will you find Yale and give this to him before you leave town?"

"How will I find him?" Rosalie took the folded message.

"I don't know." Tears slipped down her cheeks, leaving moist trails behind. "Frosty said he was looking for work at the sawmill. Maybe he was hired on." She dried her cheeks with her handkerchief. "He can't go away without reading my note. What if I never see him again?" Her voice broke, and she began to sob.

Rosalie hugged her, patting her back and murmuring soothing sounds, not knowing what else to do.

"Skylark?" Preston Danson appeared through the trees. "Papa says it's time to leave."

She didn't look at her brother. "I'm coming." She stepped

back from Rosalie and whispered, "You'll find him? You won't leave without seeing he gets it?"

"I promise."

"Thank you. Oh, Rosalie, I'm going to miss you so much." She turned and hurried after Preston.

Rosalie didn't move. An overwhelming loneliness washed over her as she considered the weeks and months ahead. Skylark had helped her through so many rough times. And now they wouldn't get to say goodbye properly. She would be gone before Skylark returned from the territorial capital. They might never see each other again.

She felt close to tears herself as she walked out of the grove of aspens and headed toward the boarding house.

Yale stared inside the house that was nestled against the mountains at the east end of the valley, not far from where Pony Creek emptied into the river. According to Vince Stanley, the old Hadley place had been vacant for three years. Two of the three glass windows were broken. Leaves and dust lay thick on the floor inside, and the house smelled of the forest creatures that had taken shelter in it.

It would take some elbow grease and sweat to make the place livable, but Yale wasn't afraid of hard work. Never had been. He figured he had a lot to prove, first to himself and then to Will Danson. He'd meant what he said the other night. If Skylark thought there was something worth seeing in him, then he meant to find out if she was right.

He shook his head. Maybe he was plumb loco. But here he was, wanting to marry Skylark Danson and settle down for good in this valley.

Going into the bank yesterday, Yale had been as uncomfortable as a camel in Alaska. He'd thought for sure Vince Stanley would tell him he wouldn't even consider loaning Yale money to buy his own spread. Instead, Vince had suggested the Hadley place as a possibility. The price was reasonable, and if Yale could come up with one hundred dollars within sixty days, the bank would give him a mortgage on the rest.

One hundred dollars. It was a lot of money. He might be able to come up with half of it if he sold his horse and saddle, but that wasn't a good solution. Without a horse and saddle, he couldn't run a ranch, and he sure as blue blazes wasn't a farmer. The only thing he knew was horses and cattle. As soon as this place was his, he meant to make a first-rate cattle ranch out of it.

In the meantime, he'd been lucky. Sigmund Leonhardt at Boulder Creek Lumber was willing to take him on at the mill. That would earn him eight dollars a week. In addition, he'd heard Zoe Paddock was looking for someone to make repairs at the restaurant and around her house. She'd told him that a widow woman with three daughters could always use a man's help to fix things up, long as he was a hard worker. He'd promised her he was, and she'd offered to pay him fifteen dollars when the work was done. Another job or two like that one, and he'd have his hundred dollars.

With a sigh, he reminded himself that this place wouldn't clean itself up. He tossed his hat aside and rolled up his shirt sleeves as he entered the house. There wasn't much to it. Just three rooms and a loft. But a good scrubbing and a bit of whitewash would make a heap of difference. Still, would it be good enough for Skylark or was he plumb weak north of his ears?

Maybe Will was right about him. If he had any sense, he'd get on his horse and leave this valley. But even as he thought how foolish it was to stay, he kept working. He was in love with Skylark, crazy or not, and he'd do whatever he had to to make her his wife.

6

Her money was gone!

Rosalie stared into her keepsake box with horror and disbelief. Her money had been there. She knew because last night she'd added the week's wages Mrs. Paddock paid her yesterday. Now all forty-eight dollars were gone.

Mark!

She felt anger boil up inside. It had taken her four months, working six days a week at the restaurant, to earn forty-eight dollars. It had taken even longer to save that much. How dare her brother come into her room, go through her things, and take her money? How dare he do this when she needed so desperately to leave Boulder Creek?

She stared at the contents of the box where she'd dumped them on the bed. A hair ribbon her mother had given her when she was ten. A marble she'd won in a game with Loring Barber when she was eleven. A poem Skylark had written and given to her. Bits and pieces of her past. Nothing of real value to anyone but her. Only the money was gone. And with it had gone all hope of escaping before her pa returned.

Whirling away from the box on her bed, Rosalie hurried from the room and down the stairs. She headed for the front door, determined to find her brother, even if she had to go into that saloon to do it. But she didn't have to go farther than the parlor. Mark was seated there, as if waiting for her.

He grinned when she stepped into the room, then reached for a bottle of whiskey and poured some into a leaded glass. "Looking for me?"

She stared at him, momentarily speechless.

"Where's Ma?" he asked. "She gone to the McNeal house for Sunday dinner?"

Rosalie still didn't answer.

"Well then, you'd best fix your brother something to eat."

Cook for him? She'd rather die. "Give it back."

"Give what back?"

"You know what." Her head pounded, and her breathing came hard and fast.

Mark drained the whiskey. "Ahhh." He set the glass on the table beside him and refilled it. His grin broadened. "Now that's smooth, I tell you. It's some of O'Neal's best stock. Expensive, too. A real pleasure going down. I don't often get to buy whiskey this good. Would you like a sip, Rosalie? Might make a woman of ya."

"I want my money back, Mark. The money you stole."

He picked up the glass, held it with the fingertips of both hands, and stared at the amber contents, his elbows braced on the arms of the chair. "Stole is a mighty harsh word. I like borrowed myself."

In a flash, Rosalie crossed the room. She reached out and knocked the glass from his hands before he could react. It broke upon impact with the wall. Whiskey ran down the wallpaper and puddled on the floor.

"How dare you?" she yelled. "How dare you take what's mine?" With another swing of her arm, she knocked the whiskey bottle from the table. It rolled across the room, leaving a stain on the rug.

Mark hopped to his feet, his face darkening, his eyes narrowed.

Rosalie paid no heed. She was too angry to care what his reaction might be. "I want my money back."

"Well, you ain't gonna get it. Besides, you just poured some of it out on the floor. A real waste, Rosalie. You shouldn't waste good whiskey."

She tried to slap him but he hit her first. She reeled from the blow to the side of her head and collided with the divan, bruising her shin on the carved birch leg. Falling sideways, she hit the floor. Her ears rang and black dots appeared before her eyes. But she scrambled back to her feet and headed toward him, again throwing caution to the wind. "I want it back." She lunged at him.

He hit her, and when she fell this time, he kicked her. "Stay down, you stupid girl."

She tried to get up. She needed to get back the money he took. She had to leave Boulder Creek. She had to get away from this place.

Mark's fingers snaked through her hair, and he yanked her head up from the floor even as his boot pressed harshly against her belly. "You need yourself a good lesson, runt. I shoulda made sure you learned how to behave a long time ago." He jerked on her hair as he removed his foot from her body. "Get up."

She couldn't have stayed on the floor, even if she'd tried.

He lifted her by the roots of her hair. She cried out in protest, though she knew it would make no difference.

"Don't you ever do that again, Rosalie. Not ever."

He raised his arm to strike again. Rosalie closed her eyes, trying to prepare herself for the explosion of pain she knew would come. But the expected blow didn't happen.

"I suggest you let go of your sister."

She opened her eyes, slowly focusing on Michael Randolph. His fingers were closed around Mark's wrist.

"This ain't your concern, mister," her brother snarled.

"I'm making it my concern. Let her go."

Mark gave her a shove. She caught herself against the wall, glad it was there to help steady her shaking legs.

She watched as her brother turned and tried to hit Michael, but Michael ducked, then brought his left fist upward, catching Mark under the chin. His right fist followed with a violent punch to her brother's middle. Mark staggered backward, the air whooshing out of his lungs. Michael didn't give him time to recoup. He followed with four lightning quick jabs. The fourth one left her brother sprawled on the floor.

After a moment, Michael turned toward Rosalie. A couple of quick strides brought him to her. His hands—hands that had dealt so harshly with Mark—closed gently around her arms. "Are you all right?"

"Yes ... yes, I'm okay."

"You'd better sit down. You're shaking like a leaf." He glanced across the room. "Let's get you out of here before he comes to."

She nodded, her gaze following his to her brother's inert form, heaped in the middle of the floor.

Fear streaked through her, mingling with her pain. She

began to shake even harder. It had been a long time since Mark hit her. She'd stayed out of his way for years, the same way she'd tried to stay out of her pa's way. She'd forgotten how much pain a man could deliver with one swing of his arm.

A wave of dizziness washed over her, and she leaned against the wall, feeling herself about to crumple. Before she knew what was happening, she was cradled against Michael's chest, one of his arms behind her back, the other beneath her knees. She clutched her hands together behind his neck in an instinctive move to prevent herself from falling. Her heart hammered, and she felt her throat close, choking her.

She'd never been held like this. She'd never wanted a man to hold her like this. It was terrifying, but she hadn't the strength to resist.

"Don't worry," Michael said softly. "You're safe with me."

She looked up into his eyes and saw only tender concern. She knew she shouldn't trust him. He was a man, after all. But for some reason, she did trust him.

She closed her eyes and pressed her forehead against his shoulder, hiding from the rest of the world. For a moment, she allowed herself to believe she was safe. That she wasn't trapped. She pretended for this moment that her brother hadn't hit her and her father wasn't coming back to Boulder Creek. For this moment, no one could harm her.

With swift, smooth strides, Michael carried her out of the parlor and up the stairs.

Mark was gone by the time Michael came back downstairs after leaving Rosalie in her room. He was sorry. It would have felt good to toss him into the street. Michael couldn't remember the last time he'd felt such a cold rage as the one that had swept through him at the sight of Mark striking his sister.

Brawling wasn't Michael's style. Nor was it usual for him to involve himself in another family's squabbles. He had enough problems with his own family. He liked to keep a cool and controlled eye on any situation. He liked to think things through before he took action. He tried never to act in haste. Controlled retaliation was more his style.

That had been impossible today.

He gave his head a self-deprecating shake. He couldn't be sure he'd be welcome in the boarding house after this. Beating up his landlady's son probably wouldn't endear him in her eyes. True, he'd protected Virginia Tomkin's daughter, but he hadn't failed to notice that the woman seemed to favor her son, despite the man's less than respectable behavior.

Worse yet was the trouble this incident could cause him if word got back to John Thomas. His father would not approve, whatever the provocation. Michael couldn't afford that kind of mistake.

But it was done now. He couldn't change it. Besides, he wasn't sorry for what he'd done. Mark Tomkin could have broken Rosalie's neck, the way he'd held and hit her.

He felt the anger returning and made a conscious effort to control it as he stooped to pick up broken pieces of glass. What was done was done, but that didn't mean he had to become more involved. He would give Rosalie Tomkin a wide berth from now on. If she was determined to leave

Boulder Creek, then he wouldn't have to worry about her for much longer. A few more days and she would be on the stage bound for Boise. He wished her well.

"Mr. Randolph, what happened?"

Michael turned to meet Virginia's startled gaze. "A little accident. A glass broke."

Her glance flicked to the whiskey bottle nearby. "I don't tolerate liquor in this house, Mr. Randolph."

"It isn't mine."

She stared at him a moment, then looked back at the bottle. "Mark." She breathed out her son's name on a note of sorrow, her shoulders slumping more than usual.

"Yes."

Virginia was nearly as petite as her daughter but without any of the stubborn strength he'd recognized in Rosalie. Mousy was the word that came to mind whenever he looked at Virginia Tomkin's thin, lined face. He suspected she looked older than her years. A hopeless air about her had earned his pity.

"Mr. Randolph." Virginia held out her cupped hands. "I'll not have you cleaning up my son's mess. You give me that before you cut yourself, then go on about your business."

He hesitated a moment before carefully placing the jagged pieces of glass in her hands. She was right. He wasn't there to clean up after the Tomkin family. He wasn't there to become involved in their problems. Virginia would have to work things out on her own—and so would her daughter.

Rosalie lay on her side on the bed, curled into a fetal position, her eyes staring blankly at the wall, her arms cradling her bruised ribs. Her body ached, and she felt the swelling begin on her bruised face. She could still taste blood. It was a bitter taste. Bitter—like her heart.

How had this happened? She'd sworn she would never allow anything like it to happen again. She closed her eyes, fighting the pain, fighting the fear, fighting the reality of what the future would bring if she couldn't escape soon.

A shiver shook her as she recalled the shattering pain of Mark's hand upon her cheek. She knew where he'd learned to hit like that. He'd learned it from their father. And Pa was coming back soon.

She groaned and sent up a silent prayer for God's help.

7

The next morning, Rosalie stood in front of her dressing mirror and stared at her reflection with her right eye. She couldn't see out of her left. It was swollen shut, and the skin around it was black and blue. Another bruise marred her right cheek. Tenderly, she touched the sore flesh, wincing as pain spread from the point of contact.

I can't go to the restaurant like this.

She remembered how often her mother had hidden inside the house so others wouldn't see her bruises. No money. No escape. Trapped.

And now Rosalie was just like her. No money. No escape. Trapped.

Moving with care, she shed her nightgown, bathed from the washbasin, then put on a faded skirt and white blouse. She found it even more difficult to bend and lace up her shoes.

Discouragement slammed into her with the force of one of Mark's fists. What was she to do? It was the same question that had haunted her throughout the night. But she refused to give in to the despair. She had things to do, and she would not cower inside her room all day.

Rosalie reached for her reticule, checking to make certain Skylark's note was inside, then headed for the door. First she would stop by the restaurant and tell Mrs. Paddock she wasn't leaving Boulder Creek any time soon. Hopefully, she would still have a job. After that, she needed to find Yale. She wasn't about to forget her promise to Skylark. Her friend was counting on her.

Rosalie quietly descended the stairs. She didn't want her mother to hear her leaving. She had avoided Ma yesterday, pretending to be tired and wanting to nap. A part of Rosalie didn't want her ma upset, another part suspected Ma would blame Rosalie for what Mark had done. It was her way. In Ma's eyes, the men of the family were in the right, no matter what.

Before opening the front door, Rosalie tied a deep-brimmed sunbonnet over her hair, tugging the edges forward to help hide her face. It was a temporary disguise, but her pride demanded she try to hide the bruises. Once ready, she opened the front door and stepped onto the porch.

Michael stood on the bottom step, his back to her. He turned at the sound of the opening door.

Rosalie stopped and lowered her gaze to the porch, unwilling to meet his eyes.

"Good morning, Miss Tomkin." There was gentleness in his tone.

"Mr. Randolph." She moved toward him, expecting him to step aside for her to pass.

He didn't.

She waited a heartbeat, then glanced up. With her on the

top step and him on the bottom, they were almost at eye level with each other—and close enough for her to notice that his lashes were surprisingly long and thick and much darker than the golden-blond hair of his head. Close enough for her to read the tender concern in his eyes.

Did she also see pity? She didn't want his pity. "Excuse me." Her throat grew tight and her words came out in a whisper.

He didn't move from her path. "Listen, about yesterday—"

"I'd prefer not to speak of it," she said quickly with all the dignity she could muster.

He looked as if he would say more, then closed his mouth and stepped back, making room for her to pass.

Rosalie lowered her gaze again and tugged at the brim of her bonnet, trying to shield more of her face. That was when the idea came to her—Mr. Randolph could help her! She looked at him a second time. He still watched her with that thoughtful gaze of his. He'd helped her. He'd saved her from Mark. He'd been gentle with her, caring, concerned. He was still concerned.

"Mr. Randolph?"

"Yes?"

She squared her shoulders and tried to stand tall. She even lifted her chin, giving him a full view of her bruised face. "Mr. Randolph, I ... I appreciate what you did for me yesterday. You've been kind. More than kind. And I ... now I need to ask a favor."

"And what is that favor, Miss Tomkin?" His expression didn't alter, nor did he seem put off by her forwardness.

A bit more hopeful, she continued, "I would like you to take me with you when you return to San Francisco."

One of his eyebrows arched. "I beg your pardon."

"I need to get to San Francisco, and I don't have the price of a ticket." She saw a frown crease his forehead. She rushed on. "I wouldn't be any trouble to you. Not a bit. I promise I wouldn't. I eat very little, and I can sleep anywhere. As soon as I find a job, I would pay you back every cent." She took a quick gasp of air. "Please, Mr. Randolph. Take me with you to San Francisco. I must get away from this place."

"I'm sorry, Miss Tomkin, but that's not possible. My plans don't call for me to return home for quite some time."

The urge to beg was strong. She had to get out of there before she embarrassed herself even more than she already had. Whispering a quick apology, she scooted by him and hurried down the walk without a backward glance.

Not wanting to be seen by anyone, she turned into the alley and made her way to the back door of the restaurant. When she entered, she found Zoe Paddock and her friend, Doris McNeal, the sheriff's wife, sitting at a table near the kitchen, sipping cups of coffee.

Zoe took one look at her, and Rosalie knew the bonnet hadn't disguised much at all.

"Mrs. Paddock. I'm sorry, but I don't think I can work today. I ... I had an accident."

"An accident?" Zoe rose from her chair. "Child, whatever—"

"I ... I fell." It was a lie she'd heard her ma tell countless times. "But I'm all right. Really. But I'd rather ... I'd rather not be seen like this."

Doris clucked her tongue softly. "If you want, I could say something to Hank and he could speak to—"

"No!" She tried to quell the rising panic. "Please. There's nothing to tell the sheriff."

"Hmm."

Rosalie looked at Zoe again. "Mrs. Paddock, I won't be going to San Francisco as soon as I thought. If ... if you haven't given my job to someone else, I'd like to stay on."

"Of course, dear. The job is yours. I told you that."

"Thanks. I'll come back to work on Thursday if that's all right." She reached for the door. "Thank you, Mrs. Paddock. I ... I really appreciate it." She slipped out to the alley again, closing the door behind her.

Yale didn't care much for sawmill work. The noise, the dust, the cramped quarters. He much preferred being out under the wide canopy of sky, breathing fresh air and listening to the sounds of nature. But the work was honest and the pay was good. That made his days seem more tolerable.

"James! There's someone here to see ya."

Yale turned and looked at the foreman, then followed the man's gesture. He saw a slight, feminine shape silhouetted in the mill doorway, daylight at her back. For a moment, he wondered if it was Skylark, but just as quickly, knew it wasn't.

His gaze returned to Ted Wesley. "Be right back."

It wasn't until he was almost to the doorway that he recognized his visitor. He'd met Rosalie once when she'd come to the Danson ranch. The morning sunlight glared behind her, keeping her face beneath her bonnet in shadows, but he still knew it was her.

"I'm sorry to bother you, Mr. James," she said as he approached, stopping a short distance away. "Skylark asked me to give you something before she left Boulder Creek."

He felt a bolt of alarm. "Left Boulder Creek?"

"Her parents took her to Boise City for a while."

"Oh."

Rosalie lifted her chin slightly. Yale had the distinct feeling she was studying him. "Mr. James, Skylark thinks she's in love with you. I guess she is, from the look on her face when she talks about you. I hope you feel the same, because if you don't, it's going to break her heart." She held a slip of folded paper out to him, dipping her head forward so that the brim of her bonnet obscured her face once again.

"Thanks." He stepped closer and took it from her.

She turned to leave without looking up again.

"Miss Tomkin?"

She stopped but didn't glance back.

"I mean to see that she's happy. You got my word on it."

Rosalie nodded, then walked away.

Yale stared down at the paper in his hand for several heartbeats before he worked up the courage to open it.

My dearest Yale,

By now you know Papa has taken me and the rest of the family to the capital for a spell. He thinks if I don't see you that my feelings will change. That isn't true.

It's my fault you lost your job at the Rocking D. I never should have told Papa how I felt about you. He doesn't understand. He's too old, I guess, to understand. I'm sure he's never felt this way or he wouldn't have done what he did. He'd know I will die without you.

Please don't leave Boulder Creek, no matter what happens. I will be back, and when I am, I'll come to you. Papa can't stop me from loving you. Nothing can stop that. I swear it on my life.

Devotedly yours,
Skylark

Yale could almost hear Skylark speaking the words to him. She was passionate, fearless, dramatic. Why had she given a man like him a second look? Odds were that a few days or weeks in Boise would be enough for her to come to her senses, the way her father wanted.

But there was also a chance that she truly loved him and would keep on loving him, like her letter said. And that was the chance Yale meant to pin his hopes on.

8

           —————

Rosalie carried the dishes into the restaurant kitchen, placed them beside the sink, and released a deep sigh. Thank goodness her first day back at work was almost over. With the careful use of rouge and powder, she had hoped to disguise the bruises, but it hadn't worked. Everyone had asked about her injuries. She'd repeated the story about falling down the stairs, but from the looks on their faces, no one believed her.

"Are you feeling all right, Rosalie?" Zoe asked, looking up from the table where she diced onions.

"I'm fine."

"Maybe you should go on home. I can wash those dishes, and Esther and Faith will be here soon to help get ready for the supper crowd."

"I don't mind staying." She went to the stove and, using a towel to protect her hand from the heat, lifted the kettle filled with water and carried it to the sink.

"Do you know what I heard today?" Zoe asked. "Mr. Randolph, the fellow staying at your mother's boarding house, bought some land and plans to build a hotel here in Boulder Creek."

Rosalie set some of the dirty dishes into the wash pan and began cleaning them. "A hotel?"

"Well, don't you see? He's a man of some importance. You only have to look at him to know he's wealthy. He wouldn't come all the way to Boulder Creek unless he was sure such a venture would be profitable. Doris says Mr. Randolph must know something we haven't heard yet. Something that'll turn Boulder Creek into a real boomtown."

Boulder Creek a boomtown? Rosalie had a hard time picturing it. But then, she didn't know what a boomtown looked like. She'd never even been down to Boise City. Imagine! Thousands of people living in one place.

And San Francisco was even bigger. If she'd been able to go there, would she have been frightened? Excited? Probably a bit of both. But she wouldn't have a chance to know if she couldn't get back the money her brother had stolen from her. And her time to escape had nearly run out.

She didn't need to go to San Francisco to be frightened. She was already afraid. Her pa was coming back, and she was trapped. She couldn't get away. She remembered him through the memory of a child—a dark, angry man with an iron fist and a gruff voice. She remembered the day she'd sat in church and thought how much she hated him. Even then, she'd known it was a sin to hate. Especially to hate one's own pa. But she hadn't cared. She'd hated him, she'd been afraid of him, and she'd wished he'd go away.

And then he *had* gone away. Like an answer to a prayer, he'd left Boulder Creek—but not before he'd killed Tom McNeal and burned down the old sawmill.

She knew he'd done it as certainly as she knew her own name, but she'd never told another soul. The child she'd been was afraid they would bring her pa back to Boulder Creek. Later, when she was told he'd been imprisoned for bank robbery, she'd thought it enough that he'd been locked up.

But now Glen Tomkin was coming back.

"Rosalie?" Zoe's hand alighted on her arm. "Rosalie, you'd better sit down. You're as white as a sheet."

She allowed the other woman to help her to a chair, not realizing until she started to walk that her legs were like rubber.

"Here. Have a drink of water." Zoe pressed a cup into Rosalie's hand.

She sipped slowly, trying to steady her shaking hands. Finally, when she'd drained the cup, she said, "I think I will go home, Mrs. Paddock, if you don't mind."

"Of course, I don't mind. But are you sure you want to go alone? Maybe you should wait for the girls to get home from school. Esther could walk you back to your place, make sure you got there all right."

"No." Rosalie shook her head. "No, I'll be fine on my own." She rose, bracing her thigh against the table to steady herself. After drawing several deep breaths, she nodded at Zoe. "I'll be fine."

"You just get home and into bed. And don't you come in to work tomorrow unless you're feeling a whole sight better."

At the top of Tin Horn Pass, Michael drew his roan gelding to a halt beneath the shade of a tall pine tree. The mid-May sun was hot, the sky an expanse of unmarred blue stretching from horizon to horizon. In the valley below, freshly turned fields and those already planted with spring crops created a checkerboard of browns and greens. Cattle and horses grazed in pastures of long field grasses. A ribbon of blue—Pony Creek—wound its way across the valley, disappearing into the next range of mountains.

He'd been impressed by what he'd seen and learned today. The farmers and ranchers in the two neighboring valleys had prospered, and the logging and mining interests in the mountain areas were thriving. There would be an influx of people when Idaho became the forty-third state to join the union. Boulder Creek was bound to see its share of newcomers.

He knew of the plans to bring a spur of the Oregon Short Line up this direction. His father hadn't chosen towns where a hotel was guaranteed to fail. No, he'd given both of his sons equal opportunities to succeed. Still, after today's outing, Michael believed he would be the one who succeeded. Palace Hotels would be his, as it was meant to be.

He couldn't deny, even to himself, that there was a new and increasing excitement inside him at the idea of making a success of this venture. It was different from anything he'd tried before. The Palace Hotels had been built to host royalty and dignitaries, not miners and loggers or farmers and traveling salesmen. But that's what made this an interesting challenge.

Michael lifted his dusty Stetson from his head, wiped his shirtsleeve across his forehead, then set the hat back in place. His gaze swept over the panoramic scenery of the valley and surrounding mountains. It was wild, beautiful, and rugged, yet serene. The sight made him feel things he hadn't felt in years—a sense of newness, of adventure, even a sense of peace.

Perhaps, when this year was over, he would have something more to thank John Thomas for than simply control of Palace Hotels.

Two men glanced up as Rosalie opened the back door of the boarding house. She saw him then—her father—and froze in the open doorway, her chest growing tight, her knees growing weaker.

"Well, I'll be," Pa said with a grin. "Look who's all growed up." He pushed his chair away from the table and rose to his feet.

Rosalie glanced toward her mother, standing near the stove. Ma seemed more faded and wan than ever.

"Come here, girly, and let me have a closer look at you."

Reluctantly, she moved toward him.

His eyes narrowed but his grin remained as he studied her face. "What happened?" He touched her cheek.

She flinched. "Nothing."

"I see you're as prickly as a porcupine." He grabbed hold of her arm, his face darkening into a scowl. "Now, I asked you what happened."

"Mark happened." Rosalie jerked her arm away and stepped around to the other side of the table.

Her pa chuckled. "Still scrapping with your brother, are you? Guess you haven't grown up as much as I thought."

The other man rose from his chair, drawing Rosalie's attention. He had wild black hair and a grizzled beard. His eyes—such a pale gray they seemed almost colorless—traveled over her.

She shivered but tried to hide her distaste.

"And who might you be?" the man asked.

Her father answered for her. "That's my daughter, Rosalie. Rosalie, this here's Jack Adams. Folks call him Mad Jack."

She could see why. There was madness in his eyes.

"You didn't tell me you had anything like her at home, Tomkin." Jack's lurid grin revealed a missing tooth near the right corner of his mouth.

Rosalie felt a sudden need for a bath.

The man stepped around the table, drawing closer to her. "I think you and me are gonna become good friends."

"I doubt it." She wanted to back away but forced herself to hold her ground.

Her pa laughed aloud. "I don't think she cottons to your attentions, Mad Jack."

"She just don't know what she's missing."

"Why don't you marry her and take her off my hands. That'd be one less female for me to worry about."

Rosalie whirled toward her father. "Marry? I don't have any intention of marrying this man or any other."

Before she could react, he was around the table, his fingers once again squeezing her arm. "You seem to forget who you're talking to. You'll do as you're told. You hear me?" He gave her a shove toward her mother. "Come on, Jack. Let's go check out that saloon. Time I said howdy to my son. Besides, I need a drink to wash down that lousy stew."

Rosalie watched them go, pain and fear congealing into a cold knot in her belly.

So this was it then. Her nightmare had begun.

Later that evening, Rosalie stood at the open window of her room. Laughter and music came from the saloon, two doors down the street. The noise had never sounded so uninviting as it did tonight.

"Don't provoke your pa."

Remembering her ma's warning, Rosalie sighed. How many times as a child had she heard the same words? Dozens, perhaps hundreds. Always Ma had defended Pa and Mark. No matter what they'd said, no matter what they'd done, she had defended the men.

Why?

Rosalie had been the one who'd stood up for her mother when Pa was at home. Rosalie had been the one who'd worked so hard in the boarding house after Pa ran out on them. It was she who'd helped support the family through the lean times by taking the job at Zoe's Restaurant. But Ma wasn't going to change. She believed this was a woman's lot in life and that they had to make do.

Rosalie gripped the window sill. She had to get away. She had to leave. She wouldn't let Pa force her into marriage. She refused to become like her mother—broken and beaten down, both by circumstances and by some man. Rosalie wanted more from life than that.

But how? How did she escape?

If only Skylark were here. If Skylark was in Boulder Creek, Rosalie could have gone to stay at the ranch or she could have borrowed money from her friend's family. But Skylark wasn't there, and Rosalie didn't know when she would be back.

She turned from the window and walked to her bed

where she lay down on her back. The evening breeze rustled the curtains.

As she watched the shadows dance across her ceiling, an unwelcome memory intruded and her cheeks grew warm. She'd had the audacity to ask Michael Randolph to help her escape Boulder Creek, and he'd refused. As was his right. Now she understood why. Mrs. Paddock said he meant to build a hotel in this small town. He must be very rich to throw his money away like that. Her ma barely had enough boarders for them to get by.

Another memory came, more unwelcome than the first. Michael had cradled her in his arms and told her she was safe with him. Tender words. Gentle words. So unexpected after her brother's violence.

And yet, still, he wouldn't help her get away.

Rolling onto her side, she closed her eyes and tried to shut out the memories. She wanted to sleep ... and to forget.

In a hotel room in Boise City, Skylark also lay on her bed, tears wetting her pillow. She understood now what the poets meant by a broken heart. Surely her own was shattered into a thousand pieces. It wasn't supposed to be like this. Falling in love was supposed to be the most wonderful thing in the world. She and Yale should be together. He should be courting her. She should be planning a wedding. Instead, she was estranged from the father she adored and separated from the man she loved.

A light tapping broke the silence, followed by her mother's voice. "Skylark, are you awake?"

She swiped at the tears on her cheeks. "Yes."

The door opened. "May I come in?"

"Yes." Skylark sat up.

Her mother paused inside the doorway and turned up the gas lamp. "Are you all right, dear?"

"Yes," she whispered.

Her mother approached the bed. She wore an evening gown of emerald-green satin, and her red hair was swept high on her head. "I wish you'd have come with us this evening. It was a wonderful play. You'd have enjoyed it."

"I didn't want to go."

Her mother sighed as she sat on the edge of the bed. Lightly, she patted Skylark's hand with her own. "You can't keep trying to punish your father this way, shutting yourself off from everything and everyone."

"He's being unreasonable."

"Perhaps so are you. You won't change his mind by acting like a child."

Skylark drew in a quick, shallow breath. She'd thought her mother was on her side. Almost from the moment they left Boulder Creek, her mother had tried to convince Skylark's father to take the family home again.

"Darling, you don't understand what it means to a father to have his little girl grow up. Will has taken care of you from the moment you got off that stage all those years ago. In his mind, you'll always be that shy little orphan who needed his love so desperately. He can't imagine that you might want another man more than you want him."

"I do love him. But I'm not a little girl any longer. I'm a grown woman."

"Then prove it. Prove to him you're an adult." Her mother slid closer to Skylark and put an arm around her back, hugging her close. "If the love you and Yale feel for each other is real, it will last through this separation. If it isn't, it's better you discover it now."

"Oh, Mother. I miss him so much. It feels like I'll die if I can't see him soon."

"I know. I know because I've felt that way myself."

Skylark sniffed. "You have?"

"Yes. I have." Mother kissed the top of her head, then stood. "You get some sleep. Tomorrow, you and I will go shopping for some new frocks. Staying in your room and crying isn't going to change your father's mind, so we may as well make the best use of our time."

"Mother?"

"Yes?"

"I really do love him. I am old enough to know what I feel."

Her mother nodded, then walked across the room, turned down the lamp, and left, closing the door behind her.

Skylark lay back on the bed, the room cloaked in darkness. Her mother was right, she realized. She wouldn't prove she was a woman by acting like a child. Tomorrow she would change things—starting with herself.

9

Morning sunlight spilled like liquid gold through the open doorway and across the kitchen floor.

Rosalie leaned her shoulder against the jamb, her eyes closed, feeling the brilliance of the sun upon her face. She listened to robins and sparrows and bluebirds singing their morning hymns of praise. The sharp scent of dew-covered pine trees filled her nostrils as she drew in a deep breath of mountain air.

She loved early mornings. They were nature's promise of fresh beginnings. She loved to watch and listen as the earth came to life. She treasured this comforting interlude before she began the business of living. For now, the boarding house was quiet, the other members of the household still asleep, although she knew her mother would join her in the kitchen soon.

Oh, Ma, why didn't we go away from here when we had the chance?

With a sigh, the pleasures of morning forgotten, Rosalie

backed out of the doorway and closed the door, cutting off the sunlight and plunging the kitchen into layers of gray.

In a practiced rhythm, she stoked the stove with wood and lit the fire, then she organized the ingredients for pancakes on the work table. In a large bowl, she mixed the milk, sugar, and eggs. Then she added a teaspoon of dissolved pearl-ash, spiced with cinnamon, a dash of salt, and a bit of rose-water. Finally, she stirred in the flour, adding it slowly until the mixture was the right texture.

There was no need to think about what she did. She'd helped her mother in the kitchen for as far back as she could remember. When Rosalie was little, her ma had let her stand on a stool and stir ingredients in a bowl, much as she did now, minus the stool. Maybe that's why she liked mornings so much. It had been a time when she was alone with Ma and the two of them were safe.

A sudden string of curses interrupted her musings. She turned as the kitchen door flew open and her father stumbled, barefooted, into the room. He jerked a chair out from the table and sat down, then lifted his foot and examined his toe.

He swore again. "Don't just stand there, girly. Get your old man something cold. About tore my foot clean off on that table in the hall. Fool place for it."

Rosalie pumped the handle beside the sink until a stream of cold water poured from the spout. She held a rag beneath the water, then wrung it between her hands, squeezing out the excess moisture before carrying it to her father. He didn't bother to look up as he took the rag from her hand and held it against his toe, muttering another sequence of vile curses.

Her stomach twisted. Why had he come back? Why hadn't he stayed far, far away?

"What you gawking at? Get back to your cooking."

She was only too happy to obey. She busied herself, cutting slices of bacon to fry in the skillet on the stove.

"Jack took a real shine to you, Rosalie." Her pa sounded amused. "Couldn't stop talking about you the whole time we was at the saloon."

The knife stilled in Rosalie's hand, and her breath caught painfully in her chest. He was baiting her, much as Mark liked to do. *Ignore him. Don't say a word.*

"I think he just may want you bad enough to marry you."

She couldn't stay silent. She couldn't. Setting the knife aside, she clasped her hands together and faced him. "He may want it, but I don't."

"You'll do whatever I tell you."

"No, I won't."

Her pa frowned as he leaned forward, resting his arms on the table. "I don't think I heard you right."

"Yes, you did. I won't marry that man or anybody else. I don't mean to end up like Ma."

He came to his feet so fast, the chair toppled backward. "Your brother told me you needed taken down a notch or two, and by heaven, I mean to do it." He took a step toward her.

Rosalie's gaze darted toward the door. Could she get there in time?

As if in answer, the kitchen door swung open, and Michael stepped into the room. He looked at her with a smile, but there was something steely in his eyes. "Good morning, Miss Tomkin." Then he turned toward her pa. "And you must be Mr. Tomkin. Your wife told me you'd returned to Boulder Creek yesterday. I'm Michael Randolph, one of your boarders." He held out his hand.

He'd saved her again. Like one of those dashing medieval knights in books and fairy tales, he'd come to her rescue— even if he didn't know that's what he'd done.

Michael's gaze didn't waver as the two men shook hands. He wondered if Mark had told his father about the fight they'd had, but Glen's handshake was friendly enough, which made him think Rosalie's brother had kept the altercation to himself.

He was glad when the contact with the man broke. He'd heard the raised voices as he'd descended the stairs, and he suspected he'd come into the room just in time to prevent Rosalie from taking another beating. It made his blood run hot, thinking about it.

Blast, there he went again, letting himself worry about something that wasn't his concern. He had to stop before it became a habit. He wasn't there to protect Rosalie Tomkin.

"I hear tell you're lookin' at building a hotel here in Boulder Creek." Glen picked up the chair where it lay on its back.

"That's right."

"Seems like a fool thing to do, if you ask me." He sat down. "You're the only boarder we've got. What makes you think this town needs a hotel?"

Michael shrugged. "Instinct. This area's going to continue to grow."

"Well, I think you're crazy, but I guess it's your money."

"Yes, it is." He shrugged. Let the man think him a fool. He was anything but.

Later that afternoon, when Rosalie returned from her shift at the restaurant, she found Michael in the parlor, reading some official-looking documents. He glanced up when she appeared in the hallway.

She hesitated briefly before stepping into the room. "May I speak with you a moment, Mr. Randolph?"

"Of course." He set the papers onto the divan beside him. "What can I do for you?"

Did she dare ask another favor of him? Especially after he'd refused the first one?

"What is it, Rosalie?"

Strange how hearing him use her given name gave her courage. "Mr. Randolph, I know now why you couldn't take me with you to San Francisco. Because you'll be busy here. But I was wondering ... I was hoping ... I'd like to ask to borrow the money for the trip from you. I'm good for it. I'd pay you back, and with interest. I'm not afraid of hard work. You've seen that for yourself. I only need enough for the train fare and maybe a week or two of lodging until I can find work."

It surprised Michael, how much he would like to agree to her request. He understood now why she wanted to leave Boulder Creek. The bruises on her face were a grim reminder of her reasons. Giving her the money would take no more effort than scribbling a bank draft. It wouldn't even matter to him if she never repaid it. But was it right to involve himself in this matter? And what if doing so put her in even more danger than she was now.

"Sit down, Rosalie."

She hesitated.

"Please."

She obliged him, taking the chair farthest from where he sat.

She was beautiful, even with the bruises marring her face. He wondered why she had turned out so differently from the others in her family. She was like a single flower—a beautiful rose—in a patch of weeds. She belonged with other roses.

"As I said before," he began, "San Francisco is no place for a young woman alone. It's dangerous."

Disappointment flashed across her face.

"I can't, in all good conscience, simply give you money and send you off to make your own way."

Her body stiffened. Fear and dread filled her pretty eyes, although there wasn't any sign of the tears he'd half expected.

In that instant, he knew that failing Rosalie Tomkin wasn't an option. He couldn't *not* help her.

She started to rise from the chair.

"Wait. I'm not finished. If you'll allow me some time to make proper preparations, I will arrange for a position for you in San Francisco. I have contacts with some of the other hotels in the city, and I'm sure I can find someone who will agree to take you on. I also know a woman who runs a respectable boarding house for young ladies. I'll see if she has an opening for you in her establishment."

"Oh, Mr. Randolph."

He raised his hand to stop her thanks. "I also will want to arrange for you to have a proper escort to San Francisco. It's a long journey, and not one to be made by a woman alone."

"Tell them I'll be a good employee. And I promise I'll pay you back every cent it costs for me to get to San Francisco. I swear it."

Before he could reply, she rose and hurried across the room. At the entrance, she glanced back at him. "You'll never know what this means to me, Mr. Randolph. You won't ever regret it. I promise you."

He already regretted it because he didn't know how he would manage to do what he'd promised. His father had stipulated that neither of his sons were to contact anyone in San Francisco. Not anyone at the hotel. Not anyone at the bank. Not the company attorney or any personal friends. Such a rule was meant to prohibit Michael and Dillon from using the family name or their positions with Palace Hotels to gain an unfair advantage. But that wasn't what he was doing.

Still, John Thomas Randolph was a stickler for details. He'd said no contact, and he'd meant no contact.

Michael would have to write to Kathleen. He hadn't been forbidden to correspond with his stepmother.

10

A euphoric cloud enveloped Rosalie that evening as she prepared supper. Soon, she would leave for California. Maybe a week. Maybe two. But before long she would escape her brother, her pa, and his disgusting, lecherous friend. Michael Randolph planned to set her free from them all.

She didn't realize she was smiling until she caught her ma's quizzical gaze. Rosalie shrugged and continued slicing the carrots for their supper, not wanting to spoil her secret thoughts with conversation.

Michael was the nicest man she'd ever met. He'd offered something better than loaning her the money. He was going to see that she had a job and a place to live.

"You'd change your mind quick enough if you ever got kissed." Her hand idled over the raw carrots as she stared into space, Skylark's words replaying in her mind.

Kissed by Michael Randolph for instance? She imagined herself, standing in the middle of the parlor. She pictured Michael putting his hands on her shoulders and drawing her toward him as he lowered his head. She would have to stand on tiptoe, and he would have to bend low.

Could a kiss be as wonderful as Skylark said?

Before Rosalie could imagine Michael's lips touching hers, she shook off the thought and began chopping carrots with a vengeance. Perhaps her friend could indulge in such fantasies, but Rosalie couldn't. A man, no matter how wonderful he might seem at times, was still a man. He had the superior strength—and the legal right—to make a daughter or a wife do whatever he wanted. Rosalie didn't intend to give a man that sort of authority over her once she escaped her father. She wanted no part of marriage or anything that went with it.

"Rosalie? Is something troubling you?"

She glanced across the work table. "No, Ma. Nothing's troubling me."

Or nothing would trouble her as soon as she stopped thinking about Michael Randolph.

Michael stopped in the entrance to the dining room. "Sorry I'm late."

"You're not late, Mr. Randolph," Virginia Tomkin said. "We just sat down ourselves."

He took his place at the table next to Rosalie.

At the head of the table, Glen Tomkin pointed at the man seated opposite Michael. "This here's my friend, Jack Adams."

Taking an instant dislike to the newcomer, Michael nodded an acknowledgment but said nothing.

Virginia held a platter of sliced roast beef toward him. "Help yourself."

He thanked her, then poked a fork into a juicy piece of meat.

"Tell me something, Randolph." Tomkin leaned forward over his empty plate. "You been in the hotel business long?"

He paused for a fraction of a second. "My family has."

"You ever been in the Palace Hotel in Denver?"

Michael didn't allow his expression to change, despite his surprise. Had Tomkin discovered his association with Palace Hotels? Knowing what an unsavory character Glen Tomkin was, he wondered how the man might use the information against him.

"I've been there," he answered at last.

"Thought you might, you being in the business and all. I was there once, before they sent me to prison. Never seen anything like it in all my born days. I guess a man could live out his life on what one of them fancy chandeliers cost." He leaned back in his chair. "Folks who own that hotel must be as rich as Midas. Got money to waste, I'd say. You suppose they throw their money away, building hotels in towns like this one, same as you?"

"I don't believe I'm throwing my money away, Mr. Tomkin." He deliberately began cutting his meat, acting as if the conversation meant little to him.

"But you're rich enough not to care if you lose it, right?"

Michael glanced up again. "No one is ever so rich they don't mind losing money."

"No, I suppose they ain't." Tomkin's grin broadened. "You a married man, Mr. Randolph?"

"No, I am not." His dislike for the man was increasing by the second.

Tomkin glanced at his daughter. "Ya oughta be. Man oughta have a wife to keep his bed warm at night and fix his meals. Take my Rosalie. She's of an age to be getting herself a husband. You interested? I'd let you have her cheap enough."

"Pa!"

"Cheap for you anyway." Tomkin laughed. "Not that she don't need herself set straight now and agin. Virginia wasn't able to keep her in line while I was away. But now I'm home, I'll be seeing that she learns the proper way to take care of a man."

Michael didn't so much as blink, but inside he seethed. Tomkin was even lower than he'd suspected. It made him glad he'd offered to help Rosalie get out of Boulder Creek. Not only for her sake, but because it would ruin her father's greedy hopes.

Tomkin helped himself to a generous serving of potatoes, then smothered them with gravy. "All those years I was gone, I'd never've guessed she'd turn out so pretty. Even Jack here's taken notice. But if you're interested, I'd give you first chance."

Michael glanced at Rosalie. A mixture of emotions crossed her face. Horror. Shock. Dread. Determination.

Tonight, he would write to his stepmother. He would ask Kathleen to do whatever she could to help. He would make sure Rosalie Tomkin escaped her father, and he would do it as soon as humanly possible.

Rosalie looked up then, and he gave her the slightest of nods, hoping it might encourage her, hoping she would know he meant to keep his promise to her.

Later that evening, Rosalie sat before her dressing mirror. Clad in a white nightgown, she stared at her reflection without seeing it, her thoughts returning to the supper table. Shame washed over her as she remembered what her pa had said, offering her like that. Like he was selling a horse or a cow or a chicken.

But then she remembered the way Michael had looked at her, and her stomach somersaulted. She didn't want to marry him or anybody. Still, there was something about him that made her wonder...

No, she wouldn't wonder. Wondering wasn't for her. Wondering was for a girl like Skylark, but not for Rosalie Tomkin.

She quickly plaited her long hair into a thick braid, rose from the stool, and walked over to her bed. Once there, she put out the lamp, bathing the bedroom in darkness.

I've gotta get out of here, God. Please help me get out of Boulder Creek before it's too late. And if You can, make Ma want to go with me. Get her to safety too.

She rolled onto her side, eyes closed. She would leave Boulder Creek soon. Once she was in San Francisco, she would make a new life for herself. A life that was all her own.

Sleep tugged at the edge of her musings, and she sighed.

A hand over her mouth jerked her back to reality. She felt a man's stubbly cheek near hers.

"It's cold out on that window ledge of yours."

She knew that voice. Mad Jack. A scream rose in her throat but was trapped there.

"About time you turned out the light so I could come in and get warm."

She fought him with every ounce of strength she had in her. She kicked, hit, and clawed.

He laughed. "I like me a girl who fights."

Terror icing through her, she brought up her knee. He grunted and cursed, his grip on her loosening. It was enough time for her to roll off the bed. She heard the fabric of her nightgown tear as he caught at it. For a moment, she thought it might stop her flight for freedom, but then she broke loose. Almost to the door, she stumbled but somehow righted herself and yanked the door open. With no other thought than to escape, she ran to the nearest room, the nearest sanctuary, the only place she might feel safe in this house.

Michael Randolph's room.

"Michael!"

He heard Rosalie's frightened cry as the bedroom door flew open, banging against the wall. He came fully awake and jumped out of bed. A second later, she flung herself at him. Instinctively, his arms closed around her.

"Rosalie?"

She shook like a leaf.

"Rosalie," he said again, his arms tightening. "What is it? What's happened?"

A heartbeat later, Glen Tomkin's gruff voice echoed his question. "What's happening here?"

Lamplight spilled from the hallway into Michael's room, illuminating the girl in his arms. Rosalie in a tattered nightgown. He put her behind him.

"Randolph, what are you doing with my daughter?" The

lamp in Tomkin's hand seemed to show a gleam of delight in his eyes.

"It's not what it appears."

"I'll bet it ain't." Tomkin turned toward his wife, who stood right behind him. "Virginia, fetch the sheriff."

"Glen—"

"Fetch him! Look at him, standing there in his drawers, trying to hide my daughter like nothing happened. He'll marry her in the morning or I'll see him in jail. One or the other."

Rosalie looked out from behind him. "Pa, you don't—"

"Shut up. I mean to deal with you later."

"Listen, Tomkin." Michael's voice was firm, controlled. "I don't know what happened to Rosalie, but I had no part in it. If you'll give her a second to explain, I'm sure we can find out the truth of what's happened."

Tomkin moved forward. "Well, then, let's just have a look at the truth." He grabbed Rosalie's wrist and yanked her out from behind Michael. "Look at her nightclothes. Ripped like that. You tried to have your way with an innocent girl. That's as plain as spit."

"Pa, please." Rosalie pulled her torn nightgown around her. Her head hung forward, the thick plait of chestnut hair trailing over her shoulder. "It wasn't him—"

"Shut up, girl!" Tomkin raised a hand as if to strike her, but put it down after a glance in Michael's direction.

Her humiliation was obvious to Michael, if not to her father. Angered, Michael turned and pulled the bedspread from the bed, then laid it over her shoulders.

She looked up at him, her eyes glittering with tears. Her face was as white as a sheet, and her lips looked blue. He knew it was fear, not cold, that caused her to shiver, and he wished he could help her. But there was nothing more he could do.

Steeling herself, Rosalie faced her father, prepared to make him listen, prepared to tell him what his so-called friend had tried to do and why she'd run to Michael for help. But then Jack Adams appeared in the doorway behind her mother. With his eyes, he dared her to tell everyone what had happened in her room. He taunted her with his presence.

What if Pa made her marry Mad Jack because of what he'd done? What if Pa found out it was Mad Jack who had torn her nightgown, not Michael? If Pa would threaten to make Michael marry her for such an offense, wouldn't he do the same for Mad Jack?

She looked down, fear silencing her.

Her pa's fingers pinched her jaw, forcing her head up, making her look at him. "Speak up, Rosalie. What happened?"

She couldn't marry Mad Jack. She would rather die than let him touch her.

"Nothing happened," she whispered. "Nothing." It was as close to the truth as she could manage.

"Get back to your room." Her pa gave her a shove toward the door. "You're getting married in the morning."

11

———

Michael didn't have to marry Rosalie Tomkin. He could have let Sheriff McNeal put him in jail and then sent for his attorney, Christian Dover, and in a very little time he would have gone free. Rosalie hadn't accused him of anything, and he knew deep in his heart that she wouldn't. For that matter, if he'd offered Glen Tomkin a handsome payoff, that would have been enough to be rid of the charge against him. But paying off Tomkin wouldn't have protected Rosalie for long. Besides, the last thing he wanted was to reward Tomkin for the wrong that had been done to his daughter. Not that Michael understood his desire to protect Rosalie. He didn't know her. Not really. And yet, protect her he would.

And so there he stood, Reverend Jacobs before him and Rosalie beside him.

Of course, requesting help from Christian Dover, he reminded himself as he made his vows, would have been a violation of his father's terms. Sending for his attorney would have cost him Palace Hotels once and for all. By that action, he would have conceded the contest to Dillon. He wouldn't do that. Couldn't do it. Not even if he had to take a dozen wives. So in addition to protecting Rosalie, he was also protecting himself.

A grim smile twisted the corners of his mouth. Tomkin—who stood somewhere behind him—thought he would profit from this union. He thought he could get money from his daughter's husband whenever he asked. He was sorely mistaken.

"And now, by the power vested in me by the church and the Territory of Idaho, I pronounce you man and wife. What God has joined together, let no man put asunder." Reverend Jacobs' solemn demeanor disappeared the moment he stopped speaking. He leaned back on his heels, looking pleased as he gazed at the couple before him.

For the first time since he'd arrived at the church, Michael glanced at Rosalie. Her face was pale, her eyes circled with dark shadows. The bruise on her cheek had faded to a sickly yellow shade, marring—but not hiding—her natural beauty.

A small voice of doubt sounded in his head. Was it possible this was all an act? Had she run into his room, her nightgown torn, in order to trick him into this marriage? She'd acted afraid of her father. But was it possible she'd joined forces with him to make this happen? If so, she was as mistaken as her father. He had no intention of making this a real marriage. When his year of exile in Boulder Creek was complete, he would arrange for an annulment. Or a divorce if that's what he was forced to do. He would leave this town—and Rosalie—and never see either of them again.

His bride glanced up at him, and he caught a glimmer of sorrow in her eyes. He wouldn't fall victim to it.

The reverend cleared his throat. "Mr. Randolph, you may kiss your bride."

No, he would rather not. Because if he kissed her, it might remove this suspicion that he'd been manipulated. He needed time to think. He couldn't undo it. The good reasons for the action he'd taken still existed. But he hated the thought that he'd been outmaneuvered by a slip of a girl and her nasty excuse for a father.

He took hold of Rosalie's elbow and turned her around. Without a word, he guided her past her parents and out the door. He strode quickly away from the church, forcing Rosalie to almost run to keep up with him. Once inside the boarding house, he said, "Pack your things. We're leaving."

"Where are we going?"

"Not to San Francisco, if that's what you were hoping. We're going to find us another place to live here in Boulder Creek."

"But—"

"I'm going over to the bank. Mr. Stanley should know if there's a residence available. Get your things and don't argue with me."

Her eyes widened, and her chin lifted. For a moment, she looked as if she might come to life, might even defy him. Then, just as quickly, the light in her eyes died.

"It won't take me long," she said softly before climbing the stairs to her room.

He hates me.

Could Rosalie blame him? No, she couldn't blame him. After all, it was she who had raced into his room in the middle of the night. It was her fault they'd been forced to marry. He'd done nothing more than try to protect her, and look what it had gotten him—

A wife he didn't want.

Rosalie sank onto the bed and hid her face in her hands. She should have told the truth. She should have accused Mad Jack. But would anyone have believed her? She'd been found in Michael's room, not in her own. Still, she should have told the truth.

A shudder passed through her, knowing her pa might have forced her to marry her true assailant instead of Michael Randolph.

"Get your things and don't argue with me."

She shuddered again. She hadn't been going to marry. Not ever. She hadn't wanted to place herself under a man's rule. Now her worst fears had come true. Married only a matter of minutes, and already her husband was ordering her around. He hadn't asked if she wanted to go on living at the boarding house or move elsewhere. He hadn't cared what her wishes might be. As soon as the vows were spoken, he'd become her dictator, her master.

To honor and obey. That was what she'd promised. Until the day she died, she was to honor and obey a man who now —perhaps rightly—hated the sight of her.

She wasn't certain how long she sat on the edge of the bed, her hands over her eyes, letting the waves of despair wash over and consume her, crying in her heart but shedding no tears. She wished now—as she had during the long, sleepless night—that she could simply curl up and die. Death would be preferable, she was certain, to marriage.

"Rosalie?"

She looked up, surprised to find her mother standing inside the bedroom doorway.

"It's not as bad as it seems." Ma came forward and sat on the bed with Rosalie.

"Isn't it?"

"He'll be good to you. I can tell. He's a good man. He's different from ... He's different. You'll be better off with him than here in this house."

"Oh, Ma," she whispered, sliding closer and resting her head on her mother's shoulder. "If only we could've left Boulder Creek before Pa came back. Why wouldn't you go with me? We could've made a new life for ourselves."

"Leaving wasn't ever right for me. I belong here."

"But Pa—"

"This is my lot."

"It doesn't have to be. Even now it doesn't have to be. *We* could still leave, you and me."

"No, we can't. I'm stayin' put." Ma stroked Rosalie's hair. "But you've got a chance for something better than I ever had. Don't lose it because you and Mr. Randolph are off to a poor start." She held Rosalie away from her. "You've always been made of sterner stuff than me. Don't give in now, Rosalie. Your marriage doesn't have to be what mine's been."

Her mother's words brought back the memory of Michael's arms wrapped protectively around her.

Was there hope?

Ma rose from the bed. "I'll help you pack. Your husband'll be waiting for you."

Her husband ... Michael.

She had a funny feeling in her stomach, half-fear, half-anticipation. Could Ma be right? Could her marriage be different? Could she be happy as Michael Randolph's wife?

~

When Michael opened the bank door, he found Vince Stanley bent over his desk, studying columns of figures. It wasn't until Michael stopped before the desk that the banker glanced up.

"Mr. Randolph, this is unexpected." Smiling, Vince held out his hand. "I understand congratulations are in order."

Michael returned the handshake, wondering how much the other man had heard. Too much, most likely. He imagined the whole town was gossiping about the reasons behind the hasty marriage of Michael Randolph and Rosalie Tomkin.

His jaw clenched. He detested gossip—especially when he was at the heart of it. "Thanks," he responded at last, certain he sounded less than grateful.

"So, what brings you to the bank today? Surely not business."

"Actually, it is business that brings me. Do you know of a place I could lease or buy. We prefer not to reside at the boarding house. You understand. A man wants a home of his own."

Vince nodded. "Of course. And as a matter of fact, I can help you. There's a house west of town that's been vacant for almost a year. Even comes with some furnishings. Belonged to the Reverend Pendleton and his sister. Reverend Jacobs and his family let it when they first came to Boulder Creek, but they wanted something bigger, having children and all, so they built that big house of theirs. But the Pendleton place would be just right for a young couple starting out. Miss Pendleton is anxious to sell it. The price is most reasonable." He returned to his desk, pulled open a drawer, and began shuffling through files. "Now where did I put those papers?" he muttered.

"The price doesn't concern me. Can we move into it at once?"

Vince cleared his throat. "Well, it hasn't been cleaned or aired since last fall and—"

"We can see to the cleaning ourselves. You draw up the papers. I'll be in tomorrow to sign them." Michael held out his hand, palm up. "Do you have the key?"

"Why, yes. I do. Of course." The banker opened another drawer and withdrew a key, then dropped it into Michael's hand. "Are you sure you don't want to look at the place first before deciding—"

"No." Impatience made his voice sharp. He forced himself to soften it when he added, "I'm sure we'll be more than satisfied."

As Michael turned to leave, the door to the bank opened and a lanky fellow dressed in dusty denims and a battered Stetson stepped inside.

The cowboy paused when he saw Michael, then nodded at Vince as he removed his wide-brimmed hat. "Mornin'."

"Good morning, Mr. James." Vince Stanley skirted his desk. "Have you met Mr. Randolph?"

"Haven't had the pleasure." The cowboy looked back at Michael, a friendly grin curving his mouth. "Yale James." He held out his hand.

"Michael Randolph," he said, and returned the handshake.

"Mr. Randolph and Rosalie Tomkin were married this morning."

"Is that a fact?" Yale's grin widened. "You're a lucky man, Mr. Randolph."

Lucky? He didn't think so. He returned Yale's smile, although his own felt tight and false. "Thank you. Now, if you'll both excuse me, I must be on my way."

"Of course. Of course," Vince replied. "Don't keep the little woman waiting on account of us. It's your wedding day after all."

Rosalie had packed all of her personal belongings into two carpetbags and was waiting on the front porch for Michael's return. She sat on the wooden bench, her back pressed against the siding of the house, her hands clenched tightly in the folds of her skirt. She stared across the street, barely noticing the golden beauty of the spring day. She wasn't sorry Michael had decided not to stay at the boarding house. She had no desire to live under the same roof as her father.

Turning her head at just the right moment, she saw Michael step through the doorway of the First Bank of Boulder Creek. He paused and glanced up the street in her direction. Her pulse quickened as Skylark's words returned to taunt her. *"You can't very well get married and not let your husband kiss you."*

Her friend was wrong about that. Michael hadn't wanted to kiss her, even when the minister invited him to do it. And that had stung more than expected.

Stung? No. It couldn't be true. She didn't *want* him to kiss her. She'd married him because she'd only had two options: Michael or Jack Adams. She didn't want to be a wife to anyone, but since she'd had to marry, she'd chosen what she hoped was the better of two evils.

Now it was the memory of her mother's words that flitted

through her mind. *"But you've got a chance for something better than I ever had. Don't lose it because you and Mr. Randolph are off to a poor start."*

Was it possible Ma was right? Was it possible to find happiness in this marriage?

She rose to her feet as Michael drew closer to the boarding house. He moved with such power and confidence, his long strides chewing up the distance that separated them. She'd never met anyone like him before, never known a man who could make her feel safe. But Michael could. Or once had.

With sudden clarity, she knew that the choices she made in the coming hours and days would set the course for her entire future. She prayed she would make the right ones.

The Pendleton house wasn't as bad as Michael had expected. Dust lay thick on the white sheets that covered the furniture, and the windows needed a good washing. But it would be a suitable home for the short time he planned to be in Boulder Creek. It would certainly be a good place for Rosalie after he was gone.

He walked from room to room, looking things over.

Downstairs, there was a modest-sized parlor and a small but adequate kitchen. Upstairs, there were two bedrooms. He dropped Rosalie's two carpetbags on the floor of the first bedroom, then carried his things into the second one. When he turned around, he found Rosalie watching him from the top of the narrow staircase.

"You can have the room overlooking the grove. I hope that's satisfactory."

"Michael." His name on her lips was little more than a whisper. Her knuckles whitened as she clung to the bannister. "I'm sorry about last night. I never meant for this to happen."

Oh, the little minx. Did she know how her voice and the look in her eyes tugged at him? He would have to work hard not to fall more of a victim to her wiles than he already had. "Rosalie, we'd better get something straight between us. I wasn't looking for a wife, and if I had been, I wouldn't have started looking in Boulder Creek."

"I didn't want a husband any more than you wanted a wife. All I wanted was to get away from ... from *him*."

What did happen last night?

Like a lightning strike, her demeanor changed in an instant. Her chin came up and defiance sparked in her eyes. "Pa *made* me marry you. Remember?"

"Good. Then we're agreed this marriage is a temporary situation."

"Nothing could please me more." She turned and descended the stairs.

"Wait." He followed after her, taking the steps two at a time.

She stood in the center of the parlor, her fists clenched at her sides. Her body was tense and her eyes wary.

Something about the way she looked caused him to pause at the bottom of the stairs. In a flash of insight, he understood she expected him to express his anger in physical terms. She could have run out the door, but she didn't. She stayed to face him, to fight him if necessary.

Shame hit him. What sort of man was he? He'd been forced to marry without evidence. Was he doing the same thing to her? Punishing her without cause.

He ran his fingers through his hair, then walked toward her. "Please, Rosalie. Sit down."

She hesitated a moment longer before doing as he'd asked, sitting on the edge of the sheet-covered sofa, her back ramrod straight, her head held high, her gaze vigilant.

He winced. Did she still wonder if he would hit her? He wouldn't. He wouldn't hit any woman, no matter the provocation. It wasn't pleasant to have Rosalie think he might do so.

As the silence stretched between them, he noticed a slight tremor in her lower lip, though she did her best to control it. Fear and sorrow were almost palpable. He felt the urge to sit beside her on the sofa and comfort her. But he wouldn't. He wanted to give her the benefit of the doubt, but he needed to remain cautious.

"Perhaps we'd better come to an understanding."

She nodded.

"My business will keep me in Boulder Creek for the next year. But when this year is up, I'll move on. Alone. I won't leave you destitute but—"

"You think I want your money." She stared at him, wide-eyed. "That's what you think, don't you? Well, I don't. Not now and not later." Up went that chin of hers. "And I won't give a whit where you go when you move on."

Her response almost made him smile. He resisted the urge. "Then we're agreed that this will be a marriage in name only. You'll have your room, and I'll have mine. You'll keep the house and prepare the meals, and I'll give you the funds you need to do so. We'll keep up the pretense of marriage for appearance's sake. And when the year is up, we'll each go our separate ways."

"That's fine with me." She sounded strong, but her lips quivered.

Michael cleared his throat and turned away, looking out the window toward town. "Since we seem to be in agreement about how this marriage will work, I suppose we'll be able to get along."

She didn't answer, and he didn't wait to see if she might do so.

"I've got some business to see to." He walked out of the house, closing the door behind him.

12

One good way to work off anger, Rosalie had learned, was to clean house. And so she attacked the kitchen floor with the scrub brush and soapy water.

Men are all the same.

What had possessed her—even for the briefest of moments—to think Michael Randolph was different? Dictatorial. Stubborn. Domineering. Imperious. Rude. So what if he didn't hit her? Maybe being hit would be better. At least it was more honest. He'd pretended that he cared enough to help her get away from Boulder Creek, offering to help her find a job and a place to live, but it had been an act. He didn't care what happened to her. Not in the least.

Maybe it would have been better to take the risk of her father marrying her off to Mad Jack. Chances were, it wouldn't have happened. Chances were, he'd have run off in the night, and she wouldn't be stuck in this house with a man who despised the sight of her.

Men!

She shoved the brush into the bucket, sloshing water over the sides, then inched forward on her knees as she continued to scrub the floor.

What on earth had possessed her to tell Michael she was sorry? It had made her look weak in his eyes. She wasn't weak. She'd wanted to throttle him. She'd been angry, not sad. And he'd as much as accused her of trapping him into marriage for his money. As if money would make marriage worthwhile. As if she were willing to give up independence for a pretty party frock or something. Such gall!

She sat back on her heels and pushed damp curls away from her forehead with the back of her wrist, a heavy sigh escaping her lips. "I'm being childish," she said aloud. "I need to think things through."

Perhaps this wasn't such a bad arrangement. Maybe a few months, pretending to be Michael's wife, wasn't such a terrible price to pay for the freedom she would gain later. She could keep house and cook for him as easily as she'd done it at the boarding house. And she supposed she owed Michael something. He didn't want a wife, but he'd married her, a stranger, saving her from both Pa and Jack Adams.

She got to her feet, picked up the bucket, and carried it out the back door. Following the path toward the outhouse, she stopped when she reached a grove of trees, then dumped the soapy water into the underbrush.

Turning around, she saw three women approaching the Pendleton house. Emma Barber led the way, followed by Zoe Paddock and Doris McNeal.

Rosalie glanced down at her water-stained dress. She felt her damp hair sticking to the sides of her face and knew she must look a sight. But there was no time to do anything about it. The women had spotted her and changed their direction.

"Rosalie!" Zoe exclaimed as she hurried forward. "My dear girl, what a stir you've caused. To think you would not tell a single, solitary soul that you were going to marry. Why, Mr. Randolph must have fairly swept you off your feet."

Emma interrupted Zoe's effusive exclamation, "We've come to see what we can do to help." Her gaze took in Rosalie's appearance. "Land o' Goshen, you shouldn't be working so hard on your wedding day. What on earth was that husband of yours thinking, to move you into this house without giving it a proper cleaning first?" She shook her head and *tsk-tsked*. "Sometimes, I don't think there's a man alive with as much common sense as God gave a goose." Emma took hold of Rosalie's arm and led her toward the back door. "You just leave things to us."

Michael returned to the house late in the afternoon. He'd left without telling Rosalie where he was going or when he'd be back. The truth was, he hadn't known. He'd simply wanted to get away, to have some time to think. He'd spent the day up on a ridge overlooking the valley, pondering the fix he'd gotten himself into.

Out of all the small towns in the west that John Thomas could have chosen for this ridiculous contest, why had he selected Boulder Creek, Idaho? Why did he have to end up in Mrs. Tomkin's boarding house? And why did he have to be so susceptible to sorrow in a young woman's eyes?

A grim chuckle escaped him. His stepmother had been

after him for a long time to get married, and he supposed Kathleen—mother to four of his five younger half-siblings—would find his current situation amusing. Thank goodness he hadn't written to her already. Dillon would find it amusing, too, especially after their rivalry for the fair Louise Overhart. His eldest half-brother would think Michael deserved whatever happened to him. In his most honest moments, Michael would agree with him. And then there was Louise herself. She would never understand why he'd married a girl he'd known little more than a week when Louise herself hadn't been able to entice him to the altar after more than a year.

He had to wonder the same. Why had he succumbed so easily?

When Michael opened the door to the Pendleton house, he was greeted by the tantalizing aroma of onions and roasting beef. His appetite sprang to life, reminding him that he hadn't eaten all day. A quick glance around the parlor made him wonder if he'd walked into the wrong place. Everything was spotless. All signs of dust and neglect had disappeared.

Then Rosalie stepped into the doorway. She paused when she saw him.

She wore a dark yellow dress with short, puffy sleeves and a scooped neckline. Her chestnut colored hair fell in a smooth cascade down her back, caught back from the sides of her face with tortoise shell combs. He'd never seen her look more lovely.

"Hello," she said softly. "I'm glad you're back."

Wordlessly, he removed his hat and hung it on a peg near the door.

"Dinner will be ready soon."

He glanced over the parlor a second time. What trick was she up to?

She drew herself up, as if she'd heard his silent question. Her voice was cool and laced with wounded pride. "I know you believe I trapped you into marriage, Mr. Randolph, but the truth is still the truth. I didn't want or plan to marry. It was forced upon me. So here we are, like it or not." She drew in a quick breath while squaring her shoulders. "You were clear about what you expect of me for the next year, and I mean to do as you said. I'll give you that comfortable home you want, and I'll cook your meals for you. I'll make sure there's no scandal to hurt your business. I won't cause you any embarrassment. I've got only one thing to ask in return. When your business here is done, you help me leave Boulder Creek, too. After that, we'll go our separate ways."

Michael couldn't think of a reply. He was still trying to figure her out. One minute she was as fragile as spun glass, the next she was as rigid as iron. He'd never known anyone like her.

She turned toward the kitchen again. "If you'd care to wash up, dinner will be on the table shortly."

Rosalie leaned against the back of a kitchen chair, Zoe Paddock's words replaying in her head. *"Why, Mr. Randolph must have fairly swept you off your feet."* The woman's romantic notions couldn't be any further from the truth, and Rosalie couldn't decide whether she wanted to laugh or cry at the memory.

She glanced down at the lovely new dress Emma Barber

had given her as a wedding gift. Michael hadn't noticed. And as much as she hated to admit it, she'd wanted him to notice.

That's what she got for letting her head be filled with silliness. Emma and Zoe and Doris all chattering on about love and how wonderful marriage was and how handsome her new husband was and how romantic it all was. That's what she got for allowing her mother to give her hope, telling her she could have a wonderful marriage and not to lose the chance for happiness.

Stuff and nonsense.

She heard his footfall on the stairs and turned to see him enter the kitchen. While upstairs, he'd put on a clean shirt and his hair had been slicked back with a comb and water.

Zoe Paddock was right. He was handsome.

He cleared his throat. "Rosalie." A frown furrowed his brow. "Let's sit down, shall we?" He motioned toward the kitchen chairs, then pulled one away from the table. "Please sit down. We need to talk."

She complied, but only because she suddenly felt as if her legs wouldn't hold her up.

Michael rounded the table and sat across from her. "You say you didn't want to marry me. Then why didn't you tell your father the truth?"

"I couldn't." She looked down.

"Why?"

It was time to be honest. Completely honest. "I ... I was afraid of what he would do ... of what he would make me do."

"What would he have made you do, Rosalie? Tell me."

She swallowed the lump in her throat as she met his gaze. "He would've made me marry Mad Jack. He'd threat-

ened it before. If he'd known Jack Adams was in my room ...
" She let the words trail off, unfinished.

Michael's frown turned to a scowl. "What did happen in
your room?"

"He snuck in through the window." She couldn't look at
him any longer. "He tried ... He was going to ... When I ran
from him, he grabbed for my nightgown. That's how it got
torn. I ran. I just wanted to get away from him." The back of
her throat burned. "I swear I never meant for any of this to
happen. I never meant for you to be blamed."

"Did he hurt you?" His voice was harsh and filled with
anger.

She shook her head.

The room grew silent except for the sound of boiling
water on the stove.

Despite himself, he believed her.

"I'm sorry, Rosalie. I judged you unfairly."

Once again, her mouth quivered, this time in a tremu-
lous smile. But in that smile he read sadness and regret and
perhaps a little fear, too. If he wasn't careful, he would take
her in his arms and tell her he'd take care of her and
promise her a bright and happy future.

He drew back in his chair. "I think we can agree to work
together to make this next year tolerable for us both. Yes?"

Wordlessly, she nodded.

"I'm sure we'll be able to get a quiet annulment when the
year is over. That way, there'll be no stigma for you. When
you find the right man to marry, you—"

"That's very kind, Mr. Randolph, but I don't intend to

marry again." Her unshed tears had vanished, and she held herself erect with a quiet dignity and an iron fortitude.

Beneath that show of courage lay a vulnerable and tender heart, and Michael couldn't shake the desire to protect and comfort it—and the woman who was now his wife.

13

Skylark leaned forward to better hear what the commissioner's son said. He was mildly amusing and pleasant enough. Still, she wished herself any place but this glittering assembly.

"Does your father intend to remain in Boise City for the summer? Idaho will be admitted to the union soon. You'll want to be in the capital city when it happens."

She glanced away from her supper companion, looking down the length of the table to where her father sat. "I'm not sure what Papa intends to do, but I can't imagine we will be able to remain much longer. There is a great deal of work involved in operating a ranch. His time is often not his own."

She hoped against hope that she was right. These past eleven days already seemed a lifetime to Skylark.

"Miss Danson." A second male voice interrupted her thoughts.

She pulled her attention away from her father, looking at the gentleman seated across the table from her. On sabbatical from a university in the east, Professor Edward Patton was traveling the western states and territories. In his thirties and quite dashing in appearance, he was a popular guest at the social gatherings the Dansons had attended since arriving in Boise. But Skylark found him a dreadful bore.

"Statehood is a landmark occurrence," he said, "and the heart of the celebrations will be here in the capital city. You should do your utmost to convince your father to remain until then." He leaned forward, and his voice lowered. "I had hoped to celebrate with you."

She didn't care what he'd hoped. She would never want to celebrate anything with him. "I wouldn't think to try to change his mind, Mr. Patton. He has many responsibilities. You had better plan to celebrate with someone else."

"I shall be an unhappy man if you leave, Miss Danson. Unhappy, indeed."

A thrumming started in her temples, and she wished for the evening to come to an end.

After her talk with her mother a week ago, she hadn't refused a single invitation. She'd gone shopping in the afternoons, and now had a trunk full of new frocks and bonnets and gloves and shoes. She'd been polite to all the men, both young and not-so-young, who'd made overtures toward her. She'd promised herself she would act like an adult rather than a petulant child, and she thought she'd succeeded. But inside, she longed for home and she longed for Yale. When she looked into Edward Patton's dark eyes, she longed for a pair of gray ones, eyes that crinkled in the corners, eyes that were warm and open, eyes without pretense or subterfuge. When she laughed at the sophisticated humor of the commissioner's son, she wished instead to hear Yale's plain speech. When she saw the fancy evening attire of those around her, she wanted nothing more than to see a tall, lanky man in a dusty pair of jeans, a plaid shirt, and a battered Stetson shading his eyes.

How long could she go on pretending?

Rosalie glanced surreptitiously at Michael, seated across the table from her. The only sound in the kitchen was the clink of utensils on plates as the couple ate their supper. It had been the same all week long.

Being married to Michael Randolph had proven to be easier—and more difficult—than anticipated. With the exception of church last Sunday, the only time she'd spent with him had been during meals. And meals were a silent affair with only an occasional word exchanged between them.

Each morning she arose in her solitary bed to wash in the basin. Then she dressed and went downstairs to prepare breakfast. Michael joined her in the kitchen, eating quickly before excusing himself, saying he had a great deal of work to be done. Then he left the house until supper time. After they ate the evening meal, Michael sat in the corner of the parlor, reading a book or studying sheaves of paper while Rosalie, in a nearby chair, pretended to sew.

The silence was torture, yet she didn't know how to broach it. Her husband had apparently made the decision that the best way for them to survive the coming year was to say as little as possible to each other. She hated to admit it, even to herself, but she wished he would share at least a small portion of himself with her.

Michael set his utensils in the center of his now-empty plate. "Wonderful meal, Rosalie."

She nearly jumped out of her skin at the unexpected sound of his voice. Her fork clattered onto her plate. She flushed, feeling his eyes upon her.

"Sorry. I didn't mean to frighten you."

She glanced up. "You didn't. I'm not frightened."

"I haven't been making things easy for you, have I?"

She shrugged.

"No, I haven't." He tilted his head to one side. "I'll try to do better. We'll both try to do better. Agreed?" A gentle smile tipped the corners of his mouth. "Tell me, Rosalie, what is it you hope to do, once you leave Boulder Creek?"

Her heart did some crazy flip-flops inside her chest. Her mouth felt dry. She'd been longing for conversation with him, and now that he was willing, the words seemed stuck in her throat.

He placed his elbows on the table, his fingers laced at chin-level, and continued to wait for her response.

"I ... I thought I might open a restaurant."

"A restaurant?"

She nodded. "I've learned an awful lot working for Mrs. Paddock. And from Ma, too. Not just about cooking, but on how to run a business. I know I could do it, if I had a chance."

"Are you still determined to go to San Francisco?"

"No. It doesn't have to be San Francisco. I don't care if it's a big city or a small town, so long as it's away from here. Someplace Ma might like, too, in case she ever wants to come stay with me."

She glanced toward the window and the direction of town. She'd only seen her ma once in the week since the wedding. And she'd been disturbed to notice a nasty bruise below the hairline on Ma's forehead. Ma insisted she'd done it herself on a kitchen cupboard. Rosalie knew better.

"Just away from here," she repeated in a whisper.

Michael watched the emotions play across Rosalie's face and couldn't blame her for wanting to get away. From the little he'd learned, this town held few good memories for her. She deserved better.

And I haven't given her better. Not really.

It had to be difficult, married to him but in name only. She had little to do except clean house and cook meals for the two of them. She spent her days alone. Zoe Paddock had assumed Rosalie would no longer want to work, now that she had a husband to take care of her. And Michael was so involved with his plans for the hotel, he was rarely at home.

When this year was over, she would need a way to support herself, no matter where she chose to live. Getting work in a new location wouldn't be easy. Perhaps running a restaurant wasn't a bad idea. He could help her out. It wouldn't be a hardship to give her financial assistance. He could make sure she was reasonably safe and secure wherever she went, even after the marriage was annulled.

"Maybe you'd like to run my hotel restaurant when it opens." As the words left his mouth, a shockwave went through him. Why had he made such a suggestion? He wouldn't want his wife working in his hotel. Would he?

"Really, Michael? You would let me do that?"

Was that the first time since their wedding day that she hadn't called him Mr. Randolph? He thought it was. Maybe that's why he answered, "It would be a good way to find out if it's what you really want to do when you leave Boulder Creek."

"Oh, Michael, I would love to." She smiled.

Forget what she'd called him. Maybe he'd wanted to see that look of hope spring to life in her eyes. Maybe he'd wanted to see the appearance of dimples when she smiled at him. He'd almost forgotten how beautiful her smile was.

He lifted his plate from the table. "After supper, I'll show you the plans for the hotel. Maybe you'll have some ideas for the restaurant."

An hour later, Michael knelt with Rosalie on the floor of the parlor, the blueprints of the Randolph Hotel spread out on the floor between them.

After listening to Michael's plans for the hotel, Rosalie sat back on her heels, tossing her thick braid over her shoulder. "I'm bothered about one thing. Can Boulder Creek support two restaurants? I'd hate to see Mrs. Paddock suffer. It's her only means of support since her husband passed. It wouldn't seem right if your restaurant caused her hardship."

"You don't need to worry about that. There'll be plenty of business for both of us."

Her eyes narrowed slightly. "You know something the rest of the town doesn't know. Mrs. McNeal said you did. She said you must expect Boulder Creek to become a boomtown. Is it true?" She leaned forward, pressing the heels of her hands against her thighs. Her braid fell forward over her shoulder again. "Please tell me."

He laughed, his mood better than it had been in ages. "Do you want me to give away trade secrets?"

"Yes."

"How can I be sure you won't tell anyone?" he whispered as he looked around the room, as if searching for a spy.

She drew herself upright. "Because, sir, I am your wife."

As quickly as the words were out of her mouth, the room became thick with tension. The twinkle in her eyes faded, and the somber expression on her face was no longer pretend.

His wife. And a very enticing one at that.

Rosalie felt his gaze upon her skin like a caress. Her lips began to tingle when his eyes lingered on her mouth. Was it horrible, to want him to kiss her, just once?

In her memory, she recalled Skylark's description of what she'd felt when Yale kissed her. Was it anything like the topsy-turvy, spinning sensation she felt now with only a look from Michael? A spell had been cast over her, over the entire room, and it pulled and tugged, urging her to lean forward, to offer herself to him.

Michael straightened, clearing his throat as he did so. "Did you have any other questions or suggestions? About the hotel restaurant? If not, I think I'll call it a night."

A strange feeling sluiced through her. Was it disappointment? Surely not.

"All right." He rolled up the plans.

As Rosalie got to her feet, she still felt the crazy racing of her heart.

"You go on," Michael said. "Don't wait for me. I'll put out the lights."

"Thank you." She hurried up the stairs without a backward glance.

Once inside her room with the door closed behind her,

she shed her clothes, donned her nightdress, and crawled quickly beneath the covers.

"Did you have any other questions or suggestions?"

Yes. Yes, she did have more questions. What would it be like to kiss him? What would it be like to have someone cherish her? What would it be like to have someone care what she thought, how she felt, someone to share her hopes and dreams?

What would it be like to fall in love?

14

Carrying a pail filled with cold chicken, biscuits and honey, and beans, Rosalie walked toward the site of what would be the Randolph Hotel. She was surprised to see the tall stacks of lumber and the many stakes pounded in the ground. Just yesterday the space had been vacant except for the long field grass and a couple of trees. Now, with the stakes marking the outline of the building, combined with the memory of the blueprints Michael had shown her last night, she could envision what the hotel would look like when it was finished.

Boulder Creek with its own hotel. It was hard to imagine. And Michael had said she could run the restaurant. It was too good to be true. If she made a success of it, she would be able to get employment almost anywhere. She would be able to support herself—and hopefully, Ma too—and she wouldn't ever again have to let a man have any say in her life. She could be truly independent.

At that moment, Michael stepped into view, and she felt the quickening of her pulse.

She would be independent just as soon as Michael allowed her to leave Boulder Creek. Just as soon as he got the annulment. Just as soon as she no longer had a husband. Didn't that sound ideal?

"Hello." His smile added warmth to his greeting.

Of course it sounded ideal. Honestly, she couldn't wait to leave Boulder Creek.

"What brings you here?" he asked.

She held up the pail. "I brought you lunch. It's leftovers from last night."

"I like cold chicken." His smile broadened. "And I am hungry." He motioned toward a long plank placed atop two sawhorses. "Care to join me?"

She shook her head but moved to stand near one end of the makeshift bench.

"This was thoughtful of you. I usually skip lunch." Michael took the pail from her outstretched hand.

"It wasn't any bother. I was on my way to the mercantile anyway."

"You sure you won't have something? Stay. Just for a minute or two."

Warmth rose in her cheeks. Why did he make her feel so flustered? "I suppose I can spare a minute."

"Good." He sat down on the wooden plank and lifted the white cloth covering the top of the pail. "I hired my crew this morning. There's five of us. We start work on Monday." He pulled out the chicken and laid it on the cloth. "I wasn't able to get as many workers as I'd hoped. Farmers and ranchers are busy this time of year." He set the can of beans next to the chicken. "But I think we'll be able to open the hotel this summer—Autumn at the latest."

"That soon?" She looked at the lumber. How could this be turned into a hotel in so few months?

As if reading her thoughts, Michael said, "I ordered the furnishings before I left San Francisco. It should all start arriving in the next couple weeks." He picked up a chicken breast and bit into it.

She watched him, noting how the sun glistened on his golden hair. A lock fell forward, curling over his forehead and brushing his eyebrow. She liked the way it looked, the way it made him look. It brought attention to the lines of his face, that long, straight nose, the firm jawline. Her gaze drifted downward to his broad shoulders beneath his blue work shirt. She could see the strength of his biceps through his rolled up sleeves.

My husband.

An odd feeling tumbled in her stomach.

Michael set aside the chicken and wiped his hand on the checkered napkin. When he looked at her that way, he seemed to see into the secret corners of her mind and soul. She didn't much care for that. It was ... confusing. It summoned unwanted emotions. She wished he would look away.

He didn't look away. Instead, he reached out and touched her cheek, a touch as light as butterfly wings. A quiver ran through her.

"The bruise is gone," he said softly as he withdrew his hand.

Her own fingers flew to the place he'd touched. Why had he done that? Why had he touched her?

"You're very lovely, Rosalie. Has anyone ever told you that before?"

She shook her head.

"That's a shame. Someone should have told you."

Panic exploded inside her. She jumped up from the wooden seat. "I'd better get my shopping done." She turned away. "Don't forget to bring the pail home." With those words, she hurried toward the mercantile.

Michael watched his wife's retreat with a sense of regret. He hadn't meant to startle or frighten her. He'd never known a woman who didn't like being told she was lovely.

He thought of Louise Overhart. Louise expected to be told how beautiful she was on a regular basis. Of course, her expectations were not so plainly stated, but they were there, all the same. But not Rosalie. She didn't expect anyone to say anything nice to her. She only wanted him to leave her alone for the next year and then let her go her own way.

That's what he wanted, too. Just to get through this next year so he could put his life back in order.

His thoughts were interrupted by the appearance of a man striding toward him, coming from the direction of the sawmill. By the time the fellow was across the street, Michael had recognized him as the man he'd met in the bank a week before. James. Yale James.

Yale stopped and bent his hat brim in greeting. "Mr. Randolph, I hear you're hirin' a crew to build this here hotel."

"That's right."

"I wondered if you'll be needing more help? I put in four days a week at the mill, but I could sure use the extra work. I can't say I've done much building, but I'm not afraid to work up a sweat and I'm a quick learner. I don't have a family to go home to, so I can keep working as long as there's daylight. I'm willing to work when I'm done at the mill, and I got two full days besides. Three if you want me to work on Sundays."

"We won't work on Sundays."

Yale nodded. "Well then, you can have me those other days and hours. You see, I need the work. I'm buying me a ranch, and I mean to take me a wife as soon as I can get her pa to agree. That won't happen until the place is mine." He grinned. "I'd guess you can understand the hurry I'm feeling about getting hitched."

My circumstances were somewhat different. He doubted the cowboy would understand if he said that thought aloud.

"I'm a hard worker, Mr. Randolph. You won't be sorry you took me on."

Michael rose from the bench, studying Yale James a little longer. He was a fair judge of character, and something told him Yale would work as hard as he'd promised. Finally, he held out his hand. "Pay's sixty-five cents an hour. We start Monday morning. You tell me when I can expect you, and you can work as many hours each week as you're willing and able."

"That's plenty generous, Mr. Randolph." Yale grasped Michael's hand and shook it, grinning the whole while. "Plenty generous."

"Call me Michael."

A few minutes later, Yale returned to his job at the sawmill, leaving Michael to finish his lunch of cold chicken, biscuits, and beans—and to wonder what made a man so eager to get married.

15

R osalie! Rosalie Randolph!"

Rosalie and Michael looked at each other, as if the sound of her name tied with his hadn't occurred to either of them. Then they turned in unison and watched Rachel Harrison hurry toward them.

"My goodness, you two left services so quickly, folks couldn't hardly say a word to you." Rachel waved her hand in front of her face as she gasped for air. "I haven't had a chance to say congratulations, me not being in town for church last Sunday." She looked from one to the other and back again. Then in a lowered voice she said, "Rosalie, perhaps you could introduce me to your husband."

"I'm sorry. Of course. Rachel, this is Michael Randolph. Michael, Rachel is Emma Barber's daughter. She's married to Norman Harrison."

"It's a pleasure to meet you, Mrs. Harrison." Michael tipped his hat brim.

"And mine, Mr. Randolph. I was so excited when I heard about your wedding. Most of the married women in the valley are older than Rosalie and me. It'll be nice to have a married friend close to my own age." She looked at Rosalie. "I'm having a quilting bee at my house tomorrow. In the afternoon. Priscilla Jacobs will be there and so will Ophelia Turner. Please say you'll come."

"Well, I—"

"Don't disappoint us. We want you there."

Rosalie had never participated in a quilting bee. She'd always felt a little like an outsider in Boulder Creek. Not that anyone had treated her that way. She knew the fault was inside herself. She'd looked at other families and wondered what it would be like to have a father who loved her, a brother who stood up for her. But she didn't have a family like others, and so she'd preferred to keep herself apart.

"Please?" Rachel prompted, drawing Rosalie's thoughts from the past.

"All right. I'll be there."

"Oh, good." Rachel grabbed her hand and squeezed it warmly. "Come at noon. We'll have a bite to eat before the others arrive."

Rosalie agreed with a nod.

Rachel turned a grin up at Michael, then walked back toward the church.

"Old school friends?" Michael asked.

"No. Not really."

"Well, she seems nice. You should have a good time tomorrow."

"I suppose so."

Together, they turned and continued toward home.

Strange, Rosalie thought, how nice it felt to be invited, to be included among friends, when she had no intention of remaining in Boulder Creek. Would Rachel want her there if she knew Rosalie was a fraud? Legally she was Rosalie Randolph, but in actuality she was little more than Michael's housekeeper. She fixed his meals and washed his clothes and cleaned his house, and in return, she got room and board. And in a year, she wouldn't even be that to him.

She remembered the night when he'd shown her the plans for the hotel. She remembered the moment when she'd thought he might lean forward and kiss her. What would it be like, to be kissed by him, to really be his wife? What would it be like to share his thoughts, his hopes and dreams ... and his bed?

A disturbing image entered her mind, but it skittered away the moment she saw her pa standing on the front porch. As if sensing her distress, Michael took hold of her arm. She looked at him, and in that moment, she felt strong and unshakable.

"About time you two showed up," Pa said. "Preacher must've been long winded today."

"We didn't expect you." Rosalie stopped at the base of the porch steps.

Michael's fingers tightened slightly on her arm. Like a reminder that he was with her.

"Thought it was time I come calling to see how you're getting along."

"Quite well, Mr. Tomkin," Michael responded.

"Good. That's good. Glad to hear it. Now, if you don't mind, I'd like a minute or two to talk to my daughter alone."

Michael glanced down at her, one eyebrow raised in question.

She wanted to refuse. But what could it hurt? Michael wouldn't be far away.

"We can sit on the porch." She motioned to a couple of chairs.

Michael guided her up the steps and to the nearest chair. After another glance down at her, he released her arm and went inside. She hated the sound of the closing door.

Her pa leaned his backside against the porch rail and crossed his arms in front of his chest. "Seems your old man did all right by you. Rich husband. House all your own."

"What is it you want, Pa?" She sat, her hands clenched in her lap.

"That don't sound grateful."

"I'm sorry if it doesn't. I can't help that. You came for a reason. What is it?"

"Well, I'll tell you. The boarding house ain't doing no business, and your ma don't seem to have the money she should. There's things we're needing from the mercantile to tide us over until we get some new boarders."

"I can't help you, Pa. Mark stole every last penny I saved."

Her pa chuckled. "I'm not talking about a few dollars put back in a tin box. Just ask your husband for—"

"No."

"Don't you smart mouth me, Rosalie. You just smile pretty and tell that man of yours that you—"

"No!"

He grabbed her arms and yanked her to her feet. There was no time to prepare for the pain as his fingers bit into her flesh. "I've told you before not to talk back." He gave her a harsh shake. "Now, I'm not asking anything unreasonable. If you don't help, what do ya think's gonna happen to your ma?"

"Ma's done fine without you all these years. If you'd never come back, we'd all be happier."

He raised his hand to slap her, but before he could strike, his arm stopped in mid-air.

Michael pulled Glen Tomkin away from Rosalie, letting go of his wrist only so he could grab the man by his shirt collar with both hands. They stood almost nose to nose, Michael leaning down toward the shorter man.

"Let me explain something to you, Mr. Tomkin. If you ever lay a hand on my wife again, I'll break every bone in your body. Is that perfectly clear?"

"A pa's got a right—"

"You gave up your rights the day she married me." He pulled up on Tomkin's shirt, almost lifting his feet off the floor. "Now get off my porch." He released his hold.

Tomkin stumbled backward, catching his balance with a hand on the post beside the steps.

Michael didn't waste a moment on the man's furious glower. He moved toward Rosalie, placing his hands gently on her upper arms. Her face was chalk-white. "Are you all right?"

She nodded.

"Let's go inside."

She glanced toward her father. From the corner of his eye, Michael saw Tomkin descend the steps and stride away, but he concentrated on the woman before him. He sensed her dread, and it surprised him. He'd seen how fearlessly she'd faced her brother. He'd known the father and son were cut from the same cloth, and he supposed he'd expected her to be as dauntless with her father as with Mark. That wasn't the case.

"Come." He pulled her toward him, pressing the side of her face against his chest. With one hand, he stroked her hair. With the other, he stroked her back, making small circles with his fingertips. "There's nothing to fear. I'm here."

"There's nothing to fear. I'm here."

Rosalie let out a shaky sigh. The fear drained away, as if obeying Michael's words. His arms around her felt strong, sure, and safe. With her ear pressed against his chest, she heard the steady rhythm of his heart. It, too, sounded strong, sure, and safe.

She didn't know how long they stood like that, there on the porch, his arms holding her close. Time didn't matter. Nothing in the world mattered beyond the circle of his arms. As long as he held her, no one could hurt her.

Her heart skipped a beat at the thought. Did she believe it? Was it possible?

She pulled her head away from him, tipping it back so she could look into his eyes. She'd never seen eyes as blue as Michael's. Or eyes that looked at her with such tenderness.

The breath left her.

His hands moved to the sides of her face, cupping her head gently, tipping it backward. She felt more than saw him bending toward her. It seemed to take forever for his mouth to draw near. When his lips touched hers, her knees lost all strength. To keep from falling, she wrapped her arms around his neck and clung to him for dear life.

The kiss didn't last long, but when it was over, Rosalie felt as if the world had changed. She had changed.

Michael lifted his head. His hands still cradled her face

with infinite gentleness. His eyes stared down, questioning eyes, looking deep into her soul. She felt more exposed now than on the night she'd run into his room in her torn nightgown.

Fear returned. A different sort of fear. Her pa and her brother could beat her. They could hurt her body in painful ways. They could leave her with bruises and even broken bones. But Michael could do something they never could. Michael could bruise and break her heart.

She stepped back from him. "I don't think we should have done that. We won't do it again."

Michael watched her, the silence hanging thick and tense between them. Finally, he nodded. "I'm sorry. We won't do it again."

Twelve months would surely be an eternity.

16

Michael left the house earlier than normal on Monday morning. The previous afternoon and evening had been uncomfortable, the memory of that kiss lingering in his mind, teasing and tempting him. Rosalie had told him it wouldn't happen again, and he'd agreed. Trouble was, he'd like for it to happen again. And often. A crazy thing to want. He didn't plan to stay married to her, after all.

And yet he couldn't shake the wish for something more.

It was shortly after ten o'clock when he looked up from the stack of blueprints he'd been studying to see Rosalie walking briskly through town headed east. It would take her almost two hours to reach the Harrison place on foot. Yesterday, he'd offered to hire a buggy from the livery, but she'd declined. She told him she enjoyed walking. He thought she simply didn't want to accept anything from him after they'd kissed.

That kiss. A simple kiss. Yet it had changed something between them. Something he couldn't define.

As she passed the building site, she didn't glance his way. Her determination not to notice him couldn't have been more obvious. And that made him smile.

She looked even prettier than usual in that yellow dress, the wedding present from Emma Barber. The color reminded him of the flecks of gold he sometimes saw in her hazel eyes. As silly as it sounded, he wished he'd been the one to give the dress to her. In fact, there were lots of things he'd like to give Rosalie Tomkin Randolph. He'd like to give her fancy dresses and glittering jewels and outrageous hats with ostrich plumes and fabric flowers. He'd like to give her the freedom to smile more often. He'd like to give her joy and laughter. He'd like to give her more than one brief solitary kiss. He'd like to give her children. He'd like to—

"I don't believe it," he whispered as he watched Rosalie disappear from view.

When was it, exactly, that he'd fallen in love with his wife?

Rosalie had never been an expert with a needle, and at first, she felt awkward, sitting around the quilt, watching the other women working with confidence, their needles seeming to fly in and out of the fabric. But before long, she relaxed and began to enjoy the easy camaraderie that pervaded the parlor of the Harrison home.

The conversation centered on familiar, comfortable topics—Boulder Creek and the families they all knew. They talked about crops and about calving. They talked about who had been ill and who was moving away and who had arrived in the valley. They talked about babies and children. Although Rosalie added very little to what was said, the other women made her feel as if her words mattered, and that felt good to her.

"Tommy McNeal fell out of a tree by Pony Creek yesterday." Ophelia Turner threaded her needle again. "He broke his arm." She bit off the thread with her teeth. "Chad had to carry him over to Doc Upton's office."

"That boy is a caution," Priscilla Jacobs replied. "I don't know how Doris manages. I'm much younger than she is, and I can scarcely keep up with my two."

Rachel smiled. "My mother used to say she hoped I'd have a daughter one day, and then I'd know what she went through." She looked from one woman to the next, her smile growing. "I just might do that, come next winter."

Silence gripped the room for a few heartbeats.

"Rachel!" Ophelia dropped her needle on the quilt and leaned over to grab Rachel's hand. "Really? A baby? You and Norman are going to make me an aunt?"

Rachel nodded again, her eyes moist.

"What a joy," Priscilla added. "I pray you'll have an easy confinement."

"If I'm anything like my mother, I'll have no hardship. She says there wasn't anything to childbearing for her but lying still and letting nature take its course."

"And my mother said childbearing is both a blessing and a curse for women." Ophelia picked up her needle and began to take slow, careful stitches. "But I wouldn't care how terrible it was, if only I could give Chad a son."

The other women murmured sympathetically.

"Not that being Chad's wife isn't wonderful, mind you,"

Ophelia continued. "I've loved him almost from the moment I first laid eyes on him at that barn dance all those years ago, but he was so stuck on Addie Danson, he didn't even notice me." She sighed.

Rachel nodded. "I know what you mean. It wasn't easy for me to catch your brother's eye. No matter how hard I tried."

"When Chad and I were first married, I wasn't in any hurry to have a baby. I wanted him all to myself. There's nothing so wonderful as sharing love with a man." Her eyes widened, as if surprised by her own words, and a blush brightened her cheeks. She quickly lowered her gaze to the quilt.

A knowing look passed between Rachel and Priscilla. A look that made Rosalie feel excluded.

"Well, it's true, and I'm not embarrassed to say so." Ophelia drew needle and thread through the fabric before her, her cheeks still flushed. "It is wonderful. The Holy Bible says the union of a man and a woman is blessed. Why shouldn't we talk about it? We talk about having babies all the time. Why should this be any different?"

Rachel leaned forward, her voice little more than a whisper. "I don't know *why* it's different. It just is."

Rosalie felt as if she were eavesdropping on a conversation spoken in a secret code. Oh, she knew what it was they meant, but she had no firsthand knowledge. Her ma said married women had to endure the needs of a man. But that wasn't what Ophelia thought.

Unbidden, the memory of Michael's embrace, of his lips upon hers, returned to taunt her. She thought of the strength of his arms, the steady pounding of his heart. She thought of the way he'd smelled of soap and water and a dash of bay rum. She'd wanted the kiss to go on. She'd wanted ... something more.

Her own cheeks warmed. Glancing up, she found Rachel watching her. Her friend smiled, somehow communicating that they shared a special knowledge.

Once again, Rosalie felt like a fraud.

For what Michael's crew lacked in experience, they made up for in enthusiasm. The men were quick to follow his instructions, and by late afternoon, they'd made a lot of headway. It wouldn't be long before the framing of the Randolph Hotel could go up.

Michael stepped back and looked around the site. With his practiced eye, he envisioned the hotel, its board siding painted a pristine white, its name in black letters emblazoned above the awning. There would be ten sleeping rooms. Most, he realized, would remain empty at first, but he'd planned so that an addition could be made later, expanding the number of rooms. The lobby would be airy without wasting space. The dining room would be the largest individual room by far. It was where the money would be made initially. Even before the influx of newcomers to the area—brought by the railroad, which would soon begin its way up from Boise City—the restaurant would be important to his profits. Later, miners and loggers, ranchers and farmers would pass through Boulder Creek on their way north, filling his hotel to capacity.

He shook his head, silently mocking himself for the pleasure he felt. When he'd dreamed of adding a hotel to those his father had built, he hadn't imagined one like this. He'd dreamed much bigger. Something like the Palace Hotel in San Francisco. Built on the grand scale of a European palace, with its sweeping staircases, its glittering chandeliers, Turkish carpets, gilded-and-mirrored assembly halls and ballroom, and its expansive dining room, which featured foods prepared by one of the best chefs in the world, the San Francisco Palace made his plans for the Randolph Hotel in Boulder Creek seem paltry, if not downright pathetic.

But this small start, this ten-bedroom hotel, would succeed. He knew it. He felt it in his bones. For the people of Boulder Creek, Idaho Territory, this hotel was important. It meant progress. It meant growth. And for travelers through these parts, it meant a comfortable place to stay and a chance for a decent meal. There was satisfaction found, knowing the work of his hands would provide all of that.

Not that he meant to stay here and watch it continue to thrive. He belonged in a place like San Francisco or New York City. Just because he'd fallen in love with a small-town girl didn't mean they had to stay there. After all, Rosalie wanted to leave Boulder Creek, too. Of course, she planned to leave alone, not with him. Convincing her to change those plans wouldn't be easy, but it would be worthwhile. He remembered his mouth upon hers. Convincing her might be pleasant as well.

"Hey, Mr. Randolph."

The shout pulled him from his reverie.

"What do you want us to do with this rock pile?"

He started walking toward Paul Stanley. "We'll have to cart them away. Bring the wagon over and we'll toss them in."

"Yes, sir."

Michael waited as the young man climbed onto the

wagon seat, picked up the reins, and guided the team of horses to the pile of rocks, cleared from the area that would form the foundation of the hotel. One day, where those rocks were now, kitchen workers would go in and out through a doorway. Perhaps he could entice Chef Petit to come out of retirement and relocate to Boulder Creek. Wouldn't that be something? His brother would never think to do the same.

He began grabbing the large stones and tossing them into the back of the wagon. Trickles of sweat soon streaked the sides of his face and the back of his neck. Despite the warmth of the day, he enjoyed the physical labor. It had been too long since he'd rolled up his sleeves and taken part in the construction of one of the Randolph family hotels.

Several smaller rocks tumbled from their high perch, rattling their way to the ground. At least, he thought that's what caused the sound. He reached in with both hands to grab a large rock at the base of the pile.

"Get back, Mr. Randolph," Paul shouted. "It's rattlers."

But it was too late. The snakes had struck him before he saw the nest.

Paul turned to the rest of the crew. "Get Doc Upton! Quick. The boss is snake bit!"

Michael staggered back a step, keeping his eye on the nest that had been hidden among the rocks. Most of the snakes were babies. They couldn't be all that dangerous. Still, his arm burned like the dickens.

"My pa says rattlers are poisonous as soon as they hatch." Paul drew Michael away from the rock pile.

Michael stared at his arm. It felt like he'd been jabbed with a hot needle. Unpleasant, but surely not dangerous.

"You'd better sit down in the shade here, Mr. Randolph.

Best thing to do is stay calm. Doc'll probably cut the bites and suck the venom out."

His arm felt slightly numb.

A bottle of whiskey appeared before him. "Have a swig of this," someone said. He wasn't sure who. "They say it's best for snakebites."

He heard some gunshots, and his pulse jumped. He looked toward the rock pile where men were shooting the snakes. The noise started a severe pounding in his head. He took a swig of the whiskey.

"Let's get him over to his house."

Michael's vision blurred.

"How long ago did it happen?"

Was that the doctor? When had he arrived?

"Ten, maybe fifteen minutes."

No, not that long. It just happened. I just sat down.

"Easy now, Mr. Randolph. We're going to get you inside where I can work on you."

It was hot, and he was thirsty. He needed a drink. And not whiskey either. Vile tasting stuff. But he'd give a silver dollar for a glass of cold water.

"That's right, sir. You lay still on the bed. Let me have a look at that arm."

Bed? Where had his bed come from? Wasn't he sitting on the ground? No, they'd put him in the wagon. Hadn't they? And he was wet. Drenched in sweat. Was May always so hot in this country?

No, it wasn't the heat of day. It was moving all those rocks. That's why he was sweating. That's why he felt so tired, so dizzy, so strange.

"Two bites. Maybe three. I'm afraid they may have hit a

vein." The doc's voice sounded so far away. "We'll have to wait and see."

Waves of nausea hit Michael as he spiraled into darkness.

"Michael? I'm here. Can you hear me?"

Rosalie. Sweet, little Rosalie. He'd wanted to tell her he loved her.

17

After Doc Upton left, called away to an accident at one of the logging camps to the north, Rosalie was grateful when Yale James stayed behind.

"You're no bigger than a mite, Mrs. Randolph," he'd told her. "You wouldn't have the strength to lift Mr. Randolph if he needed it. If you don't mind, I'll stay, in case you or the boss have need of me."

"Thank you, Mr. James. That's very kind of you."

"If it's all the same, I'd be pleased if you'd call me Yale. And I'll just bed down on the porch. You holler if I can be of help."

Rosalie told him where he could find something to eat if he got hungry, and then returned to her bedside watch. She talked soothingly to Michael. She cooled his fevered brow with a damp cloth. She worried and she prayed for him. And eventually, some time after midnight, she drifted into an exhausted sleep.

It was the ugly sound of violent retching that brought her awake again. Michael had rolled onto his side, his head hanging over the edge of the bed as he emptied his stomach. Rosalie shoved the washbasin beneath him on the floor, then grabbed his shoulders and tried to keep him from falling out of bed.

"Yale! Yale, help me!"

Michael's body seemed determined to rip itself in two. He flailed the air with one arm, nearly striking the side of her head.

"Yale!"

"I'm here, ma'am."

Yale's hands replaced hers on Michael's shoulders, and Rosalie stumbled backward, her heart racing.

Was he going to die?

"You go get some cool water for him to drink," Yale said. "He's gonna need it when he's through here."

"Yes. Yes, I'll get some water." She hurried from the room.

God, please don't let him die.

In the kitchen, she leaned her hands against the table and let her head drop forward.

He won't die. I won't let him.

Rosalie had nursed her ma and her brother through sickness. She'd cared for them, and they'd come through, right enough. Michael would come through, too.

But what will I do if he does die?

She knew nothing about his family, nothing other than he'd come to Idaho from San Francisco. Who would she tell if he died from a snakebite? And how would she live? She had no money of her own. Would what he had become hers? Or would she have to leave this house? Would she have to return to her ma's boarding house, to her pa's rule?

Shame welled up inside. Her husband could be dying, and her thoughts were only for herself. What kind of woman had she become? And besides, he *wouldn't* die. She would see to it that he didn't.

Pushing away from the table, she went to the sink and began pumping the handle until water streamed from the spout. Then she grabbed a pitcher and filled it to the brim.

"It's not right, Father. The Palace Hotels belong to me. You told me so when I was only six years old."

"I didn't know about Dillon then."

"But I'm your legitimate son."

"Dillon is not at fault for his birth. I am. If I'd known—"

"If you'd known, you'd never have married my mother, and I'd have never been born. That's how you'd prefer it, isn't it? Answer me. Isn't it?"

"No, Michael, I've always been proud of you. But I'm proud of Dillon, too. If the two of you would learn to compromise ... You were friends once. You could make Palace Hotels—"

"It's too late for that. You've made your decision. I'll go off to Boulder Creek, and I'll make certain that what's mine stays mine."

"Michael—"

"You'll hear from me in a year."

"Michael—"

Rosalie drew the cool rag across her husband's fevered brow. He was so still, his face pasty-white, his lips nearly blue, his breathing shallow. The spells of vomiting had stopped at last, replaced by moments of delirium, excessive thirst, and cold sweats.

After two nights with little sleep, Rosalie was exhausted, but she refused to leave him, not even at night when Yale was there. She wanted to be with him if he needed her. She had to make certain he got well.

Michael mumbled something, and she knew he dreamed again. Sometimes she heard him say names. Father. Kathleen. Dillon. Louise.

Who was Louise? And who was Kathleen? Strange that it was the women's names that stayed with Rosalie, that made her realize again how little she knew about the man she'd married.

When Doc Upton had been by that morning, he'd said Michael was through the worst of it. She found that difficult to believe when he was so pale and drawn.

How could a couple of days change a man so much? She remembered him on the front porch on the day he'd kissed her. He'd worn his dark suit jacket, white shirt and collar, and a black tie. No hat. He'd removed his hat, and the sun had glinted off his golden hair. She remembered the strength of his arms. She remembered the taste of his lips, and the rapid beating of her heart in response. He'd been strong and full of life. So full of life.

She reached forward and swept his hair off his brow, her fingers lingering on the crown of his head. Even with two days growth of stubble on his face, he was the most handsome man she knew.

Fearfully and wonderfully made. Wasn't that what the Good Book said? That people were fearfully and wonderfully made. And surely that had never been more true than it was for Michael Randolph.

What am I thinking?

She closed her eyes, trying to drive away the growing

attraction she felt for this man in the bed. The one she'd worried about and prayed for. The one she'd tended to day and night. But she mustn't let herself care. The year would end. Her marriage would end. He would go his way. She would go hers. She must not care for him. Only a fool would let herself care.

~

"Michael, this is Dillon." Kathleen put her arms around Michael's shoulders. "He's going to live with us. I hope you'll treat him like your own brother."

Michael eyed the other boy with suspicion, then asked his stepmother, "Why is he going to live with us? Where's his own family?"

"His poor mother died of the influenza. His ... his father ... Dillon never knew his father, but that isn't his fault. He's a good boy. Be kind to him, Michael. He's not been as privileged as you. I think you can be the best of friends."

~

"Great friends," Michael said softly, turning his head on the pillow. "I promise."

Rosalie leaned forward. "Michael?" She brushed her fingertips across his forehead. "Michael?"

"I promise."

"Michael, can you hear me? Please wake up." She leaned closer.

He did as she asked. He opened his eyes and looked straight at her, yet without recognition in his gaze. "He was my friend." His voice sounded husky from disuse. "Why did I do it?" His eyes fluttered closed again.

"Michael?"

But he had slipped away from her once more.

"Have I ever told you you're the loveliest young lady in all San Francisco, Miss Overhart?" He asked the question as they waltzed around the ballroom of the Palace Hotel. "Why waste your time on someone like Dillon when you know I'm the better man?"

"I know no such thing, Michael Randolph. And what have you against your brother?"

He ignored the question. "Palace Hotels will come to me, not Dillon. He'll have to leave San Francisco to make his fortune elsewhere."

"It's true then, the rumors I've heard? Dillon's adopted?" Her eyes widened. "But the two of you look so much alike, I never believed it."

He could have said more, but he did more damage by saying less.

"He's going to be all right, Rosalie." Doc Upton placed his stethoscope into a black leather bag. "You keep spooning broth into him and cooling him with sponge baths. Best thing for him now is rest while the poison works its way out of his system."

"But shouldn't he be awake by now?"

"He's been a mighty sick man. A snakebite isn't anything to make light of. Three of them should have killed him. If they'd hit a vein, he wouldn't have made it. He's mighty lucky to be alive. Sleep is the best medicine for him now."

Rosalie stared down at Michael, wishing he would wake up and thankful he would survive.

"And what about you, young woman? Are you getting any sleep? In a bed, I mean."

"I sleep well enough in the chair there."

Doc Upton lifted her chin with his index finger. "You let Mr. James watch over your husband tonight while you get some sleep. There's no point him being here to help you if you won't let him lift a finger. I saw there's a bed in that room across the hall. You make use of it tonight. Hear me?"

She shrugged, thankful he hadn't guessed the bed he'd mentioned was her own. "I'm all right. Really, I am."

"I mean it, Rosalie. You don't sleep in that chair tonight. You let Yale watch over your husband."

"All right. I will."

"I'll stop by again tomorrow morning. I want to see you rested by then."

"I will be."

She followed the doctor from the bedroom, down the stairs, and out onto the front porch, watching until he'd driven his buggy out of sight. Then she sank onto the porch swing with a weary sigh. A light breeze brushed her skin, refreshing her, while the sound of bees buzzing over the morning glories soothed her ragged nerves.

Doc Upton was right. She needed sleep. She would let Yale sit with Michael tonight. Yale had told her to let him do that from the very first, but she hadn't wanted to leave Michael's side. Yes, sleep would do her a world of good, especially now that Michael was out of danger.

As the morning sun warmed her cheeks, she imagined it

was Michael's hands cradling her face. The breeze brushed across her lips, and she thought of his mouth, how gently it had pressed against hers. Perhaps, when he was well, he might cradle her face and kiss her mouth once again. What could it hurt? After all, he *was* her husband.

18

Yale leaned back in the chair, his long legs stretched before him, crossed at the ankles. His gaze was fastened on the man in the bed, watching Michael's chest rise and fall in a steady rhythm. A good sign. And it seemed to Yale that there was a bit more color in the man's face. Another good sign. He reckoned he wouldn't be needed at the Randolph house after this night. He'd lay odds Michael would regain consciousness by sun-up. He was glad, for both Rosalie's and Michael's sake. He didn't know either of them well, but well enough to like them.

He yawned and thought he wouldn't mind a few winks himself. He allowed his eyelids to drift closed.

It would be good to get back to his own place. He had plenty of repairs to make in that old house, and with working two jobs in town and spending the nights here, those repairs were taking longer than he'd expected. But he supposed all of his efforts would prove Skylark's father was wrong about him. He wasn't some saddle bum moving through this valley. He had a place of his own now, plus thirty-nine dollars put back and another fifteen dollars in wages coming for this week's labors.

Michael's crew had decided to keep going while their boss was laid up. Yale had become the unofficial foreman, he supposed because he helped out at the Randolph house each night. He figured the others saw that as a sign he knew what to do.

He grinned, proud that he'd figured out how to read the blueprints. He hadn't made it much past the flyleaf of a first-grade primer, and he'd often felt as if his brain capacity wouldn't make a drinking cup for a hummingbird. But once he'd set his mind to it, reading the blueprints hadn't been all that hard.

Skylark would be plenty proud of him, too.

How he missed her. Did she miss him too? He sure hoped so because he was ready to let her hogtie him with matrimonial ropes. More than ready, in fact. Eager.

Rosalie awakened in the middle of the night, her skin covered with a light sheen of sweat, her heart hammering at an alarming rate. She'd dreamt of Michael and rattlesnakes, of sickness and death. But it was only a dream, she told herself. Michael was getting better. The doctor had said he was out of danger, and rest and time were all he needed now. Besides, Yale would have called for her if there'd been a change for the worse.

She closed her eyes and willed herself to go back to sleep. It didn't work. She needed to see Michael for herself. She wouldn't find peace until she did. After getting out of bed and donning her robe, she made her way in the dark to the bedroom across the hall.

A lamp next to the bed cast a soft glow over the room. Yale was asleep in the chair, his chin resting on his chest. Rosalie spared him only a quick glance before approaching the bed.

Michael didn't look as he had in her dream. There was no pain written on his face, no perspiration on his forehead, no restless jerking of his head. He lay still, his color normal, his breathing steady.

She released a sigh of relief.

As if he'd heard her, Michael opened his eyes. Her breath caught in her throat. He saw her. For the first time since the incident on Monday, he truly saw her.

"What day is it?" he asked in a gruff whisper.

"It's Thursday. Thursday morning." She glanced toward the window. "The sun won't be up for a couple more hours."

"You should be asleep."

"I needed to check on you." She straightened away from him.

"Don't leave."

She leaned forward again. "I won't." She brushed the hair off his forehead. The action had become something of a habit over the past few days. "How do you feel?"

A frown puckered his brow. "Not great. What happened?" He paused a moment, then answered his own question. "Rattlers."

"Yes."

Behind her, Yale said, "Mrs. Randolph."

She looked over her shoulder. "He's awake, Mr. James."

The cowboy stood and went to the opposite side of the

bed. "You had your wife clean worried, Mr. Randolph. Fact is, whole town's been asking about you."

Rosalie stepped to the washstand beside the bed and filled a glass with water from the pitcher. "Here. Drink this." She lifted his head off the pillow with one hand as she held the glass to his lips with the other.

For a moment, he simply stared at her. Then he raised his hand, placed it over hers on the glass, and drank. When he finished, he lay back, already drained of energy. He couldn't seem to keep his eyes open.

"Stay ... Rosalie."

What else could she do? She glanced at Yale. With a nod, he left the room. She sat in the chair and watched as her husband slept.

The next time Michael opened his eyes, sunlight streamed through the window. He lay still, staring up at the ceiling, trying to recall all that had happened. Piece by piece, some memories fell into place. The final one was of Rosalie, standing over his bed, her dark braided hair hanging over her shoulder as she gazed down at him. He turned his head on the pillow and found her, seated in a chair beside the bed. She slept with her arms on the bed, cradling her head.

Three days. He'd been ailing for three days. And she'd been there with him all the while. He understood that without being told.

You must care for me a little, Rosalie. What would you do if I told you I love you?

Yes, he loved her. How many days was it since he'd realized it? Also three. The same day he'd reached into that nest of rattlers. For some reason, that thought made him smile. Because he suspected that she might strike out at him too, if she knew how his feelings had changed.

I'm a sucker for underdogs who fight against the odds. Is that why I fell in love with you?

Maybe it was. And if so, it didn't bode well for the two of them. Look at the mess he was in with Dillon because of it. If he hadn't loved his brother, if he hadn't trusted him, he wouldn't be fighting for what was rightfully his. For six years, he and Dillon had been as close as any two people ever were. For the next ten years, they'd been rivals in just about every way possible.

He focused his eyes on Rosalie again. She stirred and turned her face away from him.

Falling in love with her wasn't the smartest thing he could do. He had enough trouble in his life. He didn't need another complication. But he did love her. Wrong or not, trouble or not, he loved her. And somehow, he would have to make her love him, too.

19

***

Boredom drove Michael mad. Stark raving mad. For the last two days, since leaving the delirium behind, he'd done nothing but sip broth and stare out the window at a blank blue sky. For two days, all he'd been able to do was think about things he couldn't do and the things that needed done.

"Can't you fix me anything to eat besides soup?" He looked up from the lunch tray. "A man needs real food."

Rosalie's eyes narrowed. "Mr. Randolph, you're as surly as an old grizzly bear just out of hibernation. Do you know that?"

"I need out of this bed. I've got work to do."

"Doc Upton said rest was the best thing for you." She rested her fists on her hips in a stance of defiance. "And you're going to stay right there until he says otherwise."

"I'm rested!" He looked toward the nearby chair. "Where are my trousers?"

She held her chin at a lofty angle, a smile tugging at her mouth. "They're on the dresser."

"Well, hand them to me."

"No. Not until you eat your lunch."

It was a stand-off, and Michael knew she'd won this round.

"I'm eating it." He picked up the spoon and ladled soup into his mouth.

She grinned in triumph. "I'll check later to see how you're doing."

"Don't bother," he snapped. "I'll be over at the building site."

"Of course you will." She left the room, laughter in her voice.

He ground his teeth together. If he was strong enough, he'd—

Blast her, she was right. He hadn't enough strength to leave the room to use the necessary. There was no way he could go back to work at the hotel site.

He frowned. She was right about something else. He was as surly as an old grizzly bear. A smile replaced the frown. He supposed he needed to change that. His current behavior was no way to make a woman love him, especially not one who was just as stubborn as he was.

His stomach chose that moment to growl. He looked down at the bowl of barley and beef soup. His first bite had told him how good it was, and he was hungry. If he wanted his strength back, he needed to eat whatever she put in front of him.

There wasn't a bite of food left by the time Rosalie reappeared in the doorway to his room.

He motioned to the tray. "Satisfied?"

"Yes. And I'm sorry for the way I spoke to you."

"No, it's me who's sorry. I was being unreasonable. You were right. You were right about everything."

She shook her head. "I feel guilty."

"*You* feel guilty? I was the old grizzly bear. Not you."

"I swore to myself I would take good care of you, make sure you got well. It's the least I can do after everything that's happened, you being forced to marry me and all."

He winced inwardly. Guilt and obligation weren't what he wanted Rosalie to feel when she was with him.

Michael patted the side of his bed. "The problem is I'm bored. Why don't you sit down and talk awhile? That would cure my boredom."

The request seemed to surprise her.

"I shouldn't. I've got to go into town for some supplies."

"Shopping can keep."

"Well, I—"

"Please."

Rosalie's instincts told her to turn and leave the room and ignore the pleading look in his eyes. She owed Michael Randolph plenty, but keeping him company wasn't part of their bargain. It was dangerous to be this close to him. He made her think things she shouldn't think. He made her feel things she shouldn't feel. He made her want things she couldn't have. The smart thing would be to turn and go.

She sat down on the chair beside the bed. "I can't stay long. There's work to be done."

He didn't smile, yet something about the way he looked at her felt like one. And when he spoke, the gruffness was gone, the voice turned almost tender. "Tell me, Rosalie. If you had no work awaiting you, what would you do for fun? A full day of it."

A full day of fun? A day without work waiting to be done? She shook her head. "I don't know."

"Come on. You can think of something."

The way he watched her made her feel strange on the inside. As if, with a look, he'd pulled her closer to him. Not physically but emotionally.

"All right, then. Tell me one of your favorite memories. From when you were a little girl."

She didn't have to call up the memory. It came in an instant. She pictured herself as she'd been lifted onto Skylark's horse. She could hear her own laugh of excitement. Oh, it had been a glorious day.

"Come on. Tell me."

"It was my ninth birthday. Skylark's gift to me was a ride on Dark Feather, her horse. It was the nicest gift I ever got. I didn't do much but go in a tight circle, but I thought it was wonderful. Then Skylark got up with me and we went round and round the churchyard." She thought of her friend, riding up the street to tell her Yale James had kissed her. "Skylark still rides that same horse today."

"And did you have a horse of your own?"

"No. We couldn't afford it."

"But you wanted one, didn't you?"

She shook her head, hating that he'd read her so well. She *had* wanted a horse. She'd longed to go for rides with her friend. She'd wished she could walk to the stable, saddle up, and gallop away from her unhappy home. But money had never been plentiful in the Tomkin house, not before her pa left and certainly not after. Even during the times when the boarding house had done well, there'd been too many other needs, too many improvements to the house itself—a porch to build, the siding to paint, new curtains for the windows. There'd been nothing left over for Rosalie's childish desires. Eventually, the wish for a horse of her own had been forgotten, tucked away with other wishes and dreams that would never come true.

If Michael could have done it, he'd have given her a horse right then and there. That wasn't possible. But if given the chance, he would give her a day with nothing to do but lie beneath the sky and find funny shapes in the clouds. If it was within his power, he would give her whatever would make her happy. A horse. A home in San Francisco. A restaurant to manage. He would give her the world on a platter if he could.

All of a sudden, Rosalie stood. "I must get to town. The day is wasting." Her cheeks were flushed, and she didn't meet his gaze. "Is there anything you want from the mercantile?" She picked up the tray from the washstand and left the bedroom before he could answer.

Ever since Michael's sixteenth birthday, there'd been one thing he'd wanted—to own and manage the Palace Hotels. Not even love for his family had come before that desire. The business had been his single obsession, from the moment he'd awakened in the morning until the moment he'd retired for the night. He'd expected to marry and have children one day, of course, but even then he'd known the business would come first.

How was it possible that a woman, that *this* woman, had become more important to him than Palace Hotels? He'd known Rosalie one brief month. They were married but they were also strangers. In contrast, he'd grown up in the grand hotels John Thomas had built. Twenty-six years worth of memories were of suites and ballrooms, kitchens and laundry rooms in the Palace Hotels. The hotels were his life.

Kathleen had told him that he would know when he met the right woman. Meeting that one perfect woman, she'd said, would change him in an instant. He'd thought his stepmother said it because she disapproved of Louise, but perhaps she'd said it because it was true. Kathleen had promised that when he fell in love, nothing would be more important to him from then on.

If I had to choose, would Rosalie come first or Palace Hotels?

Michael closed his eyes. What was he thinking? He didn't have to choose. Rosalie was his wife. He could accomplish the work he'd been sent here to do and still earn her love.

20

Nothing in Skylark's life had ever looked so wonderful as her first view of Boulder Creek as the Danson family carriage rolled in to town on their return from Boise. If only she could stop long enough to ask Rosalie about Yale. Was he well? Had he found other work? But her father had no intention of stopping until they reached the ranch, and Skylark had to be satisfied with drinking in the familiar town as they passed through.

"What's that?" Naomi, her five-year-old sister, asked.

Skylark looked out the other side of the carriage. There was a new building going up between the church and Sigmund Leonhardt's house. "I don't know. Mother, do you know?"

"No, dear. But it's too large to be a private home, I would think."

How could so much change in town in only a few weeks? Fear gripped Skylark's heart. And what if Yale's feelings had changed too?

When the carriage stopped at last in front of the ranch

house, Preston and Naomi hopped out and raced inside. Skylark wanted to do the same, but she waited for her father to help her down, not because she needed it but because she wanted to impress upon him that she was a grown woman. She'd learned a few things during her weeks in exile. One was that she had to restrain her more enthusiastic nature if she wanted to convince her father she was old enough to know her own mind and heart.

Without being asked, Skylark herded her brother and sister upstairs and told them to change out of their traveling clothes. She then went to her room to do the same.

Freshly washed and clad in clean chemise and open-leg drawers, she was reaching for a pink-and-fawn tartan gown when she heard a light rapping.

"Skylark?"

"Come in, Mother."

The door opened. "Frosty wasn't expecting us back," her mother said, referring to the cook, "and we are sadly lacking in supplies. Would you mind going into town with me?"

"Now?" Skylark's heart leapt with excitement. Maybe she would see Yale. "No, I don't mind."

"Good."

A suspicion sprang to life. Had her mother invented this as a reason to go to town, just so Skylark might see Yale James? She felt certain that was true.

"You finish getting dressed," her mother said. "I told Frosty to have the buggy hitched up for us. As soon as you're ready, we'll go."

"I'll be ready in less than five minutes."

She turned away and immediately slipped her arms into the sleeves of the clean gown. Her fingers, made clumsy by her haste, fought with the hooks and eyes. Even so, she was downstairs in under five minutes.

As she climbed into the waiting buggy, she wondered if her father had objected to the ruse. He'd surely seen through the flimsy excuse for the trip back to town. Frosty would never allow the larder to get so short on supplies that he couldn't feed a bunch of cowboys, let alone be unable to feed the family.

As if reading her thoughts, her mother said, "Your father and Mr. Simpson are looking over the cattle in the west range. I don't expect them back until late."

"Will he be angry with you when he finds out?"

"Maybe for a short while." Her mother grinned as she slapped the reins against the horse's rump. "But he'll come around. He wants you to be happy, Skylark. That's all he's ever wanted."

"Mother." She waited for her mother to look at her. "Papa's a lucky man."

"So is Yale James."

Rosalie stood outside of Barber Mercantile, the basket on her arm holding flour, cornmeal, and sugar. She debated stopping in to see Ma before she walked home but decided against it. She didn't want to chance an encounter with her pa.

"Rosalie!"

She glanced up as a buggy rolled to a halt before her. "Skylark?"

Her friend jumped out of the conveyance and flew toward her. In an instant, they were hugging each other. "It's so good to see you, Rosalie. It feels like I've been gone for a lifetime."

"It felt like that for me too."

Skylark stepped back. "I hoped and prayed you wouldn't be gone yet. I was going to walk to the boarding house to see when Mother and I were finished with our shopping."

"But I—"

Skylark's mother stepped onto the boardwalk. "Hello, Rosalie. How is your mother?"

"She's fine, Mrs. Danson." As she said the words, she hoped they were true. She'd seen little of Ma since the wedding, and as long as Pa was around, Ma was in danger of *not* being fine.

"Good. Tell her hello for me, would you?" Addie Danson looked at her daughter. "You two have a nice visit. Skylark, I'll come by the boarding house for you in about half an hour."

"Mrs. Danson," Rosalie said quickly, "I ... I'm not going to the boarding house."

Addie raised an eyebrow.

"I ... I don't live there any longer."

"You don't live there?" Skylark stared at her with wide eyes. "Why not? Where do you live?"

Rosalie felt a flush rise in her cheeks. "I live with my husband."

Skylark's mouth gaped. For one of the rare times in her life, she appeared to be speechless.

"His name's Michael Randolph. He's come to Boulder Creek to build a hotel." She glanced in the direction of the building site.

"My goodness," Addie said. "We were away longer than I realized."

"He bought the Pendleton house. That's where we're living."

The way Addie Danson looked at Rosalie made her want to squirm. She was afraid the former schoolmarm would guess her thoughts as she'd often done when Rosalie was one of her students.

Finally, Addie relented. "It seems you two have a great deal more to talk about than expected. I'll come by Rosalie's home in half an hour." She started to open the mercantile door, then turned, reached out, and touched Rosalie's cheek. "I hope you'll be very happy, dear."

"Thank you."

Without another word, Addie went inside the store, the door swinging closed behind her.

"Tell me!" Skylark demanded. "Tell me everything."

"There's not much to tell." Rosalie started walking along the boardwalk.

"Not much to tell. Criminy! You're *married*!" Her friend caught her by the elbow, drawing her to an abrupt halt. "I'm going to bust clean open if you don't tell me what happened. How did you meet? Who is he? Was it love at first sight?"

Rosalie stared at the wooden planks of the walkway. What was she supposed to say? Her friend expected something romantic or poetic. And the truth was anything but either of those.

"Rosalie?" Skylark's voice had softened. "Rosalie, what's wrong?"

She took in a deep breath. "Nothing's wrong. There simply isn't much to tell. Michael stayed at the boarding house when he first came to Boulder Creek. That's how we met. He's a nice man. It all happened quickly."

"When can I meet him? We saw the men building over

near the church. Is that where the hotel will be? Is he there now? You can take me over and introduce me."

She almost gave Skylark a hug, thankful for a way to change the direction of her friend's thoughts. "He's not there now, but Mr. James should be."

"Yale?" Skylark turned to stare up the street. "He's building the hotel?"

Rosalie nodded. "He's working for Michael a few days a week and at the sawmill the rest of the time. Mrs. Barber says he's buying the Hadley place, over near Pony Pass."

"Would you mind if we went by the hotel site?"

"Of course, I don't mind."

"I thought I would die of missing him, Rosalie. It was awful down in Boise. Just awful. Papa tried to give all of us a good time, but without Yale, nothing worked for me. Nothing."

What would it be like to love someone the way Skylark loved her cowboy? Did it happen to ordinary people or was Skylark one of the special few? Could it happen to her?

She pictured Michael, sick and pale in his bed. Was there more to her determination to make him well again than she allowed herself to believe? She shook her head. No, there wasn't. And she wanted nothing to do with Skylark's romantic fantasies.

But then she remembered that moment on the porch of her new home. She still felt Michael's arms embracing her, felt his lips brushing softly against her own. She recalled all the crazy, careening sensations that had raced through her at the time, feeling them as intensely now as she had then.

Should she tell Skylark the truth? The whole unvarnished truth. Should she ask her friend what to do?

Before she could decide, Skylark sucked in a breath and hurried away from Rosalie.

Yale had started climbing the ladder when he heard someone call his name. But not just any someone. Skylark. His heart turned over like a flapjack in a frying pan as he glanced down. There she stood, looking even prettier than he remembered.

"You've come home," he said.

"Yes."

"You're a sight for sore eyes, Skylark Danson."

"So are you."

"Back for good?"

"I think so." She glanced down the street. "Mother's at the mercantile getting some supplies. I've only got a moment."

He nodded. "I've only got a moment, too. The boss doesn't pay me to stand around jawing."

"Rosalie told me you're working for her husband."

"Sure am. This here is gonna be his hotel. Fancy that. A hotel in Boulder Creek."

She took a step closer to him. "I'm glad you didn't have to leave town to find work." The way she looked at him made him feel soft as bear grease on the inside.

"I won't be leaving, Skylark. I'm gonna have a ranch of my own."

"It's true? What Rosalie said. You're buying the Hadley place?"

"I am." He grinned. It felt good to tell her. It felt good to own a piece of land. It felt good to know he had something to build upon. A life he wanted to build with her. "It'll take more money than I've got now and plenty of work to make it succeed. But I can earn what money I need, and I ain't afraid of hard work."

"Neither am I." Skylark glanced down the street again. "I should go. But you need to know, I missed you, Yale."

"I missed you too." He wished he was better at words. He wished he could say what all was in his heart. "Something fierce."

"Will you ... will you come see me at the ranch?"

Yale shook his head. "I don't reckon I'd be welcome just yet. I've got things to prove to your pa."

"Then when will I see you?" Tears glittered in her eyes.

He wanted to hold her and tell her he loved her. He wanted to ask her to marry him. But he wasn't about to do that in the middle of town with a bunch of men looking on. He'd have to hope she understood all that went unsaid.

"Church tomorrow," he answered at last. "Church every Sunday. And maybe when you come to town to call on Mrs. Randolph."

"Mrs. Rand— Oh, you mean Rosalie." Her face brightened. "Of course. I'll be in town often to see Rosalie. Perhaps you and I will run into each other then."

"I reckon we might."

She stepped closer to the ladder. "Yale James, I love you." With a smile as bright as a June sunrise, she turned and walked toward her waiting friend.

Watching her go, seeing the gentle sway of her pretty plaid dress, tempted him to go after her, throw her across the saddle of his horse, and light out for parts unknown. But then, that wouldn't prove he was the right kind of man to ask for her hand in marriage. No, when Yale married Skylark, her pa would be right there watching them do it. Her pa was going to know without a doubt that Yale was the man for his daughter.

He chuckled as he climbed the ladder. Never in a thousand years would he have thought he'd be domesticated by a pretty little filly named Skylark.

21

The act of getting fully dressed left Michael exhausted. He sat down on the chair beside the bed and drew in slow, steady breaths, glad Rosalie hadn't returned from town. If she saw him the way he was now, she would order him right back to bed. And if she ordered him back to bed, he would say something he'd regret later. He didn't want to give her another reason to call him an old grizzly bear.

Sure, he was a lousy patient. There was no getting around it. He hadn't been sick more than a few days in his life and those back when he was a youngster. He wasn't used to doing nothing for days at a time. He hadn't been aware of the first few days, but the past two had crawled by. All those hours alone in his room gave him too much time to think. To think about his father and Dillon. To think about anger and rivalry and the mistakes he'd made. Too much time to begin to doubt.

Take this competition with his half-brother, for instance. He'd been sure he was in the right. He'd known what he wanted and he'd pursued it. He wasn't the sort of man who doubted his decisions once they were made. But now it seemed some of his actions hadn't been noble. He had cause to regret more than one of his choices.

He shook his head, trying to drive off the thoughts that plagued him. He couldn't change anything right now. He needed to be up and about. He needed to get his strength back, and that couldn't be done in this bedroom. He rose and walked to the door. Leaning against the jamb, he listened for sounds coming from the kitchen. The house was silent. Good. He wanted to be out on the porch before Rosalie got back.

He made his way down the stairs, gripping the handrail the entire way. A wave of lightheadedness washed over him as his feet touched the main floor, and he paused to steady himself. The dizziness soon passed so he continued on. Not long after, he sank onto the porch swing and drew in a deep breath of the fresh spring air. A smile curved his mouth as he closed his eyes. A breeze rustled the leaves in nearby trees. Song birds chirped in their branches. Enjoying the sounds, he felt his strength returning. Being outside was exactly what the doctor should have ordered for him, not more time in bed.

When he opened his eyes several minutes later, he saw Rosalie round the bend in the road. Another young woman was with her. Someone he didn't recall seeing before. He gave the stranger a cursory glance, then returned his gaze to Rosalie. She looked pretty in her dark pink gown. It was a color she wore regularly. No, come to think of it, it was the dress itself that was familiar to him. It dawned on him that his wife had few dresses to choose from.

That wouldn't do. She was his wife. She should have whatever she needed. Or, for that matter, whatever she wanted. As soon as possible, he would order her a dozen new gowns.

Pleased with his decision, he was smiling when Rosalie looked his way. He saw her eyes widen with surprise, then narrow with displeasure. He was in for a scolding. She'd warned him not to get out of bed until the doctor had said it was all right, and she would be fit to be tied over his disobedience. He would be in for a thorough tongue lashing the instant the other young woman went on her way.

Michael would never admit it to Rosalie, but he'd grown fond of her feistiness.

He rose from the swing as the two women climbed the steps onto the porch.

"Michael, I didn't expect to find you outside." Her tone was mildly censuring and very wife-like.

Wife-like. He liked the sound of that too.

"You remember that Doc Upton wanted you to stay in bed a few more days."

"The doctor is wrong." Michael looked at the other young woman. "Perhaps you could introduce me to your friend.."

"I'm Skylark Danson," she said before Rosalie had a chance to reply. "I trust you intend to make Rosalie happy."

"Skylark!" His wife's eyes widened.

Michael smiled. "I intend to do my level best, Miss Danson."

"Good." She held out her hand. "Then we can be friends."

Michael took measure of the young woman as they shook hands. She was attractive with golden skin, dark brown eyes, and shiny black hair. Judging by the gown she wore, her wardrobe probably wasn't as limited as his wife's.

But if she'd been spoiled by wealthy parents, he didn't perceive it. There was more to her than that, he would wager.

"Michael." Rosalie took hold of his arm. "Please sit down."

He heard the tender concern in her voice, and that alone made him feel stronger. Without a word of objection, he did her bidding.

"Oh, look. There's Mother already." Skylark glanced from the road to Michael. "Don't get up, Mr. Randolph. Rosalie told me about your accident. I'll explain to Mother that she can meet you another time." She gave Rosalie a quick hug. "I'll come back to town as soon as I can." Skylark hurried down the steps and out to the road. A moment later, the two women in the buggy disappeared from view.

"She must be a close friend," Michael said, his gaze returning to Rosalie.

"Yes."

"Then I'm glad she decided she could be my friend, too."

Rosalie felt that wonderful-terrible trembling in her stomach, and her lungs seemed starved for oxygen. "It's Skylark's nature to be friendly with everyone."

His mouth tipped. "I see. Well, then I'm glad I didn't make her go against her nature."

The teasing tone of his voice made her heart feel funny.

"Sit down and join me, Rosalie." He patted the seat on the swing beside him.

She shook her head. "I've got baking to do."

"Just for a moment."

Why was it so difficult to tell him no?

"You can spare a minute or two."

Their agreement had been for her to keep his house and cook his meals. He hadn't said anything about sitting on a porch swing and wasting away an afternoon.

Despite herself, she eased into the seat beside him.

He smiled at her a moment before looking toward the mountains. "It must have been nice, growing up in this valley. It's beautiful here."

He needed a haircut. Was that something a wife was expected to do, too?

"More quiet than the city. Peaceful. San Francisco is all noise and bustle, people rushing from here to there."

Who cut his hair when he was in San Francisco?

"I didn't think I was going to like it here, but I was wrong."

"Why did you come to Boulder Creek?"

"You know why. To build a hotel."

"But it's more than that. Isn't it?"

A shadow passed over his blue eyes. "I needed to prove something."

"What?"

"I'm not sure anymore."

The rattle of a wagon disturbed the silence and drew their attention from each other and back to the road to see who was passing by. But the wagon was coming up the lane. Rosalie recognized Norman Harrison as the man who held the reins, but the woman beside him wasn't his wife Rachel.

"Louise?" Michael stood.

Dread fluttered in Rosalie's stomach. He'd called that name while he was deathly ill.

Michael stepped toward the porch rail as the wagon halted below him.

"Here you go, Miss Overhart." Norman hopped to the ground, then offered his hand to help their visitor descend.

Rosalie couldn't detect a trace of dust on the woman's striped lavender and white gown nor was there a strand of her silvery-blond hair out of place beneath her bonnet.

Louise Overhart held onto Norman's hand and leaned toward him. "Thank you so much, Mr. Harrison. I should have been lost without you."

"My pleasure, miss." He grinned, then touched his hat brim in the direction of the porch in a silent greeting to Michael and Rosalie.

Louise approached the porch. "Michael, they told me in town that you had an accident. They said you'd been deathly ill. I came the moment I heard."

"I'm all right, Louise."

As she arrived at the bottom of the porch steps, she finally noticed Rosalie, still seated on the swing. Her pale eyes widened in question as she returned her gaze to Michael.

"I wasn't expecting to see you in Boulder Creek," he said.

"I wanted to surprise you."

"You did."

Louise arched her eyebrows. "Have you forgotten all your manners, Michael Randolph?" She held out a hand, clearly a signal that he should come forward and assist her up the four steps.

Rosalie's anger came out of nowhere. She rose from the swing and stepped to Michael's side, effectively keeping him from moving away from the rail. "This is Michael's first day out of bed, and he shouldn't exert himself."

Holding her skirt and petticoats out of the way, Louise

climbed the steps unaided. "Michael, perhaps your nurse can wait inside while you and I talk."

"I am no one's nurse, Miss Overhart." Rosalie lifted her chin, trying to mimic the look of disdain she'd seen in Louise's own eyes. "I am Michael's wife."

22

Michael would have found the situation amusing if it had happened to someone else. Especially if it had happened to Dillon. But it wasn't happening to someone else. It was happening to him—and to Rosalie.

"Michael?" Louise's voice was filled with disbelief.

He turned toward her. "Miss Overhart, may I introduce you to my wife, Rosalie Randolph. Rosalie, this is Louise Overhart, a ... *friend* from San Francisco."

Rosalie's fingers tightened on his arm. "Sit down, Michael. You look ghastly."

He wasn't surprised. He felt ghastly. His legs wobbled, and there was a sick knot in his stomach that had nothing to do with snakebite. He complied with her request.

"I don't ... I don't believe it." Louise grabbed hold of the porch railing as if it were a lifeline. Her cheeks had lost all their color.

Michael glanced over at Rosalie. The anger in her eyes had died, leaving behind that sad, haunted look he'd seen too often in the past. He'd hoped he'd seen the last of it, but now he was responsible for its return.

"Rosalie," he began, "perhaps I should—"

Rosalie released his arm. "I will leave you two alone. When you're ready to go up to your room, call for me." She turned and disappeared inside the house.

He continued to stare at the door long after it closed behind her.

"Michael?"

Reluctantly, he turned toward Louise. A wave of regret washed over him. It wasn't her fault that he didn't love her, but he had been careless with her feelings. He could have paid special attention to any number of young women of San Francisco society, but he'd chosen Louise because of Dillon. Dillon had been smitten with her, and Michael had wanted her for that reason alone. Not for marriage. Not forever. But he'd allowed her to think he meant to propose one day. Perhaps he would have if he hadn't met Rosalie, if her father hadn't forced them to wed.

Forced? At the time, it had seemed he'd had little choice. Not without breaking the rules of this blasted competition. But he no longer regretted this unusual union. It wasn't an inconvenient match. He wanted to be married to Rosalie.

But that didn't solve the hurt he'd caused Louise. It didn't excuse him for what he'd done.

"It's true, isn't it?" she asked in a whisper. "You've married that girl?"

"Yes, it's true."

"Why would you do it?"

He sighed. "It's a long story, Louise. I should have written to you. I meant to. We haven't been married long, and then the accident happened. I had no idea you would come to see me. I wouldn't have expected your father to allow it."

"Father doesn't know I'm here." Tears pooled in her eyes. "Oh, Michael, why?" She turned away from him, pulling a handkerchief from her handbag to wipe away her tears.

Michael rose from the swing and moved to stand beside her. Rather than looking at Louise, he stared at the rugged mountains that ringed the valley. "I was unfair to you, Louise, and I'm sorry. You have every right to hate me. I wish there were words to say, something I could do. But there is nothing." He shook his head.

She grabbed his arm. "Come back to San Francisco with me. Mr. Dover will be able to help you. He's a fine attorney. Surely an inappropriate marriage can be easily broken."

"I don't need Christian Dover's help." He covered her hand with his own. "Louise, I love my wife."

She jerked her hand away from him. "I don't believe it."

"But it's true."

She slapped him.

He deserved it. It didn't matter that he hadn't intended to hurt or betray her. There wasn't anything he could say that would change the truth. He'd been unkind, unfair. Cruel, even.

"You, sir, are a cad."

"True enough. There's no excuse for what I've done." He took a deep breath. "But I was never the right man for you. And even less so now."

"What do you mean?"

"I mean the hotels and society balls and everything that was my life in San Francisco. They're no longer as important to me as they once were."

"You surely don't mean to stay here in this little town."

He shrugged. "That will be up to Rosalie."

"I see. Then I shall leave you." She looked in the direction of town.

He wanted to offer to take her to the boarding house. But his head spun and he quickly realized that he'd expended the last of his energy.

"Sit down. I am perfectly capable of finding my own way."

"I know you are." He settled onto the swing again. "You might not believe it now, but I am truly sorry for hurting you."

"Your father will hear of this," she said with a toss of her head before hurrying down the porch steps.

Rosalie waited, but Michael never called for her. Finally, unable to keep herself from doing so, she went to the parlor window and glanced out between the curtains. He sat alone on the swing, his elbows resting on his knees, his head held between his hands. Louise was nowhere in sight.

She went to the door. "Michael?" He didn't answer, and she felt a sting of alarm. She approached him, placing her hand on his shoulder. "Michael?"

He looked up. "Rosalie, did you ever take a good long look at yourself and hate what you found there?"

"Come with me. You need to get back in bed. It won't seem so bad once you've rested." She drew him to his feet, then put her arm around his back. "Help me get you upstairs."

They moved slowly and without speaking. It seemed a

long time before they reached his bedroom. Once he was on the bed, she started to back away.

"Don't go yet. I owe you an explanation."

"No, you don't. You don't owe me anything, Michael. I understand." Her chest and throat felt tight, so tight it hurt to speak.

What was there to explain? She had eyes. With one look at Louise Overhart, Rosalie had known she was the reason he'd wanted an annulment at the end of a year. Why wouldn't he?

"Please, Rosalie."

She didn't want to hear about the woman he loved, the reason why he didn't want a scandal, the woman for whom he would leave Rosalie. She didn't want to hear any of it. "Not now, Michael. I can't just now."

She turned and fled the room.

Lying on his back, Michael stared up at the ceiling of his room. What a mess he'd made of everything. What a fool he'd been.

Oh, he knew plenty about business and industry, about building and operating a successful hotel. He was a master at making deals, and he was a shrewd judge of character. He'd earned the respect of his employees. He could be a charming escort and a popular host. He was benevolent to those in need. He was seen as a pillar of society.

But his private life was somewhat less than stellar. He'd failed the people who should have been most important to him. He'd turned his back on Dillon because of something that wasn't Dillon's fault, something out of his control—his paternity. He'd fought his brother, and he'd blamed his father.

Blamed them and fought them for what? Pieces of real estate.

He'd hurt Louise, too. He'd been careless with her feelings. Dillon had been fond of her, so Michael had done everything he could to take her away from him. Not because Michael had wanted her. Not because he'd loved her. No, he'd done it out of spite. He'd done it to prove he could best his brother.

And what about Rosalie? Was it too late to make things right with her?

He closed his eyes. He wasn't sure how it happened, how he'd lost his heart to her so completely. He knew he was a better man for loving her. He couldn't explain it but he knew it was true. For many years, his only goal had been to become the heir of the Palace Hotels. That was no longer what he wanted most. More than anything, he desired to earn the love of Rosalie Tomkin Randolph.

23

By Monday morning, Michael knew what he had to do. His decision would change his life, but he believed he would be a better man for it. Hopefully, he would be the kind of man Rosalie could love, now and forever. Before noon, he posted two letters—one to Dillon Randolph in Newton, Oregon, the other to John Thomas Randolph in San Francisco, California—then he walked to the boarding house and asked to speak to Louise.

His mother-in-law eyed him suspiciously. "She's not here. She left this morning. Hired a rig and a driver to take her down south. Said she was gonna take the Oregon Short Line out of Nampa. Go back to California."

"I see. Thank you, Virginia." He placed his hat back on his head, prepared to leave.

"Michael? I don't know what this is about, but I hope you're not gonna hurt my Rosalie. Life's been hard enough for her."

He shook his head. "I promise you. I have no intention of hurting your daughter."

"I'm glad to hear it." She looked at him hard for several more heartbeats. "And I reckon I believe you."

"You can believe me, ma'am." With a nod, he turned and walked away from the boarding house.

His next stop was the hotel site. He had to admit that he was pleased with the headway his crew had made while he was recovering from the snakebites. Yale had told him how things were progressing, but seeing it with his own eyes brightened his spirits considerably.

He spoke briefly with the men, then excused himself and returned home, his pace much slower than when he'd left the house. The outing had left him drained of energy. His health was much improved, but he wasn't himself yet.

The front door opened as he climbed the steps, and Rosalie came out. He stopped, his hand grabbing the post. Neither of them spoke. In truth, they'd spent the previous day in silence, and he hadn't seen her that morning before he left the house.

How do I win your heart, Rosalie? You guard it so closely.

It wasn't that he didn't know how to woo a woman. But never before had a woman resisted his wooing like this one. And never before had that woman's response mattered as much as it did now.

"I had to post some letters," he said, as if she'd asked him to explain. He moved forward, wanting to be near her. He wanted to see her expressive eyes. He wanted to take her into his arms and kiss her sweet lips.

Her eyes widened, as if she'd guessed the direction of his thoughts. Like a wild horse boxed into a narrow space, she looked ready to bolt.

He stopped still. He would have to go slowly. He would have to win her trust before he could win her love. "I know you have good reasons to question what I tell you, Rosalie, but I hope you'll give me a chance. I plan to be here for you, whenever you need me."

"Michael, don't make promises you can't keep."

Unable to stop himself, he reached forward and gently touched her cheek with the tips of his fingers. "Just give me a chance. I won't let you down."

Rosalie's skin tingled beneath his touch, and a terrible wanting welled up inside her. A strange and foreign sensation. Her heart ached for things she couldn't have. Things she couldn't allow herself to want.

He pulled his hand away. "Tomorrow, let's go for a drive, up to the ridge." He pointed toward the mountains to the north. "There's a spectacular view of the valley. I was there a few weeks back and saw it for myself. Would you join me tomorrow? I'll hire a rig. I'm not up to a horseback ride yet."

There were at least a hundred reasons why she should decline. Instead, she said, "I'll pack a lunch. We can picnic up there."

He smiled.

She felt wonderful and confused and warm and scared all at the same time.

"I'm rather partial to your fried chicken."

"Then that's what we'll have." For a moment, she thought he might lean down and kiss her. Alarmed that he might think she was waiting for him to do so, she took a step back. "I'd better get on with my chores." Quickly, she turned and went inside.

～

Riding astride, Skylark cantered Dark Feather toward the east. Her destination was a section of land known as the old Hadley place. Yale wouldn't be there. He worked at the mill on Mondays. He worked hard all the time, and he did it for her. She loved him all the more for it, although she missed him something fierce.

The small Hadley house came into view, and she slowed her mount as they drew closer, then reined to a halt when they reached the yard. She stared at the log house. It was a single story with two, maybe three rooms. There were three windows that she could see, but two of them were covered with shutters. A simple, ordinary place in the mountains, the kind of house young families lived in all over the western territories and states.

She smiled. Yale had bought this for her. He'd taken the jobs at the mill and with Mr. Randolph in order to buy this house and land. And he'd done all of that so he could marry her. Not that he'd said so in so many words. Not that he'd actually proposed. But there were some things that didn't have to be said out loud in order to be understood.

She nudged her mare forward with her heels, stopping when she was close enough to peer inside through the only uncovered window. Through the wavy glass, she saw the sitting room. It was clean but nearly empty. Only a chair and a wooden footstool near the fireplace. Beyond the sitting room was a kitchen. A wall separated the first two rooms from the bedroom, a bed in view beyond the open door.

That would be her bed once they were married. Hers and Yale's.

Prickles of excitement shivered up her spine. She wasn't

entirely certain what went on beneath the covers on a marriage bed, but she had a fair idea. She'd grown up on a ranch, after all.

As heat rose to her cheeks, she backed Dark Feather away from the house.

"I'll make pretty curtains for all of the windows," she said aloud. "And the rug in my bedroom at home will fit in the sitting room. Mother has some paintings in the attic that I can hang on the walls."

Dark Feather huffed.

"I suppose I should ask Frosty to teach me to cook so we won't starve to death."

She laughed at the thought. Although it wasn't funny. She didn't know how to do anything in the kitchen. Would Yale be disappointed with her as a wife because she couldn't fix him a decent meal?

"I'd better get home and start those lessons right now." She turned the mare's head away from the log house, and they lit out toward Rocking D.

24

As the hired rig moved along the road, Rosalie took note of the changing season for the first time. Wild-flowers—purple and yellow and white—dotted the gently rolling floor of the valley. The air was fresh. The sky was an unmarked canopy of blue, stretching from mountain top to mountain top. A perfect day for a picnic.

"Have you been to that ridge up there?" Michael pointed toward their destination as the horse started up the steady slope of the mountain.

Rosalie shook her head.

"Quite a view. It's a good place to think. A good place to consider your future."

She cast a sidelong glance at him. What had he meant by that?

"I'm famished," he continued. "I could smell that chicken frying earlier, and it's made my mouth water ever since."

She relaxed. What could a picnic with Michael hurt? They would sit on a blanket and have their lunch, and then they would go back to Boulder Creek. It was a harmless way to spend an afternoon. Why not savor it? When was the last time she'd taken an afternoon to spend in such a pleasant way? She took a deep breath of air. Yes, an afternoon to not worry about anything, a few hours to simply enjoy herself, was exactly what she needed.

She glanced once again at the man by her side. Would it be so awful to take pleasure in being with him, too? She had no future with him. That had been decided at the first, even if he seemed to be trying to change the bargain now. Still, it made good sense to be on friendly terms with him.

Above the rattle of the harness and the clipping of the horse's hooves, she became aware of some sort of whining sound. She glanced around, trying to figure out where it came from.

Michael grinned at her. "When I hired the rig, I was warned to keep an eye out for bears. Have you ever had trouble with bears?"

"On occasion. They come down out of the mountains at night now and then."

"I wouldn't want to see one. Not when I'm having a picnic with such a beautiful lady. Good thing I brought something to scare bears away."

What on earth did he mean? She was about to ask when the road they'd followed through the pines burst into the open. Michael pulled back on the reins, bringing the buggy to a halt, then hopped down to the ground. He turned and offered his hand to Rosalie. "Come on. Let's have a look at the view."

She allowed him to help her down. Side by side, they walked to the edge of the table-flat ridge. Below them, Crescent Valley stretched for miles. Long, curved, and narrow, the valley held fields of green dotted with cattle and horses and smaller sections in shades of brown, the earth tilled and planted with crops. Pony Creek unfurled like a ribbon from one end of the valley to another.

She heard the whining sound again. "What *is* that?"

"Our bear protection."

"Our what?" She frowned up at him.

He responded with a grin. "Come have a look." Taking her hand, he pulled her toward the buggy. When they reached it, he dropped her hand and reached beneath the seat, pulling out a wicker basket.

Again, she gave him a questioning look.

He slipped the closing loop from its button and opened the lid. Inside was a gold and white puppy.

"Mrs. Barber assured me she would be great at keeping away bears with all the racket she makes." He pulled the puppy from the basket, then held her toward Rosalie. "She's yours."

"Mine?" She took the furry bundle from his hands. "A puppy?"

"I wanted to give you something special, and the mercantile was fresh out of diamond necklaces. I thought Princess might be a good choice."

"Princess."

The puppy's whines grew louder, and Rosalie drew her close, nuzzling her with her chin. "You're precious."

"So you like her?"

Rosalie glanced up, and her heart skipped, as it so often did when she looked at him. "She's perfect. I always wanted a pet, but Pa wouldn't have it. Not even a cat to keep mice away."

"Then I'm glad I got her. Forget bears. It's enough to see you smile."

~

Michael and Rosalie sat on the blanket spread in the shade of tall ponderosa pines and ate their picnic of fried chicken, biscuits with honey, cooked green beans seasoned with bacon and onions, and rhubarb pie, all the while trying to keep Princess from grabbing food from their plates. They laughed often and said little, making the puppy the center of their attention, yet never more aware of each other than they were right then. Occasionally, they reached for something at the same time, and their hands touched for an instant. Only an instant. Yet the sensations lingered long after they'd pulled back their hands.

Time melted away. Place became unimportant to Michael. Boulder Creek seemed on the opposite side of the world rather than a wide patch in the valley below. Problems and worries and fears and disappointments belonged to others, not to them.

Eventually, appetite sated, Michael lay on his back on the blanket, the puppy curled into an exhausted ball beside him. Idly, he stroked her satiny coat. "My little sister has a dog that looks a lot like Princess."

"You have a sister?"

He turned his head to look at her. She, too, lay on her back on the blanket, but she stared up at the sky.

"Yes. A half-sister. Her name's Fianna, and she's ten years old. I also have four half-brothers. Sean is eleven. Colin is twelve. Joseph is thirteen." He paused, then added, "And then there's Dillon. Have I mentioned him to you before? He's closer to my age than the others." He rolled onto his side, cupping the side of his head with his palm while bracing his elbow on the ground. "Fianna looks like Kathleen, my stepmother. Dark auburn hair and green eyes. Very beautiful. Kathleen's the reason I have so many younger siblings. The moment my father—he'd been a widower a few years by then—laid eyes on her, he was smitten. I never knew a man could lose his head so thoroughly over a woman until I saw John Thomas with Kathleen." His voice softened. "Now, I know it for a fact."

He sat up and lifted the sleeping puppy out of the way. Then he took hold of the blanket and pulled it toward him, drawing Rosalie along with it.

"I never had time ... or the inclination ... to memorize love poems, but right now, I wish I had." He reclined again, bracing himself with his elbow and forearm. Their faces were mere inches apart. "I wish I could tell you how beautiful I find your hair, that it's like the richest furs." He touched her hair with his free hand. "I wish I could tell you how the gold in your eyes has a light of its own, and how I can see your joy and your sorrow so clearly in them." He moved his fingers to trace the curve of her mouth. "I wish I knew the words to describe what I feel when we kiss."

Her lips parted, and he heard her tiny gasp.

"Maybe you feel it, too."

Their mouths touched, and instantly desire spread through him. Somehow he forced himself to proceed slowly. With infinite care, he slid his hand around to the back of her head and deepened the kiss. He waited, half-expecting her to push him away. She didn't.

His fingers deftly pulled the pins from her hair. He wanted to see her dark chestnut locks spread across the blanket, glimmering in the sunshine, but he dared not break the kiss for fear she would remember to shove him away, to resurrect the wall between them.

She sighed, her breath warming his lips.

He longed for more. They were, after all, husband and wife. But he couldn't allow himself to shatter the fragile trust she'd placed in him. It was too soon. When she was ready, she would let him know. He had to wait for her signal.

And perhaps that signal would have come that very afternoon, if not for a particular Princess. But at that precise moment the puppy scrambled over Michael's back, landing on their faces.

Rosalie drew back from Michael, and Princess dropped the rest of the way to the blanket. There was a moment of absolute silence, and then the puppy lunged toward Rosalie, licking and nipping in her endearing, aggravating puppy manner.

Rosalie laughed. "You silly thing." She sat up, drawing Princess into her arms like a beloved child.

Michael gave a half-hearted smile when she glanced at him. He wasn't quite as enamored with the puppy as he'd been before.

After a few moments, he got up and walked toward the edge of the grassy plateau to stare at the valley below. Not that he needed to look at it. He simply wanted a moment to bring his emotions under control.

"Michael?"

He turned.

She stood at the edge of the blanket, her thick, tousled hair spreading in a dark mass over her shoulders, looking every bit as beautiful as he'd known it would. She cradled the puppy against her chest and looked entirely too fetching.

"It's been a beautiful day, Michael. I'm glad you brought me here." She looked down. "Thank you for giving me Princess."

He drew in a deep breath and let it out. "You're welcome. I want you to be happy, Rosalie." *I want you to know that I love you. I want to win your love in return.*

Color flushed her cheeks. "Perhaps it's time we went home."

Understanding dawned. She was afraid of her feelings for him. She was unsure of herself and of what she wanted. But Michael would give her the time she needed to discover he was the right man for her. He hoped to give her a lifetime to love him in return.

"Sure." He stepped toward her. "Let's go home."

The easy camaraderie Rosalie had felt with Michael on the mountainside didn't vanish with their return to the house. Nor did the strange swirl of emotions his kisses had ignited inside of her. Remnants remained right up until the moment Michael announced it was time to retire for the night.

"Allow me to escort you upstairs." He bowed.

No one had ever bowed to Rosalie before. Not in such a manner. And it left her feeling awkward and unsure. And more than a little out of control. She glanced toward the kitchen. "I should check on Princess one more time."

"And wake her? Don't you dare."

With a nod, she turned to put out the lamp.

Just as the light flickered and died, a loud knock sounded at the door. Rosalie's gaze darted to her husband's silhouette. A visitor at this time of night could only mean trouble.

Michael opened the door. There was a moment's silence, then, "Mrs. McNeal?"

"May I speak to Rosalie? There's been an accident at the boarding house."

She felt an icy chill. Had Pa finally gone too far? "Ma? Is it Ma?" She hurried to the door, grabbing hold of Michael's arm when she reached him, needing it to steady herself.

Doris McNeal shook her head. "No, dear. It's not your mother. It's Mark. He's fallen and broken his neck." Her voice lowered. "I'm afraid he's dead. Your mother's beside herself."

It surprised Rosalie, the sharp sadness she felt. Sorrow for what she'd never shared with Mark rather than for what they had shared.

"She needs you," Doris continued. "You'd best come straight away."

"Yes. Yes, of course." She glanced up at Michael.

"I'll come with you," he said softly.

"Perhaps you shouldn't. You've been up a long time today and—"

"I'm well enough to be with my wife when she needs me."

His words and the strength behind them sent a strange quiver coursing through her.

He placed his hand over hers where it still gripped his arm. "Whatever you need from me, I'll do."

"Thank you," she whispered.

Then, together, they followed Doris McNeal to the boarding house.

25

The next week passed in a blur for Rosalie. It wasn't mourning her brother that consumed her. It was worry over her mother. After Mark's burial, Ma shut herself in his old bedroom and refused to come out. Rosalie braved her pa's foul moods and drunken insults to sit beside her mother for long hours every day, coaxing her to eat, bringing her hot cups of tea and cold glasses of lemonade. Michael returned to work at the hotel site across the street from the boarding house, and several times each day, he crossed that street to ask about Rosalie and her ma. The gesture touched her heart more than he knew.

On this mid-afternoon, the air warm and still, not even a hint of a breeze to stir the curtains at the open window, Rosalie opened a book and began to read aloud to her ma. "'You don't know about me without you have read a book by the name of The Adventures of Tom Sawyer; but that ain't no matter. That book was made by Mr. Mark Twain, and he told the truth, mainly. There was things which he stretched, but mainly he told the truth.'"

She glanced up from the page. Ma stared, unblinking, at the ceiling. Was she listening to the story? Rosalie couldn't tell.

"'That is nothing. I never seen anybody but lied one time or another, without it was Aunt Polly, or the widow, or maybe Mary. Aunt Polly—Tom's Aunt Polly, she is—and Mary, and the Widow Douglas is all told about in that book, which is mostly a true book, with some stretchers, as I said before.'"

Rosalie smiled as she read, enjoying the cadence of the words.

"He'll see us all dead," Ma said into the brief silence.

"What?" She looked up from the book again.

"It's my fault. All my fault."

"Ma, what are you talking about?"

"It's the drink." Ma turned her head on her pillow. "I wasn't the best mother to you, Rosalie, and I'm sorry about that."

"Oh, Ma."

Tears glittered in her mother's eyes. "I wanted Mark to be the sort of man I could be proud of, but he had too much of his pa in him. The drink and the meanness. I should've known it'd come to this."

"I don't understand, Ma. Come to what?"

Ma rolled onto her side, turning her back to Rosalie. "You go away. You leave me be. If he thinks I've been sayin' things I shouldn't, he'll make us pay."

"Ma, come home with me. Don't stay here. You don't have to stay here. Not now."

"I can't leave. This is my home. I won't be taken from it."

She laid a hand on her mother's arm. "No one's going to take you from it if you don't want to go." She stood and set the book on the nearby stand. "You try to get some sleep."

She waited until her ma's breathing became even, then she left the room and went downstairs, glad her pa was nowhere in sight. Stepping outside, she leaned her shoulder against one of the posts that supported the porch awning. Her gaze moved across the street to the two-story building taking shape. Michael stood near the rear of the hotel, calling instructions to one of his workmen at the top of a tall ladder.

She felt oddly content, looking at him. She thought of all the tender, considerate things he'd done ever since they'd learned of her brother's death. No, even before that. Even before her pa had forced him to marry her. He'd been there for her in so many ways.

Am I falling in love with him?

She sat on the top step.

Is this what it feels like?

She looked across the way again, watching Michael as he moved with those long, confident strides of his. He was a strong man, yet he'd never used that strength to threaten or hurt her. She'd seen him angry, but he'd never allowed his anger to control him. As those thoughts ran through Rosalie's mind, Princess got up from her place in the shade and ambled after Michael. The puppy scratched at his pant leg, begging for attention. Absently, while he talked to another of his workmen, Michael bent low and scratched the puppy behind her ear.

Does he love me? Is that what he's been trying to tell me all this time?

There was so much to lose. Could she trust him not to hurt her? If she let herself love him and admitted her feelings, she would never be free. Her life would belong to him rather than to herself.

Is loving him worth the risk?

She thought of Ma, lying upstairs in Mark's old bedroom, curled up on the bed, afraid of her husband's anger, afraid of life itself. If Rosalie made a mistake, if she was wrong about Michael, could that be her future?

He turned and looked in her direction. She saw him smile. Then he leaned down, picked up Princess, and started across the street. Before he reached her, she rose to her feet, one hand gripping the post.

What if it's too late? What if I love him already?

Michael saw the weariness stamped on Rosalie's face, and his heart ached for her. It frustrated him, how little he could do to help.

"How's your mother?" he asked.

"The same."

"You need to rest. Let Mrs. McNeal or Mrs. Barber sit with Virginia for a few hours. They've both offered."

"I can't."

"Yes, you can, and I think you should do it. Now."

She stiffened. Not the reaction he'd wanted.

He set Princess down and watched as she scampered up the steps to scratch at her mistress's skirt, begging for Rosalie's attention the same way she'd begged for his minutes before. Rosalie reached out and pulled the puppy into her lap, laughing when Princess licked her face.

Michael lowered himself onto the step below her.

She met his gaze and her smile vanished. "I'm afraid, Michael."

"I know you are."

"It's too hard."

"No, it isn't. You can trust me."

"How do I know? How can I be sure?"

"Try me and see." He took hold of her hand. "I'm here for you, Rosalie. Nothing's going to change that."

She stared into his eyes for a long time before pulling her hand free and rising. He stood, too.

"I'll be home to fix your supper," she whispered, then turned and went inside.

Michael stared at the closed door. What could he do to help Rosalie and her mother? He had to do something.

He swung his gaze toward the Pony Saloon. "That's something I can do." With long, ground-eating strides, he headed for the saloon. He found his father-in-law just where he'd expected, sitting at the bar, downing a glass of whiskey.

"What do you want?" the man asked as Michael approached the table.

"I want to make a deal with you."

Tomkin's eyes narrowed. "What sort of deal?"

"How would you like to make five hundred dollars?"

"Doin' what?"

"Sell me the Crescent Valley Room and Board."

Tomkin snorted. "It's worth more than that."

"No, it isn't." Michael sat and leaned his forearms on the table. "It isn't worth that now, and it'll be worth even less when the hotel opens. I can undercut whatever price the boarding house charges. I can do it for as long as it takes. You know I can. And I will as long as you hold any claim to it or live there."

"What're you talking about? You gonna throw me and my wife out—"

"Not Mrs. Tomkin. Just you." He lowered his voice. "I can have the money for you tomorrow. You sign your name to a piece of paper and move out, and I'll give you five hundred dollars." He reached into his pocket and pulled out twenty dollars, tossing the bills onto the table. "There'll be a bonus if you agree to it tonight."

Tomkin stared at the money lying on the scratched table surface.

"Oh, there is one more condition."

The older man glanced up. "What?"

"You stay away from Mrs. Tomkin from now on. The same way you stay away from Rosalie. You don't talk to her. You don't go to the boarding house. You don't ever ask her for money again."

Anger flashed in Glen Tomkin's eyes, but greed apparently made him cautious. He narrowed his eyes. "A thousand. I'll do it for a thousand dollars."

"Seven fifty," Michael countered. "That's my last offer. I won't make it again." He stood up.

"You've got yourself a deal." Tomkin slapped the palm of his hand against the table and barked a laugh. "You're an idiot. That hotel of yours ain't gonna make you a plug nickel, and now you've bought yourself a boarding house to boot." He took a quick drink of whiskey, then wiped his mouth with his sleeve. "And because you call yourself a gentleman and won't go back on your word, I'll let you in on a little secret." It was his turn to lower his voice. "I wasn't planning on staying in this two-bit town much longer anyway." He laughed again.

Michael didn't let his face reveal his thoughts. It didn't

matter to him how long Glen Tomkin planned on staying in Boulder Creek. As far as he was concerned, it was seven hundred and fifty dollars well spent as long as he stayed away from Virginia and Rosalie. The boarding house had little to do with it.

He shoved his chair up to the table. "You get your things together and be out tonight. I'll meet you at the bank at ten o'clock in the morning."

26

Stratus clouds, stained pink against a pewter sky, drifted above the mountain peaks as Rosalie walked home from the boarding house. When she opened the door, she could hear the sizzle and pop of meat frying on the stove. Normally, the odors wafting from the kitchen would have been tantalizing, but she wasn't feeling hungry at the moment.

"Michael?"

He appeared in the doorway to the kitchen, Rosalie's apron tied around his waist.

"Is it true?" she demanded.

"Is what true?"

"You've bought the boarding house?"

He nodded, looking pleased. "It's true. I was hoping to tell you myself."

"Why would you do it?" Her voice rose, and her hands clenched into fists at her sides. She shook with rage as she glared at him. "What will Ma do now? It's her home. It's her business. And you're putting her out."

"Wait a minute. I'm not putting her out. The place is hers."

"But Pa said—"

"I'm buying it to give to your mother." He crossed the parlor in several quick strides. " I told your father to pack up and get out. Did he?"

Her anger drained away. "Yes, he—" She stared up at him. "He left. He moved into Mark's old room above the saloon."

"Is your mother alone at the boarding house?"

"No. Mrs. Barber said she'd stay with ma tonight."

"Good. I'm glad she's not alone." He brushed wisps of hair off her forehead.

A shiver of pleasure passed through her, but she ignored it. "Why did you do it, Michael?"

"For you, of course." He tipped her chin upward with an index finger. "I did it for you, Rosalie. I'd do anything for you."

They sat across from each other at the kitchen table, eating the beef steaks. Michael smiled, enjoying the way the lamplight played across Rosalie's hair.

"How did you get your scar?" she asked as she set down her knife and fork.

"What scar?"

She pointed. "I saw it when I was nursing you through your sickness."

"Oh. That one." He touched the place on his left side. "A boyhood accident. Dillon and I took a silver tray from the butler's pantry and used it to slide down the staircase. We crashed at the bottom. Broke an expensive vase. Mrs. Jergens, our housekeeper, was not pleased." He laughed at the memory.

"Tell me about your family. Where you come from. Everything."

"Everything?" He smiled again. In fact, he couldn't keep from smiling when they were together like this. "Where do I start?"

"Start at the beginning."

He envisioned his father and stepmother, Dillon and the rest of the Randolph children, Mrs. Jergens and Mr. Harvey, the butler. He saw the Randolph home in San Francisco and the Palace Hotels in some of the biggest cities in the country. They were his family, his home, his past. The memories were bittersweet.

"I guess the beginning would be when John Thomas, my father, came to America from Ireland. He was poor, had nothing at all, except for a willingness to work hard and a dream to make something of himself. He made his way across the country to California and began mining for gold."

Michael felt a tugging at his heart as the memories multiplied, some good, some not so good.

"My father was one of the lucky ones. He found enough gold to buy his dream. He built a hotel fit for kings and queens. He called it the Palace Hotel."

His jaw clenched, as if resisting the continuation of the story, but he went on. It was time he went on. It was time he told her the whole truth.

"For a number of years, my father kept a mistress, an Irish woman of common birth. Like my father." He paused, trying to recall her name. Had he ever known it? Perhaps not. "When he met my mother, a woman whose family was from the cream of American society, he knew he wanted to marry her. He had great plans for the Palace Hotel in San Francisco, and she was a part of those great plans. Three days before his marriage, he gave his mistress some money and sent her away."

Michael pictured his father—handsome, proud, determined, ambitious. He wondered if John Thomas had loved his mistress. He wondered if it had been easy for him to be rid of her or if he might have suffered from what he'd done. Michael had never asked him. He'd been too angry to ask.

"I was born nine months to the day after my mother and father wed. My mother died while I was still an infant. Mrs. Jergens, the housekeeper, was the closest I had to a mother in those early years. When I got a little older, I traveled with John Thomas as he began building other Palace Hotels. Denver. Chicago. New York. It was quite an experience for a young boy."

"But you were lonely," Rosalie said. It wasn't a question.

"Yes, I was."

"Why do you call him John Thomas?"

He thought for a moment. "To punish him, I guess. To put distance between us. It started when I was sixteen."

She was silent for a while before saying, "Go on. You said you were lonely."

"Yes, and I guess my father was lonely, too, because I remember how very different he seemed after he met Kathleen O'Hara. They married the year I turned ten. Five months later, Dillon came to live with us."

"Dillon? But I thought—"

"That he was the son of my stepmother? No, he was born to my father's mistress after he sent her away. Dillon's birthday is just a few days after mine. His mother sent him to my father when she knew she was dying."

"Oh, Michael."

"I didn't find out the truth until we were sixteen. After that, I resented him. Dillon, I mean. But my father too."

Rosalie reached across the table and covered his hand with hers.

"There wasn't any good reason for my antagonism toward Dillon. I didn't feel the same way about my other half-brothers and sister, the children born to my father and Kathleen. But I resented Dillon. I resented any affection John Thomas showed to him and I resented every one of his successes in school and in business. I resented everything that went right for him."

He stopped speaking, not wanting to look at those things again. He'd put his thoughts on paper. He'd sent his letters. He'd done what he could to put the past behind him. This wasn't a night for old memories. He wanted this to be a night of new beginnings.

"You don't feel that way anymore, do you." Again, her words were a statement of fact rather than a question.

He sent her a tender smile, loving her all the more for understanding. "No, I don't feel that way anymore." Then, to change the subject, he pointed to a small line of puckered flesh on her arm. "Now it's your turn. Tell me how you got your scar?"

She answered without hesitation. "I used to fight with Mark a lot. When I was seven, he shoved me into a tree. There was a broken branch with a sharp point. It only took about five stitches to close it up."

"I'll bet you've been fighting someone most of your life."

"Most of it."

Holding her hand now, he rose and came around the table, then drew her up to stand before him. "You don't have to fight anymore." He nuzzled her earlobe.

Rosalie's insides went all aflutter and her heart hammered in her chest. She tried to look away from him but couldn't. He didn't hold her there. He wasn't even touching her except for his finger beneath her chin. Yet she was powerless to move. She could only stand and wait for his mouth to brush against hers.

And, at last, it did.

She wrapped her arms around his neck and gave herself over to his kisses, savoring the taste of him. Her senses reeled. She felt both weak and strong. It was too much like a dream and yet more real than anything she'd ever felt.

"Rosalie," he whispered.

She silenced him with her lips, wanting to feel the fire of his kisses, wanting to drown in his arms.

Michael lifted his head slightly. "Maybe we should—"

"Let's not talk anymore."

With a swift but gentle movement, he had her cradled in his arms, his mouth once again delighting hers. Her eyes were closed, but she felt him taking the stairs two at a time and knew it was into *his* room that he carried her.

There was still a faint light coming through the bedroom window, enough to let her see his face when he lay her on the bed and straightened above her. He stood motionless, looking down at her, as if waiting for something. She didn't know what. She didn't care what. She only knew she felt a terrible loss now that she was no longer in his arms.

"Michael."

"I love you." His voice was low and ragged.

Her heart hammered. Had he said he loved her? Could he mean it?

"I love you, and I want to be your husband." He paused, letting the words sink in. "But only if you want to be my wife."

"I do," she whispered, knowing it was true, no longer caring what else it might mean to surrender to him.

"I'll leave if you tell me to." But the tremor in his voice said it was the last thing he wanted to do.

"Don't leave." She lifted her arms, beckoning him closer. "Please don't leave."

"I'm going to give you good memories, Rosalie. Only good ones."

27

Rosalie was in the mercantile the next morning when the news arrived in Boulder Creek.

"The railroad's coming!"

Within a matter of minutes, it seemed every citizen of the town was packed into the store, voices buzzing excitedly.

"This will mean more to us than statehood," Doc Upton proclaimed. "Think how much faster I can get medical supplies when they're needed."

"Be a whole sight easier to ship our crops to market, too," Ted Wesley stated.

Emma Barber could scarcely contain her exhilaration. "The town'll grow faster than ever. Business will boom for certain. Everyone of us'll benefit."

Rosalie caught sight of Michael. He stood near the entrance and watched her with a secret sort of smile, his gaze gentle and loving. It made her feel all strange inside, flooding her with memories of their night together, making her forget those around her or the excitement about the railroad. Slowly, he made his way to her through the crowd. Her pulse quickened as he drew near.

When he reached her, he said, "Big news for Boulder Creek."

That was when she remembered it. She pictured the two of them on the parlor floor, bent over the blueprints of the hotel. "This was your secret, wasn't it?"

He raised an eyebrow, as if he didn't understand her meaning.

"This is why you knew the hotel would succeed."

He grinned. "You found me out."

"Will it make as much difference as they say?"

"It will make even more than they imagine." His arm went around her shoulders, and he drew her close against his side.

The day would come, she feared, when her heart would be broken, when Michael would realize he didn't love her, couldn't love her, and then it would be over. He was from a wealthy and privileged family. She was a small-town girl with few refinements and fewer illusions of what life had to offer. His father's mistress had been a common woman, like her, and he'd cast her aside. Wouldn't Michael do the same one day?

But she didn't want to think about that now. She returned her attention to those around her. The townsfolk were planning a celebration for that very night. Before long, the women were scurrying away from the mercantile, on their way to their individual homes to bake their favorite dishes for the festivities.

That night, seated against a far wall in Doc Upton's barn, Skylark—along with her parents—observed friends and neighbors as they stepped through the wide doorway. Skylark didn't care who else came to this celebration. She was waiting for Yale.

Her mother leaned close to her. "I remember the first barn dance I attended. It was after the harvest. The dirt floor had been swept clean, and the air smelled of fresh hay." She pointed toward the opposite wall. "The long tables looked just the same as they do now. White cloths with platters and bowls of food everywhere. That night there were Chinese lanterns hanging from the rafters."

Musicians stepped onto a makeshift riser and began to play.

Looking at her mother, Papa asked, "Remember our first dance?"

"Of course I remember. I remember everything about that night. Especially you."

"And I, you." He kissed her mother's temple.

"Papa," Skylark whispered, horrified. "Someone will see you."

Papa ignored her. "Care to dance with me again, Mrs. Danson?" He stood and offered Mother his hand.

"Delighted, Mr. Danson." She stepped into his waiting arms.

Skylark watched as her parents whirled away and disappeared amidst the other dancers. Sometimes she loved the affection they showed each other. But not tonight. Didn't they realize they were too old to behave that way in public?

Her gaze returned to the entrance to the barn in time to see Yale stride in. He stopped, removed his hat, and looked around the assembly. She could hardly breathe as she waited for him to find her. When he did, he gave her one of those lazy smiles of his as he started her way, skirting the dancers in the center of the barn.

"Evening, Skylark," he said when he stopped before her.

"Good evening, Yale."

"Nice night."

"Yes."

"Railroad comin'. Good reason to celebrate."

"Yes, it is."

"But I don't reckon that's why I came here tonight."

Her pulse fluttered. "You don't?"

"No, miss. I reckon I came here to dance with you."

"Funny, isn't it. I came here to dance with you."

The music stopped. Some people returned to benches around the circumference. Others went to the refreshment tables. While she didn't look away from Yale, she could be certain her father knew the two of them were together. She smiled. Perhaps he didn't care what others thought when he kissed his wife in public, the same way she didn't care what others thought about her and Yale.

The musicians began playing another song, and Yale held out his hand toward her.

"Are you ready, Miss Danson?"

"I am, indeed."

Yale James couldn't care less what other folks thought of him. Not even Skylark's father. What mattered was what she thought, and right now, the way she looked at him made him feel as handsome as a new rope on a thirty dollar pony, half again as tall as a bull buffalo, and as wise as a tree full of owls. Her luminous eyes never wavered from his face as he whirled her around the barn, her long dress popping like the crack of a whip.

"You reckon dancing with me will let folks know I'm courtin' you?"

"Is that what you're doing?"

"Yes'm, it is."

"About time."

"Don't suppose it'll impress your pa much."

"Papa's coming around."

"You think so?" He cast a quick glance in the direction of the refreshment tables, but didn't see either of her parents.

"I think so."

"Two more weeks, and I'll have the last of the money I need to give Mr. Stanley. The old Hadley place will be the new James place, free and clear."

"That's wonderful, Yale."

It took everything in him not to tell her he loved her, to speak the words out loud, to ask her to marry him. Oh, there was that understanding between them, but the way wasn't clear yet. It wasn't enough to buy the old Hadley place. He needed to stock it with horses and cattle. He needed fencing materials. He needed more furnishings for the house besides the bed and chair that was in it now. He needed a whole lot more before he could offer Skylark the life she deserved.

The music stopped. For a moment, Yale stood in the middle of the crowded barn, his arms still holding Skylark.

"Yale?" There was a world of wanting in the way she spoke his name.

With his eyes, he told her the time wasn't right.

"Oh, Yale." Tears welled in her eyes.

Before he could think better of it, he turned and pulled

Skylark across the barn and through the open doorway, past the group of men enjoying their cigars and cigarettes beneath the star-studded heavens, and into the mass of tethered horses, buggies, and wagons. He stopped as quickly as he'd begun, this time pulling her into his embrace. He kissed her, like he'd been aching to do for an age and a day. It had been far too many weeks since she'd led him into that grove of cottonwoods and aspens and offered her lips to him, and Yale felt like a starving man faced with a sumptuous banquet. He intended to indulge and not think about the consequences.

Rosalie had watched as her friend was whisked out of the barn.

"Looks like Yale's as much in love as I am," Michael said, leaning close to her ear as he spoke.

A shiver ran up her spine in response.

"It's our time to dance, Mrs. Randolph. You've stood behind that punch bowl all evening, and I'm ready to hold you in my arms."

"But I—" she began to protest.

Much as she'd seen Yale do with Skylark, Michael took hold of her hand and drew her from behind the table and toward the dance floor. Once there, she slipped into his embrace as if she'd been doing it for years. He guided her around the barn in time to the music, so expertly, he made her feel graceful and refined, even though she knew full well she had two left feet. Looking up to meet his gaze, she felt her insides turn all soft and warm.

"Randolph!"

Her pa's shout caused her heart to stop a moment before her feet did the same.

"You knew about this, didn't you?" Drunk as usual, her pa swayed as he shook his fist at Michael. "The railroad. You knew when you bought the boarding house."

The music stopped. The crowd quieted around them.

"I don't think this is the time to discuss business, Mr. Tomkin."

"You ain't gettin' away with it." He swung a wild fist in Michael's direction.

Michael took a step back, sheltering Rosalie with his body even as he avoided the punch.

Before her pa could gather himself, the sheriff appeared. Hank McNeal grabbed her pa by his wrist and hauled it up behind his back, eliciting a cry of protest. "That's enough of that for one evening, Tomkin. You'd better come over to the jail and sleep this off."

"I'm not the one you should be arrestin', sheriff. It's him. He had his way with my girl and then he cheated me out of the boarding house."

Rosalie felt many pairs of eyes turn her way. No one would believe Michael had cheated her pa. But the other accusation? Coupled with the haste of their nuptials, they might believe it. She felt the heat rise in her cheeks.

Michael took a quick stride forward and grabbed her pa by the lapel, nearly lifting him off his feet. "Say what you want about me, Tomkin, but be careful what you say about my wife. Now, you let these good people know that what you implied wasn't true before the sheriff has to arrest me for breaking your stinking neck."

Rosalie felt the icy-heat of her husband's fury.

"Tell them," Michael said again.

"It ain't," her pa managed. "It ain't true."

"How much did I pay you for the boarding house?"

"Seven ... seven hundred and fifty dollars."

"And did you or did you not sign the bill of sale?"

Her pa looked around the barn, finally answering, "I did."

Michael nodded. "Thank you. Now let me tell you something. I love your daughter, and I won't allow you or anyone else to hurt her. Do I make myself clear?"

Pa nodded.

"Good."

Michael released her pa's shirt and gave a small shove, sending her father toward the waiting sheriff. Michael took a moment to look at the people around him, then his gaze went to the musicians. They understood his silent command and resumed playing the song that had been interrupted.

Her husband's eyes returned to her. "I believe this was our dance."

"I love your daughter, and I won't let you or anyone else to hurt her."

He'd spoken those words so easily. He'd said them for all to hear. No one in Rosalie's family had ever declared their love in private, let alone in public. But Michael had.

As his words repeated in her mind, she stepped into his embrace and allowed him to guide her around the floor.

Let it be true. Please God, let it be true. Nothing good's ever lasted. Let this be true forever.

28

Yale rode his gray horse into the yard of the Rocking D the following afternoon. Almost as if he'd been expecting him, Will Danson stepped down from the porch and waited for his arrival.

Yale stopped his horse about half dozen yards away from where Will stood. He touched the brim of his Stetson. "Mr. Danson."

"Yale."

He dismounted. "I've come to talk to you about Skylark."

"I figured as much."

"Guess you already know that I'm in love with her. I'm here to ask for your permission to make her my wife."

"And why would I do that?"

Yale cleared his throat. "I've been working two jobs since leaving here. I'm buying a place of my own on the east end of the valley. I'll own it free and clear in another couple weeks. I've cleaned it up. Been making repairs to the house."

"So I've heard."

He bumped the brim of his hat, pushing it back on his head. "Skylark tell you?"

"And other people." Will gave him a nod. "I only hear good things about you, cowboy."

Yale grinned. He couldn't help it. He'd expected more of an exchange of words. Without that happening, some of his nerves drained away. If he wasn't mistaken, he saw a measure of respect in Will Danson's eyes and that felt good. "I love your daughter, sir, and I mean to provide her a good home. I don't pretend that I'll be able to give her what she's had here. At least not real soon. But I'll see that she's never in want, and I'll see that she's happy."

"It's not always easy to deliver on that promise. Making a woman happy."

"Maybe not. But I reckon I'll give it all I've got. If she ain't happy, it won't be for lack of me trying."

"Fair enough."

Yale wasn't quite sure what to make of Will Danson's replies. This encounter was a whole lot different than the last time he was on the Rocking D. In fact, it was all he could do not to rub his jaw where his former boss had punched him.

Was that a hint of a smile he saw on Will's face? Was he remembering that same moment?

Will cleared his throat. "Why don't you take a seat in the shade while I let Skylark know you're here to see her."

"You're gonna let me talk to her?"

"Isn't that why you came? If I understand correctly, you have a question to ask her." Will turned and looked up toward a second-story window. "But she probably knows you're here and what you've come for. You shouldn't have to wait long."

"Thanks, Mr. Danson."

Will looked at him again. "Just don't ever call me Pa."

"No, sir. I wouldn't think of it."

Rosalie was hanging laundry out to dry when Skylark came galloping Dark Feather down the road to Boulder Creek. Skylark must have seen her standing near the clothesline, for she turned the little mare abruptly, slowing her in time to prevent a cloud of dust from covering the just-washed bed sheets. Judging by her friend's joyous expression, Rosalie knew something good had happened.

Skylark hopped down from the saddle. "We're engaged!" She threw herself into Rosalie's arms. "Yale asked me to marry him, and I said yes!" She backed away and twirled in a circle, her arms thrust heavenward. "Oh, I'm so happy I could burst!"

Rosalie laughed. "Calm down a minute and tell me all about it."

Her friend stopped spinning and grasped Rosalie by both hands, drawing her toward the shade of a tree where they dropped to the ground. "Yale rode out to the ranch today. He told Papa he wanted to ask for my hand, and Papa said he could. Do you believe it? After Papa was so stubborn and all. He even punched Yale before we went to Boise. But now he seems happy about it. We're going to get married in September. Mother has all sorts of ideas for the wedding and my dress. Oh, Rosalie, I can hardly wait."

Rosalie smiled, knowing her friend well enough to wait until her outburst had run its course before she tried to speak.

"Yale has his own place now. Did you know that? I went out there once when he wasn't home, to see what it was like. It's small and plain, but I can fix it up really nice. And we'll be all alone out there with no one to bother us. He can kiss me all night long if he wants to and no one can tell him to stop."

She thought of Michael's kisses. She thought of his kisses and so much more.

"What's it like, Rosalie?"

Heat rose in her cheeks. "I'm sorry. What did you say?"

"What's it like? You know. To be married."

She looked down at her hands and plucked at blades of grass. "It's very ... special."

"Rosalie." There was a note of surprise in Skylark's voice. She didn't look up.

"You love him, don't you? You didn't act like it before, but I can see it now." Skylark took hold of her by one hand. "I'm glad for you. You deserve to be happy." She leaned forward and kissed Rosalie's cheek. Then she flopped backward onto the ground, her hands tucked beneath her head, her eyes staring up at the cloudless blue sky. "Remember when we used to come sit in the shade, just like now, and talk and share our hopes and dreams? I was so shy and afraid back then. I scarcely talked to anyone but you. Remember?"

It was hard to believe that was ever true.

"You were always fighting with Mark because he said such mean things to me. Remember how he used to call me —" Abruptly, Skylark sat up. Her eyes widened. "What if Yale doesn't know?"

"Know what?"

"What if he doesn't know about my real parents? Maybe

he doesn't know I'm adopted. What if he doesn't know I'm part Sioux?"

"It won't matter to him."

"But what if it does?"

Rosalie remembered well the way her brother had tortured Skylark about her heritage, always calling her names. For a while, others had joined him, but now she doubted anyone remembered that Skylark wasn't actually Will and Addie Danson's natural daughter.

"I'll have to tell him," her friend said as tears filled her eyes. "Why didn't I think of this before?"

Rosalie put her arms around her friend and hugged her close. "Because it doesn't matter. It doesn't matter at all."

Skylark had never been as afraid as she was now. She didn't ride Dark Feather very hard or fast on her way to Yale's place. She wasn't in as great a hurry as she'd been earlier that afternoon. She saw him before he saw her. He was digging post holes, his muscles straining, his arms moving in a steady rhythm as he scooped the dirt up and tossed it into a pile.

Oh, to be as sure of Yale's feeling as Rosalie seemed to be. Skylark remembered too well the way some people had treated her after her parents died. First at the orphanage and then here in town. Not all people were as understanding as Will and Addie Danson or Rosalie.

Yale raised an arm to wipe his forehead, and that's when he saw her approach. His mouth turned up in a grin as he reached for his shirt and put it on. By the time she'd pulled her mare to a halt, he was ready to help her to the ground.

"I didn't expect to see you again today." He hesitated a second, then leaned forward to kiss her lightly on the lips. "Does your pa know you're here?"

"I ... I needed to tell you something before ... before Mother goes any further with the wedding plans."

His smile vanished. "What's wrong?"

She took a deep breath. A sick knot had formed in her stomach, and her knees felt weak. Even her voice quivered. "There's something you don't know about me, Yale. I ... I never thought to say anything before now."

He took hold of her upper arms, forcing her to look at him. "What is it? Don't go worrying me like this."

Once started, the words tumbled out of her mouth quickly. "My grandmother was full Lakota Sioux. She married a white man, a trapper, and their son was my father. And he married a white woman, my mother, who was Will Danson's sister. After my parents died, Will and Addie adopted me. I was eight years old." She drew a quick breath. "I couldn't let you marry me without knowing."

His expression softened as he drew her close, wrapping her in his arms. With his mouth near her ear, he said, "Skylark, I figure I'm the luckiest man west of the Mississippi. I hope we have us enough kids to start our own school, and I'm gonna love each and every one of 'em, especially if they look like their ma." He kissed the crown of her head. "I've been working the range near on half my life. I knew you didn't get your looks from Will or Addie, and I figured out the rest on my own."

"And you don't care?"

"Care? Yeah, I care. I care that I'm not good enough for you. But I'm not about to let you go now. It don't matter what excuse you come up with. We're getting married come September."

She raised her head to look at him. "Oh, Yale, I love you so."

"I reckon you better, because I sure as shootin' love you." He cradled her face with his callused hands. "And don't you ever doubt it again."

He kissed her, just the way she liked to be kissed. He kissed her until he'd stolen the last shreds of doubt from her mind, the last scrap of fear from her heart. And by the time he was finished kissing her, Skylark's only thought was how far off September was.

29

Michael looked up from the papers in his hands, glancing across the room at Rosalie. The lamp cast a soft yellow glow over her, gilding the chestnut hair that fell in a smooth cascade about her shoulders.

The past week since the barn dance had been one of the best of his life. The townsfolk treated him like a long-time resident rather than a stranger. The hotel construction was right on schedule. Furnishings for the hotel were expected to arrive this week. And every night his wife lay beside him in their bed, snuggled in his arms. He marveled at his own contentment.

At the moment, Rosalie was mending the shirt he'd torn on a nail earlier in the day. The house was quiet except for the ticking of the clock on a nearby table. Beyond the open window, a soft breeze rustled leaves in a nearby tree, and he heard the occasional *jug-o-rum* of a bullfrog.

A few months ago, this type of quiet evening would have left him restless. In the city, he had dined in the opulent homes of friends, attended balls and plays, and talked business deals in smoke-filled rooms into the wee hours of the night. He'd never considered a different kind of life—until now. Here in Boulder Creek, he'd found a happiness he hadn't known he lacked. Only one thing was needed to make it all perfect. He needed Rosalie to admit she loved him.

What must he do to teach her to trust him? He believed she loved him, and yet she kept her heart closely guarded. A part of him understood the reasons. She'd been hurt by the people she should have been able to trust. By both her father and her brother. Perhaps even by her mother, although in a different way.

Instinct told him she didn't see herself worthy of love. And telling her that he loved her would never be enough. He suspected she was merely waiting for him to take the words back.

Yet, when she was in his arms …

He smiled. Yes, he was vastly contented. He could be patient. He would be patient. He would prove his love, one hour, one moment, at a time.

The next day, Michael sat at the kitchen table, eating his lunch, when a knock sounded at the door.

"You eat," Rosalie said. "It's probably Skylark." She left the kitchen.

He took another bite of his sandwich. Then he took up the pencil and made a note to himself in the small book he carried with him at all times. He was startled from his thoughts by a brusque voice. A familiar one.

"Is Michael Randolph here?"

He got to his feet. He'd expected a letter, perhaps even a telegram. But not the arrival of his father.

"And you must be Rosalie," came a much sweeter voice. "This is John Thomas, Michael's father, and I'm Kathleen. How good it is to meet you."

In a few strides, Michael reached the doorway. "Father. Kathleen. I didn't expect—"

"What on earth *did* you expect?" his stepmother asked with a smile. "You are the first of our children to marry. Of course we had to come at once." She stepped forward and gave him a warm hug and a kiss on the cheek. Then she whispered, "She's lovely."

He returned Kathleen's embrace, but it was his father's reaction he awaited as varied emotions surged through him. Old angers. Insecurities. Hopes and expectations. Admirations. Disappointments.

John Thomas looked around the sitting room. "You purchased this house?"

"Yes, sir. I did. A married man needs a home."

"Hmm."

Michael motioned toward the settee. "Please. Sit down."

His father released a soft grunt of disapproval, then moved to the sofa. Kathleen joined him there.

"When did you arrive?" Michael asked.

When John Thomas didn't answer, Kathleen did. "Within the hour. We took lodgings at the boarding house, and then came here straight away."

"And the children?"

"They're all with us. All but Dillon, of course."

Michael looked toward Rosalie, still standing by the door. He lifted a hand toward her. She hesitated a moment before coming to him. He nodded, hoping to give her some encouragement. Then he drew her toward two chairs.

"Sir, I have yet to introduce you to my wife, Rosalie Randolph."

"We met at the door."

"That's hardly an introduction." He glanced in her direction again. "And knowing her name is hardly enough either. You need to know that she has a kind and giving heart and is a blessing to those around her. And although she didn't mean to and probably didn't want to, she made me fall in love with her before I knew it was happening."

His father muttered something beneath his breath while Kathleen smiled with tears in her eyes.

"Before you say anything, sir, I would also like to say that I won't change my mind. I'm glad you've come. I'm glad I'll be able to show you around Boulder Creek and let you see the progress that's been made. But I've made my decision about my future."

"Balderdash. You've never wanted anything more than Palace Hotels. You've fought with your brother over it for years."

"Did you read my letter?"

"I read enough of it."

It suddenly occurred to Michael that he wasn't tied in knots on the inside. How long had it been since his father hadn't worked him into a lather with a few words? Ages. But this time Michael wasn't anxious or angry as he addressed the man. He had nothing to prove, and he no longer was desperate to inherit the ownership and management of Palace Hotels. Nothing his father could threaten would touch him. Knowing that, he smiled.

"What is wrong with you?" John Thomas demanded. "You're behaving like a fool."

"I'm a happy man, sir. That's all." His grin broadened. "Happy men smile."

~

Rosalie didn't understand the words exchanged between the two men. What she did understand was that Michael's father disliked her. She didn't blame him. No man of means wanted a son to be forced to marry a girl like her. Michael would be better off without her.

"And although she didn't mean to and probably didn't want to, she made me fall in love with her before I knew it was happening."

The memory of those words warmed her in ways she didn't understand.

"Son, you cannot give up everything you've worked for on a whim." His father shook his head, a frown furrowing his brow. "Kathleen was right. I let this thing with Dillon and you go too far. I should have found another way to settle matters. Forget Boulder Creek and the plans for this hotel. Come back to San Francisco with us. I'll send for Dillon and we can find a solution."

Suddenly chilled, Rosalie glanced at Michael. Would he leave her? Not long ago she'd wished he would leave. But not now. Not yet.

"Palace Hotels needs you," his father continued. "And you need them. You'll never be satisfied, living in the territories, running a small hotel."

Michael's hand tightened on Rosalie's, but his gaze was glued to the man opposite him. "You're wrong, sir. Palace Hotels doesn't need me. You're going to be around for a long time to come, and when you retire, Dillon or Joseph or Colin or Sean can take over. Maybe all four of them. And you're wrong about something else. I *can* be happy here. I'm happy now, happier than I ever knew I could be. Maybe if I get tired of it, I'll buy some land and raise cattle or horses. I've got friends here who can help me learn to be a cowboy, if it comes to that." He turned to look at Rosalie. "My wife and I will decide on our future together."

Her heart hammered with frightening intensity.

"You see, sir, I've found something more important than running a successful business. I found Rosalie."

His image swam before her as she fought unwelcome tears. The wall she'd so carefully constructed to shield her heart was crumbling about her. She felt stripped, exposed, unprotected.

But she couldn't stop herself from loving him. Not now. Not ever.

30

Rosalie stood before the mirror, staring at her reflection. She couldn't believe the woman she saw in the glass was really Rosalie Tomkin. Then again, she wasn't Rosalie Tomkin. She was Rosalie Randolph. And for the first time, the image in the mirror seemed to fit the name.

The striped dress of dark blue satin and fawn silk net had arrived on yesterday's stagecoach, along with more than a dozen other dresses, all of them of the latest fashion. They'd been delivered shortly after John Thomas and Kathleen Randolph returned to the boarding house. Michael had watched her open the parcels, awaiting her response to each and every one of the gowns. And there were other things besides. Frilly undergarments. Matching gloves, parasols, and purses. Shoes made of satin and kid; real shoes, not boots with buttons to be hooked and unhooked. Silk stockings in various shades. Hats with ribbons and plumes, even fur.

"Why, Michael?" she'd asked while staring at the bounty

spread on the floor before her. "Why did you buy so much? I don't need it. Not here in Boulder Creek."

"Because Rosalie, you're lovely and you deserve lovely things."

Mercy, how she'd wanted to give in to the tenderness in his voice. How very much she'd wanted to believe him. Wanted to believe him still.

She blinked away the memory, bringing her attention back to the young woman in the mirror. She hadn't time for woolgathering. Not today. She had to prepare tonight's supper for Michael's entire family over at the boarding house. It had been his idea. He wanted to show his father what a successful restaurant the hotel would have with Rosalie in charge.

She wondered how her mother was doing with a house full of Randolphs. Rosalie thought Ma's emotional and mental state had improved since Michael purchased the boarding house and put her father out. But there was still a haunted look in her eyes that made Rosalie uneasy.

A shiver ran through her. Could John Thomas be as harsh and dangerous as her own father? He'd looked at Rosalie with such contempt when he'd met her. Did a cruel streak run through him too? But then she thought of Kathleen, of her easy smile. She had such an air of contentment. Would that be possible if John Thomas was a tyrant?

She took a deep breath and lifted her chin. She would make Michael proud tonight. She owed him that much after all he'd given her. And because she loved him.

She turned away from the mirror and left the bedroom. Her pace didn't slow as she passed the hotel site, not even when she saw Michael showing his father around. She walked on toward the mercantile, ticking off the things she would need to prepare the meal she had in mind. She was concentrating so hard, she didn't see her pa until it was too late. By that time, he'd grabbed hold of her arm and hauled her into the shadowed alleyway between the saloon and the livery.

"Pa!" she cried as his fingers pinched into her arm.

"Well, at least you remember who I am."

She recoiled from the smell of whiskey on his breath. Memories of the way he used his strength when he drank washed over her, but she refused to react in fear. "Let go. You're hurting me."

He didn't comply. Instead, his grip tightened. "You think you're something with that rich husband of yours. Look at you, all gussied up like some fancy woman. Well, you watch your step, girly, because I'm still your pa." He yanked her toward him, leaning his face down toward hers. "It's only because I don't aim to stay in this town that he's getting away with taking what's mine. He stole the boarding house from me. And you helped him cheat me outta it."

"The boarding house was never yours. Ma's paid for it with her own pain and sweat. It belongs to her."

"You watch your mouth or you might be the next one to fall down a flight of stairs." He shoved her away from him.

Her eyes widened, and her breathing quickened. "What are you saying?"

"You just watch yourself, Rosalie." He pointed at her. "And keep an eye on that man of yours, too." Then he stumbled away.

Rosalie leaned against the wall of the livery. Had he done something to Mark? Isn't that what it sounded like? He could have. She knew he was capable of it. She'd always believed it was her pa who'd killed Tom McNeal and set the sawmill ablaze the night he'd left Boulder Creek. But would he kill his own son? No. No, he couldn't have. Even her pa wouldn't do that.

His warning whispered in her head, and she shuddered. *God, please keep Michael safe.*

Michael was proud of what had been accomplished since he'd arrived in Boulder Creek. He showed it all to his father without hesitation or apology. No, it wasn't a Palace Hotel, but it was his hotel. He'd designed it, and he knew it would succeed. It would be important to the people of Boulder Creek. His friends. His neighbors.

John Thomas's approval came begrudgingly, but it was there all the same. "You've done a fine job, son. You've proven your point. Now it's time to come home."

"Father, I thought I'd made myself clear in my letter. I don't intend to come back. Rosalie and I are happy here."

"But don't you—"

He interrupted his father's words by placing a hand on his shoulder. "I'm not doing this out of anger or spite or revenge. It's my choice. It's what I want to do. I discovered I didn't care much for the man I'd become. But here in this place." He motioned toward the town. "Here I've found something better. Here *I'm* better."

John Thomas stared at him a moment, then shook his head. "I don't understand."

"Stay awhile. Get to know the town. See what I see. Then you'll understand." Michael glanced across the street at the boarding house. "And give Rosalie a chance, too. She deserves it."

His father scowled. "You haven't told us how you met her or what caused you to marry so quickly."

"I met her at the boarding house when I first came to Boulder Creek. I married her so quickly because ... because it seemed the right thing to do. And it was."

"You really think you're in love with the girl?"

He turned a steady gaze on his father. "I don't *think* it. I *know* it."

John Thomas looked as if he would try to dispute Michael's statement, then pressed his mouth together, holding back the words.

Michael breathed a silent sigh of relief. He didn't want to argue with his father. Especially not about Rosalie. "Let me show you the dining area," he said, then led the way.

Rosalie worked alone in the boarding house kitchen. She had refused both her mother's and Kathleen Randolph's offers of help. Tonight's meal was something she wanted to prepare alone. It was important to her. She had something to prove—to herself, to Michael, to his family.

Besides, the solitude gave her time to think about her confrontation with her pa. After some careful reasoning, she'd decided she needn't fear his threats. Michael was more than capable of taking care of himself. He'd dealt with her pa on several other occasions. He could handle him in the future if necessary.

With the back of her hand, she pushed stray wisps of hair away from her face. The kitchen was warm this late in the afternoon. Perspiration beaded her forehead. She could have done with a moment outside in the shade of the poplars, but there was too much to be done before supper. Still, she'd accomplished a great deal already. Potatoes boiled on the stove and a fine cut of beef was roasting in the oven, along with carrots and slices of onion. Two pies cooled on the windowsill, along with some freshly baked bread.

She heard the kitchen door open behind her as she removed the potatoes from the stove. "I told you to relax, Ma. I'll take care of supper tonight."

"So your mother told me."

Rosalie almost dropped the kettle. She set it down, then turned to face her father-in-law. "Mr. Randolph. You surprised me." She wiped the sweat from her brow with the back of her hand, then, embarrassed, she dried her hand on her apron.

"Smells good." He moved into the center of the kitchen, stopping at the table.

"It should taste the same."

He cleared his throat. "Young woman, I believe my son is making a grave mistake that he will one day regret. However, he doesn't seem inclined to listen to my advice. I'm hoping I might engage your cooperation."

A knot formed in her stomach. She no longer felt the heat of the kitchen. Instead, she felt the chill of trepidation seeping through her veins. "What is it you want from me, Mr. Randolph?"

"I think you know. I think that's why you married my son. Will five thousand dollars be adequate?"

"Five thousand dollars?" She felt desperately short of breath. "For what?"

"Why, to leave my son, of course."

All her anxieties, all her fears, all her uncertainties seemed to pile up and explode. It showed itself in a spurt of temper. "I didn't marry your son for his money, sir, and I don't want any of yours either." She stepped forward, stopping opposite him, the table between them. "I wasn't looking to be married when Michael came to Boulder Creek. In fact, a husband was the last thing I wanted. He'll tell you that himself. All I wanted was to leave here, to get away, go anywhere. But then ... but then Michael married me. He's been nothing but good to me, and I won't do anything to ... to hurt or betray him. It'll have to be him who tells me to go away. I won't do it for you or for your money."

He watched her in silence for a long time. Finally, he inclined his head toward her. "I believe I may have judged you unfairly, Rosalie. I beg your forgiveness."

Her strength left her like air from a punctured balloon, and she grabbed onto the back of the chair at the table, praying her legs would continue to hold her upright.

Mr. Randolph might be right. Michael could be making a mistake. He might one day tire of her and send her on her way. He might want to return to his real life in San Francisco. He might want to go back to the Palace Hotels and to refined society women like Louise Overhart. What affection he felt for Rosalie might not last despite his assurances to the contrary. And still she wasn't ready to let go. She'd done all she could not to fall in love with him, but she loved him now and always would.

"You won't mention this conversation to my son."

"No, sir, I won't."

"Thank you." Then he left the kitchen.

Lying in their bed that night, Michael drew Rosalie close. He kissed the top of her head and stroked her back and hoped she could feel his love even when he didn't speak it.

Something had upset her tonight, but he seemed unable to ask what was wrong. Maybe he didn't need to ask. Maybe he already knew.

It didn't have anything to do with his family, although he suspected something had happened between Rosalie and his father. John Thomas's initial attitude toward her had been less than cordial in the beginning. That had changed this evening. By the time Michael and Rosalie left the boarding house, he'd known she'd won over John Thomas as thoroughly as she'd won Michael himself.

Neither did it have anything to do with her own family, although he suspected her pa would continue to cause her grief whenever the opportunity arose.

He didn't doubt that Rosalie could do an admirable job of holding her own with either of their fathers. She was a fighter, his Rosalie.

But Michael didn't want her to fight any longer. Especially not him. He wanted her to trust him, to trust her own feelings for him. He wanted her to say the words aloud. He wanted her to tell him she loved him.

You will tell me one day. He kissed her head again and breathed in the soft scent of her hair. *Somehow I'll make you admit your love. I'll wait as long as it takes.*

31

The next week was the most confusing and wonderful week of Rosalie's life. Michael's family, it turned out, was a noisy, fun-loving group who thrived on laughter and more than a fair share of practical jokes. With the exception of John Thomas, they showed their emotions openly, hugging and kissing each other with some frequency, and it didn't take long for them to include Rosalie in their candid displays of affection. They made the boarding house come alive as it never had before. Even her ma came out of her shell a little. And with each passing day, Rosalie's feelings of awkwardness around the Randolph family eased. They seduced her with their stories of Michael's childhood and tales of his triumphs in the world of business. They charmed her with their protectiveness, with the way they squabbled amongst themselves, yet would brook no criticism by others. They teased and joked with her, treating her as if she'd always been one of them.

And then there was Michael. He continued to treat her with love and tenderness, chipping away at her fears, wearing down the last shreds of her defenses. Against her better judgement, she began to believe in a love that lasted, not only for people like Kathleen and John Thomas, but for someone like her. She began to believe that Michael could love her, not just now but for all the tomorrows to come. She began to believe that she could have the happiness that had eluded her.

She began to believe in Michael.

On the first day of the following week, Michael walked into the kitchen at the boarding house, took Rosalie by the hand, and announced, "Rosalie will have to miss lunch." Then he led her out to a horse and buggy that waited at the gate.

"Where are you taking me?"

He grinned. "You'll have to wait and see."

"But I don't have time for this. I need to prepare lunch for your family."

He helped her onto the seat of the buggy. "I'm tired of sharing you with others." He joined her in the buggy and picked up the reins. "I want an afternoon with you for myself." He looked over at her. "And I've got a surprise for you."

They traveled in silence for a while, and it wasn't long before she guessed their destination. The trail they followed led up to the ridge where they'd picnicked the day he'd presented her with Princess. But she couldn't imagine what another surprise might be. There weren't any packages in the back of the buggy, no more wicker baskets under the seat. He obviously wasn't giving her another puppy or more hats and shoes and dresses.

Michael flicked the reins against the horse's back as they started up the incline. "Close your eyes."

She obeyed, feeling a silly excitement.

After a while, she felt the warmth of the sun upon her face as the buggy moved from the shade of the trees into the clearing on the ridge. "Can I open my eyes?"

"No, not yet."

They slowed, then stopped. The buggy rocked as Michael hopped down. She listened to the crunch of pebbles beneath his boots as he walked around to her side.

"Keep your eyes closed," he reminded as his hands closed around her waist and he lifted her to the ground.

His kiss was unexpected. Her heart jumped, and her breath quickened, as it always did when he kissed her. Then his arm swept beneath her knees and lifted her feet off the ground. She clung to him, enjoying the taste of his mouth and the feel of his arms cradling her against him.

She opened her eyes and gazed up at him as he lifted his mouth from hers. "What was that for?"

"Just because I love you, Mrs. Randolph." He grinned. "Now, close your eyes again."

"Michael—"

"Close them."

"But—"

"Humor me."

With a sigh, she obeyed. She lay her head against his shoulder as he carried her across the clearing. To be honest, she didn't care where he was taking her or why.

He stopped again. His lips brushed her hair. "I know your birthday isn't for another three months, but I couldn't wait until then." He set her on her feet, then turned her to face away from him. "Open your eyes."

She obeyed, but at first she didn't understand what she saw. It seemed unreal.

"You're not ten anymore, but I hope ..." His voice drifted into silence.

Rosalie stepped toward the golden horse that was tethered to an aspen. The gelding bobbed his head, then pawed the ground. Rosalie touched the animal's neck, at the same time glancing behind her.

"He's yours," Michael said, answering her silent question.

"Mine?" She looked at the palomino again.

"Now you can go riding with Skylark whenever you want."

How could he have known? How could he see into those secret corners of her heart, those old hurts, those buried hopes and dreams? Somehow, he understood the child who'd felt so different from everyone else, the girl who had no one to love her, the young woman who worked so hard and had so little. She'd denied ever wanting a horse, and yet he'd guessed the truth, guessed that she'd wanted one still.

His hands closed over her shoulders. "I want to give you whatever will make you happy, Rosalie. Tell me what you want, and I'll get it for you. Name it and it's yours."

"He's beautiful."

Michael turned her toward him. "But not as beautiful as you." He cradled her face with the palms of his hands. "Nothing is as beautiful as you." He kissed her, a kiss as sweet as dew in the morning, as gentle as a summer breeze.

I love you, Michael.

She wanted to tell him. She wanted to say it aloud. She wanted to announce it to the world. But the words caught in her throat, words too foreign, too strange to be uttered. So she told him the way she felt in other ways, the only way she knew how.

Michael glanced at his wife, seated beside him. She, in turn, was twisted around to look behind her at the gelding, which was tied to the back of the buggy.

"I can't get over that he's really mine," she said, catching him watching her. "I can't wait to ride out to the Rocking D and show him to Skylark."

"Just so long as I'm with you. Maybe next Sunday after church."

"But I don't want to wait until Sunday."

"He's still a little green, Rosalie, and you aren't exactly an experienced horsewoman." He recognized the stubborn set of her chin. "Promise me you won't take him out alone. Not until you're both familiar with each other, and he has a bit more time under the saddle."

He could almost tell what she was thinking as she pondered his request. Should she promise never to go alone and then chafe against it? Or should she say she couldn't promise, even though he was trying to protect her?

He turned the horse off the road, following the drive up to their home. That's when he saw a man standing on the porch. Even before they drew closer to the house, he recognized his brother's stance. Rosalie must have felt him tense, for she too looked toward the house. She didn't ask the question aloud, but he answered anyway.

"It's Dillon."

His brother stepped down from the porch. His dark hair was tousled, his clothes dusty, his face closed, revealing nothing. Michael pulled in on the reins, drawing the horse to a stop. Without comment, he passed the reins to Rosalie and stepped down from the buggy.

"Dillon."

"Hello, Michael." His brother cracked a half-smile. "Not an easy trek from Newton. I had a devil of a time getting here as soon as I did."

It surprised Michael, how glad he was to see Dillon. He wondered if his brother felt the same.

"I hear tell the family's in town."

Michael nodded. "Yes. They arrived a week ago."

"Father accepted your decision?"

"I think he has."

"Are you sure it's what you want?"

"I'm sure."

Dillon glanced toward the buggy. "I never thought you'd let pleasure get in the way of business, but now I understand why you changed your mind." He stepped forward, his smile broadening. "You must be Rosalie. I'm your new brother, Dillon." He took her by the hand and helped her down from the buggy.

Rosalie glanced from Dillon to Michael and back again. "It's amazing," she said.

Dillon chuckled and leaned close to Rosalie's ear. "I used to put boot black in his hair so it looked like mine. Folks thought we were twins ... unless he rubbed up against something." He winked at her. "But as we got older, it became clear I was by far the more handsome of the two."

Michael didn't know whether to laugh with Dillon over the memory or hit him for flirting with Rosalie.

His brother looked at him, and his smile faded. "I'm glad

you wrote to me, Michael. The past few months have given me a chance to think through a lot of things. Father wasn't all wrong to send us off to prove ourselves." He shoved out his hand. "I've missed you. Let's forget what came between us."

Michael felt a swelling of emotion in his chest. He grabbed Dillon's proffered hand, giving it a couple of hearty pumps. Then, realizing that wasn't enough, he yanked his brother forward and hugged him. When they stepped back, each held the other by the shoulders.

"I've a lot to make up to you," Michael admitted.

"No more than I have to you. Let's put it behind us." Dillon jerked his head toward Rosalie. "For now, I think I'd like to get acquainted with my new sister." He grinned again, that irrepressible grin that spelled mischief.

"Just remember she's *my* wife," Michael warned, only half joking.

Dillon Randolph was as charming a reprobate as Rosalie ever knew. He had the same sparkle, the same enjoyment for living that all the Randolphs exhibited. But she liked Dillon best. Perhaps it was his uncanny resemblance to Michael. Or perhaps it was because she knew how much her husband loved his half-brother.

That evening, as she quietly observed the two men, listening to their stories, watching as they mended bridges once burned, Rosalie knew a moment of envy, wishing she might have had a brother who'd loved her as these two loved each other. And then she realized that she'd been given that chance. Dillon was her brother now. Dillon and Joseph and

Colin and Sean were all her brothers. She even had a sister in young Fianna.

I'm part of his family now.

Her gaze turned to her husband.

And maybe we'll have a family of our own soon.

The thought made her pulse quicken, imagining a son or daughter who would look like Michael. He had already given her so much she'd never had before—an adorable puppy, a beautiful horse, a pleasant home, pretty dresses, freedom, and a new family—but most of all, he'd given her love. It would be wonderful to share that love with their children.

She said a silent thanks to God for bringing Michael Randolph to Idaho before joining into the conversation and laughter.

32

———

Statehood! July third had arrived at last.

For all their talk that the railroad meant more, the citizens of Crescent Valley turned out for a celebration that wouldn't soon be forgotten. They came on horseback. They came in their buggies and their wagons. They came on foot. They came with elderly parents who were bent with age and with infants carried in their mothers' arms. They came alone, in pairs, and in bunches—parents and children, married and single. They came with blankets and picnic baskets, fiddles and bows. They came to celebrate and celebrate they did.

The townsfolk served up a bounty of food. They dined on fried chicken, sliced ham, potatoes, baked beans, and breads. There were cookies and cakes and pies and puddings. They drank sweet punch and hot tea. Everyone shared their bounty with their neighbors. For this night, they all shared the same hopes and dreams.

As night fell, the women of Crescent Valley put away the leftover food while the men gathered wood and built a bonfire in the center of an open field. Fiddles and mouth organs appeared, and the musicians commenced to play lively, foot-stomping tunes. Ted Wesley's baritone voice shouted commands to the dancing couples.

For Rosalie, it was a magical, wonderful night. She leaned into the crook of Michael's arm, resting her head against his shoulder while watching the dancers, enjoying the warmth of his body against hers, enjoying the way they fit together as if made for each other.

Michael stroked her hair with his hand. "Boulder Creek's going to become an important link for logging and mining in these mountains, once the railroad comes in here. The town's going to grow. We probably ought to think of buying more land now, while we still can."

She turned her head, looking at him. "Do you really mean to stay here? Are you sure you won't want to go back to San Francisco?"

"Why? Do you still want to leave Boulder Creek?"

She thought about that for a moment. Did she want to leave? There weren't a lot of happy memories associated with this town. Yet the thought of leaving no longer tempted her, no longer promised more happiness elsewhere.

"Look at that sky." Michael drew her even closer to him. "The sky's not the same in California. The mountains aren't the same either."

Was that the truth? The sky was the sky. It had to be the same everywhere. Mountains were mountains. Weren't they? Yet, this was home. This was her sky, and these were her mountains. Perhaps he was right after all.

A rocket shot upward and burst into a shower of blue and white sparkles, startling her from her reverie. The ground shook and the noise was deafening as charge after charge was set, the fireworks shooting into the sky to challenge the stars. A sense of joy seemed to explode within Rosalie with the same brilliance—and with it came a burst of courage.

"I love you, Michael."

The words were lost in the din of the night.

Michael hadn't heard her, but she was content for now. There would be other times to tell him, more opportunities to say the words. It was enough to know she'd spoken them at last, that she'd set the words loose and given them life.

Rosalie awakened the next morning before dawn, her heart singing with joy, her body quickened by emotions too wonderful, too foreign to name. She felt a strange energy that made her restless, even though she knew she should be exhausted after so few hours of sleep.

She gathered her clothes, then, on silent feet, made her way downstairs where she dressed in the kitchen. She thought about stoking the fire in the oven and baking something, then discarded the notion. It wasn't the sort of day to be stuck in a hot kitchen.

She opened the back door, letting in a rush of fresh morning air and an excited puppy. Unfastening the rope that held the gold and white dog captive at night, Rosalie lifted Princess into her arms, then leaned against the door jamb and watched as the sky above faded from black to gray, the stars winking out one by one.

Princess wiggled impatiently. "All right. All right." Rosalie set the puppy on the floor. "You're getting too big to hold like that anyway. Come on. Let's go for a walk."

The path led them to the shed where the two horses were sheltered, Michael's tall roan and Rosalie's flaxen-maned gelding. Princess tried to scramble through the stall railing, but Rosalie grabbed her in time.

"I think you'd be sorry," she whispered to the rambunctious pup.

The gelding thrust his head over the stall door.

"Look. You're both the same color." She stroked the horse's neck. "I'll call you Prince."

Prince bobbed his head as if in agreement, and Rosalie laughed, the overwhelming sense of joy returning.

"You know what I'd like to do." She stroked the horse's neck. "I'd like to go for a ride. I'd like you and me to become friends."

Michael had warned her that the gelding was green-broke and made her promise that she wouldn't ride alone. Prince looked calm enough to her now. The more she thought about it, the more she wanted to take her horse for a ride. She wanted to make all those silly, girlhood dreams come true. She wanted to feel the wind in her hair. She wanted to gallop him across the grassy fields, maybe even let him soar over a bubbling brook.

She shook her head. She supposed galloping and soaring would have to wait until she became more confident in the saddle. Besides, as tempting as it was to go for a ride on her own, she'd made a promise to Michael. They'd come so far, she wasn't about to break a promise to him now.

Still half-asleep, Michael stretched out his arm ... and found an empty spot where Rosalie should have been. He opened his eyes, squinting against the morning light that was brightening the bedroom. He moaned softly. It was Independence Day, and he'd given the work crew the day off. For a change, he didn't have to be over at the hotel site at the crack of dawn, and he'd hoped to spend a good portion of the morning in bed with his wife.

"Rosalie?" He braced himself on one elbow and glanced about the room. "Come back to bed."

There was no answer.

He sniffed the air experimentally. Breakfast wasn't ready, he decided. He smelled nothing but the fresh morning air.

With a sigh, he tossed aside the bed covers and slid to the edge of the mattress, lowering his legs over the side. After dressing quickly, he checked the other rooms throughout the house. His wife wasn't anywhere to be found. Where had she gone so early in the morning? He opened the back door. Princess's rope lay near the step, but neither puppy nor mistress were in sight.

"Rosalie?"

Again, no answer.

Why would she take Princess for a walk instead of lingering in bed? There was no understanding that.

Letting out an aggrieved sigh, Michael started down the path to the shed, deciding he might as well take care of his morning chores before he went searching for Rosalie and her puppy. Then, halfway to the shed, he had an alarming thought. What if she'd taken her horse out for a ride, despite her promise that she wouldn't?

He broke into a run, unsure whether to give in to anger or fear. If she'd done something foolish, if she'd rejected his advice and gone riding without him, if she ended up getting hurt because she hadn't done as promised, he would regret ever thinking of giving her that gelding, no matter how happy it made her.

He rounded a curve in the path and came to an abrupt halt. Rosalie had taken the palomino from his stall and tied him to a hitching post where she was now brushing his coat while singing softly to herself. Relief swept through him. Relief—and regret that he hadn't given her more credit.

"Good morning."

The brush paused in mid-stroke. Rosalie peered at him over the horse's back. "Good morning."

"You weren't in bed when I woke up."

"I know." She laughed softly. "I was out here."

He resisted smiling back at her. "Have I been abandoned for a horse?"

"Maybe." She began running the brush over the gelding's back again. "But Prince needed a good grooming."

"Prince?"

"That's his name." She looked down at the puppy playing near Michael's feet. "Every princess needs a prince. Right?"

Was it possible to fall a little bit more in love with his wife every day for the rest of his life?

"I gave my men the day off," he said.

"I know. You told me yesterday."

He took a few steps forward, bringing himself to the side of the horse opposite her. "So, do you want a riding lesson before breakfast or after?"

Her hand stopped for a second time, and her smile brightened even more. "Before?"

"Somehow I knew you would say that." His stomach growled, probably loud enough for her to hear. "I'll get the saddle and bridle."

33

———

Rosalie sank down beneath the warm water in the tub with a sigh. She wouldn't admit it to Michael, but she hurt in unexpected places on her body.

"Feels good?" he asked from the doorway.

Her cheeks warmed, although she didn't know why she should suddenly feel shy or embarrassed. Michael knew her body well by this time. Still, never before had he watched her bathe. It felt unexpectedly intimate for him to be in the same room.

His smile told her he'd guessed her thoughts. "I promised to take the family out to the Rocking D. I don't plan to stay long. They can find their own way back. Do you want to come with me?"

"Would it be awful to say no?" She closed her eyes and sank down a little deeper in the water.

"No." He chuckled softly. "There's more to learning to be a good rider than you thought, isn't there?"

"I wouldn't admit it, even if it's true."

Another chuckle, then he said, "I'll take Prince into town

when I go and leave him at the livery so he can be shod. You can rest until I get back. And if you keep feeling sore, use some of that liniment. It'll help."

If she'd had a sponge, she would have thrown it at him.

Laughter, louder this time, trailed behind him as he left her to bathe in peace.

Two hours later, Rosalie had grown tired of resting and waiting for Michael's return. The hot bath had relieved her soreness, and a walk sounded inviting. So she set out for the boarding house and a visit with her mother.

"You look happy," Ma said as they sat in the kitchen a few minutes later, sipping cups of tea.

"I am, Ma."

"I'm glad, child. I wish I could've done that for you myself."

"But you did. You told me not to throw away my chance for something better. You told me my marriage didn't have to be like yours. And it isn't. I love Michael. Love him more than I thought possible."

"I'm glad for that. Real glad."

Rosalie leaned forward. "And, Ma, you don't have to be afraid anymore. Pa will leave Boulder Creek soon. There's nothing to keep him here."

"Your pa won't leave me be. I know too much."

Rosalie felt a tiny shiver of alarm. "Why would you say that? What do you know?"

Ma shook her head. "Too much. I just know too much."

"Ma."

"I've not been a good mother to you. I'm sorry. I'm more sorry than you'll ever know." She stood, whatever pleasure she'd taken in Rosalie's confession of love had already dissipated. "I'm tired and I'm gonna lay down before the

Randolphs return and the house is full of noise again. You see yourself out."

Rosalie sat in the kitchen for some time, wishing she knew what to do. Ma had never been a strong woman, and she'd retreated into herself since Pa's return from prison. If only Rosalie knew how to help her.

With a sigh, she rose and went to the front door. She still didn't feel much like going home, only to wait there alone for Michael's return. Instead she would go to the restaurant and treat herself to a piece of pie, along with some of Zoe's friendly conversation.

Several school-aged boys ran down the street, shouting and laughing, and a few seconds later, another string of fire-crackers rattled the air. Rosalie jumped, even though she'd known what was coming. She'd better get used to it. Children in town were either not tired of celebrating statehood or were getting an early start on celebrating Independence Day. Firecrackers served both purposes.

She was passing the livery stable when two loud bangs erupted. She heard the frightened cry of horses. If those boys were lighting firecrackers in the livery, Chad Turner would flay them alive. Then she remembered that Prince was at the livery to be shod. If anything were to happen to him—

She stepped through the open door. "Who's in here?" she demanded. Before her eyes could adjust to the dim light, she felt strong fingers clasp her wrist and drag her arm up behind her back.

"Don't you say a word," a gruff voice whispered in her ear.

"Pa?"

She would have turned and looked at him, but that's

when she saw Sheriff McNeal lying next to one of the stalls. There was blood on his head, more on his shirt.

"Pa, what did you—"

Her father jerked her arm. "He had it coming. And if you don't keep your mouth shut, you'll get the same thing."

"Is he—"

"Never could stand that family. Working for his son when it was me that kept that mill going. Tom was as big a fool as his old man."

Icy terror seeped through her veins. "You did kill Tom McNeal."

"I don't think you wanna say that." He pushed her toward the stalls. "You and me are gonna saddle up a couple of horses and get out of here. And if you don't cause me too much trouble and that husband of yours is willing to pay the price, you might live longer than your brother."

Rosalie knew then without a doubt. Her pa had killed Mark, just as he'd killed Tom and Hank McNeal. He would kill her, too, if she gave him the least provocation.

She tried not to let fear reveal itself in her voice. "They'll come looking for you. Someone else must have heard the shots."

He merely laughed as he wrapped a gag around her mouth, then tied her hands behind her back, securing her to a post. Once he was certain she couldn't escape or cry for help, he strode over to the sheriff, dragged him into an empty stall, and covered the body with straw.

No wonder her father could laugh. Even she'd thought it was firecrackers she'd heard. By this time, everybody in Boulder Creek had grown accustomed to hearing the bangs and pops, mixed with children's laughter. If Chad didn't find

Hank's body tonight when he came to feed the livestock, Rosalie might never be found.

She didn't fool herself. Her father wouldn't keep her alive any longer than he thought it served his best interests. If she became a hindrance to him rather than a means of gain, he would fire one of those bullets into her head without so much as a blink of an eye.

Michael was eager to return from the Danson ranch and get home to Rosalie. He wanted to see how she was doing after the morning's ride. If his father hadn't announced yesterday that it was time for the family to return to San Francisco, Michael would have postponed his promise to take them all out to the Rocking D.

But when he got home, he found the house empty. Rosalie didn't answer his calls. Princess was tethered on the back porch, so wherever his wife had gone, she'd gone alone.

Michael shook his head. To think he'd expected her to stay there and rest. He should have known better. She was probably at the boarding house, telling her mother about her riding lesson that morning. He'd have to go see for himself.

34

Michael didn't find Rosalie at the boarding house. She'd been there, Virginia told him, but must have left when Virginia went to lie down. He'd tried both the mercantile and Zoe's Restaurant before he heard the news about Hank McNeal.

"Sheriff was found in the livery stables. Shot, he was, a couple of times."

Along with a number of others, Michael ran to the stables. The doctor was there, tending to the injured man. Doris McNeal knelt near her husband's head, gently stroking his gray hair, hair that was streaked with blood from a head wound.

When Hank saw Michael, he motioned him forward. "Glen ... Tomkin," he said in a near whisper. "He killed ... my boy."

Michael looked at Doris. There were tears streaking her cheeks.

"He took ... Rosalie."

Cold fingers of dread closed around Michael's heart.

"Tomkin took Rosalie?"

Hank nodded.

"How long ago? Where?"

The sheriff didn't answer. His eyelids had drifted closed, and Michael could tell the man was beyond hearing.

"I'll spread the word," Chad Turner said from behind him. "We can have a posse together in no time. Don't worry. We'll find her."

Michael straightened and looked around the stables. "Where's Prince? In the corral out back?"

"No," the blacksmith answered. "He was in that stall there. Tomkin must've took him along with one of mine."

Michael didn't know whether to be comforted that Rosalie was riding her own horse or concerned that Prince was only green-broke. But that was the least of his worries. His wife had been taken hostage by a killer.

"If he hurts her, I'll hunt him down if it takes me the rest of my life." He spun on his heel and left the livery stables. Walking with long, determined strides, he headed for home and his horse.

And his gun.

For the first hour of her pa's flight from justice, Rosalie was terrified. She clung to the saddle horn, her wrists bound together, and prayed she wouldn't fall from the saddle. Michael's instructions during her lesson that morning hadn't prepared her for the speed of this journey. At least she could be grateful that Prince caused no problems, probably because he was being led behind her father's mount.

By the second hour, she marveled that no one had

noticed her leaving town with Pa. Had everyone, except the children, stayed inside on this hot fourth of July? Was there no one who would think it odd for her to go riding with the man who'd been so cruel to her and her mother?

By the third hour, she decided she wouldn't cower in his presence. She wouldn't let him use her fear to manipulate her. Not ever again.

As the horses picked their way along a trail that followed a frothy, swift-flowing river, she called to him, "Why are you doing this? Why take me with you? You could go faster without me."

"Because, girly, that husband of yours owes me, and if he wants you back, he's gonna have to pay plenty."

Sawing her wrists back and forth, trying to loosen the rope that bound her, she studied the passing countryside. If she could get away, at least she wouldn't get lost. She could follow the river back toward Boulder Creek.

Hoping to keep her father talking so he wouldn't notice her attempts to free herself, she asked, "How do you know he'll even want me back?"

"He will."

"But he didn't want to marry me. You forced him to. He'll be glad to be rid of me."

He laughed. "I've seen the way he looks at you. He'll pay. He bought the boarding house because of you, didn't he?"

"No, he didn't. He did that for himself, so he'll have a monopoly once the hotel is built. He's interested in making money. That's all." She didn't believe a word she'd told him. Michael loved her. Might even give his life to save her. But she would say anything to try to distract her father.

"I should've burned down your ma's place before I let him have it."

Perhaps silence would have been better than distraction. Making him mad wouldn't do her any good.

A shiver ran through her as a new thought took hold. He'd killed Tom McNeal years ago, he'd killed her brother, and he'd killed the sheriff a few hours ago. He was ruthless, even when not angry. He wouldn't hesitate to kill again.

As if reading her thoughts, he said, "You better hope your husband's willing to come through with enough money to get me out of the country or your life won't be worth a hill of beans."

But that was a lie. She knew it was. He would kill her anyway, even if he got money from Michael. She had to get away from him. She had to get away before they traveled too far. "How can you ask him for ransom if you're where he can't give it to you?"

"Shut up and let me think."

Yes, he planned to kill her. She could hear it in his voice. He didn't have any intention of turning her over to Michael. Hank McNeal was dead, and she was the only one who knew her pa had done it. And he no doubt knew she would put two and two together and know he'd also killed the sheriff's son—and his own flesh and blood. Pa wouldn't let her live to tell about any of it.

Rosalie shivered as cool air brushed the skin on her arms. Dusk had come early to the deep river canyon. The tree-filled mountains, rising sharply on either side, cut off the sunlight long before sundown came to the valleys.

When darkness did come—an inky blackness that made it impossible to see more than a foot or two ahead—her pa was forced to stop. "Get down and rest. We'll wait until the moon comes up, then move on."

Clumsily, her wrists still bound despite her efforts to slip free, Rosalie slid from the saddle. Her knees crumpled as soon as her feet touched the ground, and only her grip on the saddle horn kept her from falling down. Forcing herself to breathe slowly, she waited for strength to return to her legs before letting go.

The sounds of the night seemed strange, almost eerie. The rushing river tumbling over boulders. The hoot of an owl. The rustle of forest animals as they moved through the trees and underbrush. The distant howl of a coyote, the answering cry of another.

"Best stay by your horse," Pa said. "Don't want you turning into dinner for a mountain lion."

Rosalie subdued a shudder. He was more dangerous than a cougar or a bear or even a rattler.

"Pa, I need you to untie my hands."

"Not a chance."

"I need to relieve myself. I can't manage with my hands tied."

He grunted.

She held her breath, waiting, hoping.

A few quick strides brought him through the dark to her side. He grabbed hold of her left arm with one hand. His other hand held the barrel of a gun to her throat. "Don't you do nothing foolish. You hear?"

"I hear." But a plan had formed, and foolish or not, she would try to see it through.

The gun moved away from her throat. A few moments later, the rope loosened and slipped from her wrists.

"You stay close."

"I will. You're the brave man with a gun."

He glared at her. "That's right. That's exactly who I am."

Rosalie moved a short distance down the trail, then stepped behind some underbrush. With fingers made clumsy by fear, she wrestled with the satin tie of her petticoat, but finally it was free, sliding down to pool at her feet. As quietly as possible, she stepped out of it, picked it up, and held it behind her back.

"Hurry up over there," her pa snapped.

"I'm hurrying. It isn't easy in a dress."

Her eyes had adjusted a little more to the darkness. She could make out Prince's golden rump. Her father stood between the two horses, holding them by the reins. She prayed nothing went amiss. She would get only one chance.

She moved quietly forward, holding her breath, until she was close enough to do some good. Then, with a shriek, she whirled the white petticoat over her head. She struck Prince with one hand, then sent the petticoat flying into the air. Both horses reared up, terrified squeals shattering the once peaceful night.

Rosalie didn't wait to see what happened next. She tripped, stumbled, and slid her way down the steep bank to the river. There—the sounds of her escape hopefully covered by the rushing water—she ran as best she could, crouching low, her heart thundering in her ears. Dark skeletons of trees and brush reached out to scratch at her face and arms. The river splashed over rocks, splattering her, making her feel twice as cold. She felt starved for air, yet didn't dare open her mouth to drag in more for fear she would give herself away.

Her strength had been drained during the hours of their flight from town, but fear kept her moving. She tripped once, nearly falling face first into the water. Only a desperate grab for an anchor saved her. She lay there, holding onto the bush, the river tugging at her skirts. Was he looking for her? Had he followed? Did he know which way she'd run?

She listened to see if he was nearby, but the same rushing water that had covered her sounds also covered those of her pa.

I can't just stay here to see if he finds me.

She pulled herself up and continued on. She had to find shelter before the moon rose.

Panic built in Michael's chest with every passing hour.

"We've gotta stop," Yale called to him. "It's too dangerous for the horses."

Michael reined in beside the cowboy. His father and Dillon did the same right behind them. They'd been riding hard, and all were exhausted. But Michael wasn't willing to stop for long.

While it had still been daylight, Yale had pointed out signs of recent travel—two horses moving fast, he'd said. Michael's gut told him Yale was right. They'd found the right trail. Rosalie was somewhere ahead of them. In the dark. With her murderous father.

"If we can't see," Yale added, "neither can Tomkin. Not until the moon's up."

Michael dismounted. "I'll go on ahead on foot. You bring my horse when you've got the light. Catch up with me when you can."

His father said, "Michael, be reasonable—"

"I can't afford to be reasonable! He's got Rosalie. She

needs me and I've got to find her. There's only one way he can go now. He's got to follow the river. Catch up with me when you can." He yanked the rifle from its scabbard and set off at a jog, listening to the sounds of the river off to his right, using that to guide him when sight wasn't enough.

As the canyon narrowed, the darkness deepened, forcing him to slow to a walk. At that very moment, he heard a distant squeal of a frightened horse. At least, that's what he thought it was.

Rosalie, he mouthed, then started off again.

He felt the thunder of hooves beneath his own feet. Instinct made him step into the underbrush moments before a riderless horse galloped past him. Prince! He'd know that palomino anywhere. Even in a dark canyon.

He took off at a run. Desperation clawed at him. Where was she? Had she fallen off Prince or had something even worse happened?

He caught sight of something out of place on the trail and slowed. What was that? He held the rifle at ready as he moved on. Whatever it was looked white in the surrounding night. When he reached it, he swooped down, his heart almost stopping when he realized what it was. A woman's petticoat.

Rosalie.

Like an unwelcome omen, the moon crested the eastern ridge of mountains, shedding its white light over trees and rocks, forest and river. It made the night nearly as bright as day.

Rosalie, I'm coming.

35

Rosalie pressed herself against a tree trunk, her legs drawn tightly against her chest. She could see her pa on the stolen horse, following the trail in her direction. Even from that distance, she felt his rage. Moonlight glinted off the revolver in his hand. If he saw her, he would kill her.

Suddenly, he jerked back on the reins. Her heart leapt in fear as he jumped down from the saddle and waved at his horse, turning it back the way he'd come. He crouched by the side of the trail and waited.

She followed the direction of his gaze. This time her heart nearly stopped. It was Michael, on foot with a rifle at his side. And he didn't know her pa had seen him.

She reacted, jumping out from behind the tree. "Michael, look out!"

Did she feel the bullet graze her arm or did she only hear the sound of the gun's report? Not that it mattered as she tumbled backward, rolling down the steep embankment, headed for the river.

Michael saw Tomkin dash for the spot where Rosalie had disappeared, and he took off running, too. Tomkin got there first and vanished from view.

Protect her, God. Please keep her safe.

He reached the ridge and looked down. In an instant, his gaze found Rosalie, lying at her father's feet. But Tomkin was disinterested in her. His attention—and his revolver—were pointed at Michael.

"Don't move, Randolph."

Michael gritted his jaw.

"Put down your rifle. Real slow like."

He did as he was told, all the while silently commanding Rosalie to move so he would know she was okay.

"Now the revolver. Unfasten the gun belt and let it drop. No sudden moves."

"Why don't you just shoot me now, Tomkin, and get it over with?" He loosened the buckle of the gun belt.

"Because I think your old man will pay good money to get you back alive." He nudged Rosalie with the toe of his boot. "I don't think you'll pay anything for her now."

Rage boiled in his chest, but he didn't let it take control. If Rosalie was dead, he wouldn't feel much like living anyway. But he meant to take Glen Tomkin with him first.

A sixth sense kept Rosalie still. First she heard her pa say something, then Michael's strong voice broke through. Without opening her eyes, she understood that her pa had his gun trained on Michael and that he wouldn't hesitate to shoot him if she made the wrong move.

"No point leaving her here like this." Pa pressed the toe of his boot against her stomach. "Might as well let the fish have her." He gave her a little push.

"No!" Michael yelled.

She grabbed her father's leg and jerked with all her strength just as the gun exploded. She opened her eyes in time to see Michael flying through the air toward her pa. As Michael rammed into the older man, Pa's leg was wrenched from Rosalie's grip, and the two men fell into the tumbling, racing river.

"Michael!" She scrambled to her feet. "Michael!"

She saw the two of them bob to the surface once, then disappear again.

"Michael!"

She ran along the bank, searching the river for any sign of them. She wasn't aware of the thundering hoofbeats until the noise seemed to surround her. She stopped, not knowing whether to be frightened or relieved, and glanced up toward the trail and the three horsemen.

Michael's brother launched off his horse and raced toward her. Dillon, who looked so much like Michael. The pain in her heart was unbearable.

"Michael," she gasped, grabbing his brother by the arm. "He's in the river. Pa shot at him. I don't know if he's hit."

"Where's your father?" Yale shouted from the trail above.

"He's in the river, too."

"Stay here," Dillon ordered, forcing her to sit down. "Don't move until we come back." He ran up the incline.

"No!" She was back on her feet in an instant. "I'm going

with you." She grabbed the reins to Michael's roan, clambered up into the saddle, and lit out in front of the others.

The two men struggled with each other and with the water, refusing to let go or give up, even as the river sucked them beneath the frothy surface and slammed them into submerged boulders.

One thing, more than any other, gave Michael strength. Rosalie was alive, and he was determined to get back to her. He managed to get his hands around Tomkin's throat, pressing his thumbs against the man's windpipe. Tomkin scratched and clawed at him, dragging them both under again. Michael's grip came loose, but he managed to grab hold of the other man's shirt as he surfaced. Gasping for air, he hauled Tomkin toward him. Then the river slammed them against another boulder.

The wind rushed out of Michael's lungs as his body rolled over the boulder and plunged down a short fall. He no longer had a hold on Tomkin's shirt, nor did he know where the river had taken him. But it didn't matter. Now Michael needed the last of his strength to get to shore. He swam and sank, swam and sank.

Finally, when he knew he had few chances left, he managed to grab hold and hang on to a shrub on the bank. Gasping and coughing, he dragged himself halfway onto the bank.

He closed his eyes, exhaustion making it impossible to move any farther.

From the trail, Rosalie saw something on the river's edge. In the shadows, it looked like nothing more than another large, dark rock, the same as others that littered the bank. But somehow she knew it was Michael.

She pulled hard on the reins, causing the roan to slide to a stop, his head flying up in the air. Before the horse had gathered himself, Rosalie was out of the saddle and sliding her way down to the water's edge. "Michael." She fell to her knees. "Michael." She reached for his arms and tried to pull him the rest of the way out of the river.

He coughed up water and groaned. "I'm all right, Rosalie," he said in a hoarse voice.

"Oh, Michael." The tears came then. Tears of relief. Tears of joy.

She pulled on him again, this time drawing his head into her lap and rolling him onto his back.

I love you. Don't die.

He opened his eyes and stared at her. She heard other voices behind them. His father and brother and Yale, she supposed.

"Are you all right?" Michael asked. "Did he hurt you?"

She nodded, then shook her head, answering both questions at once.

He took her head between his hands and drew her toward him. "I thought I'd lost you." Then he kissed her.

"I'm here. I'm all right." She returned his kiss and finally said the words so he could hear. "I love you, Michael."

36

They returned to Boulder Creek with the sunrise, Rosalie cradled in Michael's arms, her pa's body draped across the saddle of his horse. Yale had found her father, drowned and battered, several miles downriver from the spot where Michael had dragged himself ashore.

Most of the town waited for them at their home—or so it seemed.

The first thing Ma said as she wrapped Rosalie in a tight embrace was, "It's my fault. If I'd only said something."

"It wasn't your fault, Ma. It's the way he was. You couldn't have stopped him."

Doc Upton shook Michael's hand. "Hank McNeal's going to be fine. He'll be mighty glad to hear that Rosalie's okay too."

Skylark was the next person to hug Rosalie. "How could I have a wedding without you?" she asked tearfully.

The embraces continued. Zoe Paddock and her daughters, Emma and Sam Barber, the reverend and his wife, Vince Stanley, and more. All the people she'd known most of her life, all there because of Rosalie, because they cared, because they'd been searching for her, because they wanted her to know she was important to them.

When the last of the well-wishers were gone and the door closed behind them, Michael took hold of Rosalie's hand and led her up the stairs to their bedroom. Exhaustion made each step an effort, but she followed him willingly, all the same. In their room, he wrapped her in his arms and held her close against him. His clothes were stiff and scratchy from his episode in the river, but Rosalie didn't mind. She didn't mind anything as long as he was with her.

They didn't move for the longest time, just stood there, holding each other. She heard the steady beat of his heart as she pressed her head against his chest. She felt the tautness of his muscles beneath her hands on his back. She knew this man, knew his heart, his body. She knew him so well she'd become a part of him and him a part of her. Above all else, she loved him.

He kissed the crown of her head, then tipped her chin with the tip of one finger, forcing her to look up. "I expect you know that I mean to renege on our agreement." He leaned in and kissed her mouth, kissed it long and leisurely and thoroughly.

Her heart pounded in her ears by the time he drew his head back. She took in several deep breaths of air before asking, "What agreement?"

"That our marriage would be temporary. That it would only be for one year."

"Oh. That."

"A year won't be long enough." He pulled her close against him and lay his cheek upon the top of her head. "Not nearly long enough."

"No," she replied breathlessly. "It won't be long enough."

"I want forever, Rosalie. I love you. Promise me forever."

She drew back and stared up at the man she'd grown to love. Eyes the blue of a summer sky. Hair the color of spun gold. A face more perfect than any she'd ever known.

"I love you, too." She lifted her fingers and caressed the side of his face. "I love you so much, Michael, that even forever won't be long enough."

A NOTE FROM ROBIN

Dear Reader:

Awhile back, I was going through files on my computer, and I found the document that contained an old story that would become *Even Forever*.

As I read the document, I remembered how much I'd liked the concept, so I decided to rework the story. I cut and revised and cut and rewrote. Then I sent the manuscript off to be edited by Deborah Raney (a wonderful author and editor). By the time I worked my way through the changes she suggested, I knew I was even more excited to share this story with readers.

Even Forever is what some writers and readers call "clean fiction" or "sweet historical romance." Meaning it doesn't contain sex scenes or foul language. Still, it isn't my usual Christian fiction with a strong faith thread. All the same, I hope readers will be carried away by Rosalie and Michael's love story

If you want to stay up-to-date on new releases, specials, and more, please consider signing up for my newsletter. I promise not to overwhelm your inbox, and your information will never be shared or sold. To subscribe, follow this link.

Happy reading,

Robin

For even more information, visit my website at https://robinleehatcher.com

YOU MIGHT ALSO LIKE . . .

You might also like . . .

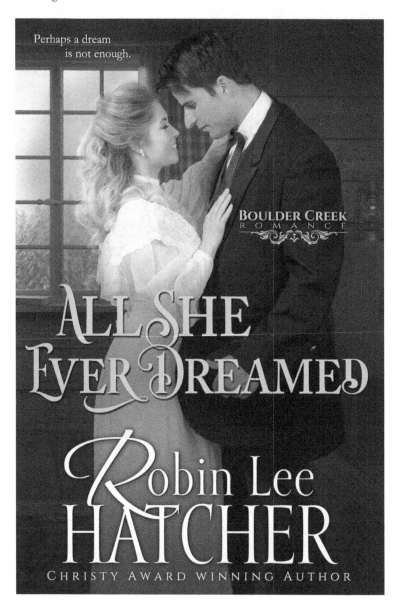

Perhaps a dream
is not enough.

BOULDER CREEK
ROMANCE

ALL SHE
EVER DREAMED

Robin Lee
HATCHER

CHRISTY AWARD WINNING AUTHOR

DECEMBER 2022

All She Ever Dreamed
Boulder Creek Romance #2

274

A dream sometimes comes at great cost.

Betrothed in a sensible match, even if the man isn't the love she's always imagined, Sarah McNeal relies on the advice her late grandmother gave as well as her own common sense. Dreams of a mysterious European count who rides in and sweeps her off her feet are the stuff of girlhood. And she's a woman now. But when her fiancé's older brother, Jeremiah, returns to Boulder Creek, he unknowingly awakens that discarded dream.

Nine years ago, Jeremiah West lost his wife and newborn son in an epidemic, and he's been wandering ever since. A survivor of the Spanish-American War, he finally returns to Boulder Creek to settle on the farm he inherited from his father, an inheritance his younger brother still begrudges.

When a blizzard threatens Sarah's life—and her reputation—Jeremiah is there to rescue her. But the pain of his past remains a stumbling block. Then fate brings Jeremiah and Sarah to a crossroads, and love demands a decision that will change the course of their lives.

ALL SHE EVER DREAMED

PROLOGUE

Cuba, July 1898

The Stars and Stripes fluttered in the hot breeze above the captured trenches of San Juan Hill. Jeremiah West, his thigh bleeding, dropped to the ground beside the other Rough Riders and doughboys, all of them panting and sweating. Numbly, he looked back at the way they'd come.

The wounded and dead littered the slope. Everywhere, Spaniards and Americans lay in pools of their own blood. A gray haze hung over the earth, and Jeremiah's nostrils burned with the acrid scent of gun smoke. A humming sound filled his ears. The moans of the wounded. There had to be a thousand of them.

He caught sight of the colonel standing over a Spaniard's body and knew Roosevelt was reveling in the victory and the gore. Jeremiah had expected to feel the same. He didn't.

Instead, he felt empty, the same haunting emptiness he'd felt for years.

A voice whispered in his heart, *Go home, Jeremiah. It's time you went home.*

Yes. It was time. Finally, he would go home again.

CHAPTER ONE

Boulder Creek, Idaho, December 1898

Bundled against the frigid day, Sarah McNeal hurried along the boardwalk toward the train station. Her younger brother was due to arrive today, and she needed to be there when he stepped off the train. Tom had been away at boarding school for three years, but it seemed longer to Sarah. She missed him more than she'd expected. And come spring he would leave again, this time for Boston where he would begin his medical training. The next time he returned to Boulder Creek, he would be a doctor.

How proud she was at that thought. Her brother, a physician. Tom was young—only eighteen—and already he was on his way to achieving something meaningful, something he'd dreamed about since he was a boy. She envied him.

When she stepped onto the depot platform, she saw Doc Varney standing close to the building, out of the icy wind that stung her cheeks. She raised her hand and waved.

Doctor Kevin Varney was a distinguished looking man with glasses, gray hair, and a bushy beard. It was he who'd encouraged Tom to pursue higher education so he could practice medicine. Many were the nights when her brother, only eleven or twelve at the time, had gone to Doc Varney's home. He'd studied the medical books that lined the doctor's shelves and had asked the older man question upon question. The physician had been impressed by Tom's intelligence and eagerness to learn, and he'd gone to great lengths to help her brother be admitted to the Elias Crane Science Academy for Boys in San Francisco. Sarah would always be grateful for his kindness.

"I didn't know you'd be here," she said as she stopped beside the doctor.

He smiled at her. "Not come and welcome Tom home? You know me better than that, young lady." His expression sobered. "How's your grandfather?"

"Ornery as ever. It was all I could do to make him wait at home. He kept saying a little fresh air would be good for him."

"Catch pneumonia is what he'd do." The doctor tugged at the collar of his coat. "I can't say the two of us won't do the same."

She nodded in agreement, then gazed down the length of track that stretched toward the southeast end of the valley. She hoped the train would be on time. If it was even a few minutes late, her grandfather might disobey her orders and come to the station after all.

Hank McNeal, at seventy-four, was as strong-willed as he'd ever been. It was only his body that had weakened. At one time a tall, barrel-chested man, he was now much thinner and somewhat bent with age. He lacked the energy that used to carry him through each day. Still, he refused to retire from his position as sheriff. Sarah had been after him for months to hire a deputy, but so far, according to her grandfather, he hadn't found anyone suitable.

After Sarah's grandmother—Hank's wife of fifty-one years—passed away the previous summer, it had become

Sarah's responsibility to make sure her grandfather got the rest he needed. That was never an easy task. Perhaps he would be better behaved while Tom was home. After all, her brother would be a doctor one day. Grandpa would have to listen to him. Wouldn't he?

"There she comes," Doc Varney said.

Sarah focused her gaze once again on the ribbon of track. She saw the billowing cloud of soot shooting into the air moments before the engine came into view. Her excitement surged to the fore once again.

"Do you suppose he's changed much?" She rose on tiptoe, her eagerness making it difficult to stand still.

"Of course he's changed. He left a boy. He's coming home a man."

Doc Varney was right. Tom McNeal *had* become a man. Sarah almost didn't recognize him when he stepped down from the train ten minutes later. Taller by a good eight inches or more and sporting a mustache, Tom looked up and down the platform before his gaze came to rest upon her.

She rushed forward and threw herself into his arms. "Tommy!" She gave him a kiss on the cheek, then stepped back. "Look at you!"

"Like it?" Wearing a cocky grin, he turned his head so she could view the mustache from another angle.

She frowned. "I'm not sure."

Doc Varney stepped up behind her. "I like it, young man. Gives you a look of distinction." He held out his hand. "Welcome home."

"Thank you, sir." Tom shook the older man's hand.

"I've heard good reports about you," the doctor continued, his voice oddly gruff.

"I've done my best, sir."

"I knew you would." Doc Varney cleared his throat as he released Tom's hand. "I won't keep you. It's too blasted cold to stand about, and your grandfather's anxious to see you. When you get settled, come to my office and we'll have a long visit."

"I'll do it."

Sarah slipped her arm through her brother's. "You're home. I can't believe it. You're finally home."

Tom looked at her again, and his grin returned. "You got even prettier. No wonder Warren's been pestering you to marry him." He shook his head. "It's hard to believe you'll be a married woman in a few weeks."

It was hard for her to believe, too, and she'd rather not think about it. Thoughts of her impending wedding left her feeling unsettled.

Her brother tapped the end of her nose with a gloved finger. "And I always thought you'd wait for that English lord to ride in on his white horse."

She playfully slapped his shoulder, then smiled as she tugged on his arm. "Let's go home. Grandpa can't wait to see you, and I've got lunch ready for you both. I made all your favorites. I know you must be hungry after your long journey."

"You bet I am. Just let me get my luggage."

As Tom turned to pick up his bags, Sarah noticed a man standing in the passenger car doorway. His face was obscured by the deep shadows of the car, yet she sensed he watched her, had been watching for some time. A shiver ran up her spine.

"I'm ready," Tom said, abruptly pulling her attention back to him. "Let's go eat that feast you've worked so hard preparing for your little brother."

~

Jeremiah felt a sting of envy as he watched the jubilant homecoming. No one would be on the platform to welcome him back to Boulder Creek the way that young man had been welcomed. Of course, no one knew Jeremiah was coming, but he doubted things would have been different even if he'd sent word ahead.

Hunching his shoulders inside his coat, he stepped to the platform, walked the length of it, then stared toward the center of town. Boulder Creek had changed in the many years he'd been away. He shouldn't be surprised, but he was. Instead of a single street, the town had several. New houses and businesses had sprouted up. From where he stood, he saw a second church at the opposite end of town. There was even a hotel and a bank.

Have I done the right thing coming back?

He turned toward the train again and went after his belongings. There wasn't much. He'd packed everything he owned into a couple of carpetbags. He hoisted them, one in each hand, and headed into town.

Snow crunched beneath his boots as he made his way to Barber Mercantile. Four years ago, Sam Barber, the proprietor, had written to Jeremiah to tell him of his father's death. The news had killed his dreams of ever finding a way to prove himself to his father. Perhaps that was why the rest of Mr. Barber's letter had surprised him. His father's will had left the farm to Jeremiah. Even now, it was difficult to believe. Why him and not his younger brother? Perhaps Sam's wife, Emma, would be able to answer that question. As he recalled, Mrs. Barber knew everything about everybody in the valley.

A bell chimed above his head as he opened the door to the store. A wave of nostalgia washed over him at the familiar sights and smells. The town might be different, but nothing had changed in this establishment. He could have been a kid again, stopping by the mercantile on his way home from school. He knew where the pickle barrel would be and the jar of licorice, too.

A woman behind the counter turned from the shelves. She was too young to be Emma Barber, yet there was something familiar about her.

"Hello. May I help you?" she asked.

He set his carpetbags on the floor near the door, then removed his hat as he strode forward. "I'm looking for Sam Barber."

"I'm sorry." She shook her head. "Mr. Barber died almost two years ago. Is there something—" She stopped and stared. "Why, you're Jeremiah West." She placed a hand on her collarbone. "I'm Leslie. Leslie Barber. Well, it's Leslie Blake now. I don't suppose you remember me at all. I was a child when you went away. How long has it been?"

"Close to fourteen years."

"Land o' Goshen! Is it really? I can hardly believe it. You must not recognize the town. Boulder Creek isn't like it used to be when we were children. The railroad's come through and we've got our own hotel and that new Methodist Church. The school's about bursting at the seams, what with all the children everybody's got. I was saying to Annalee... You remember my sister, don't you? Well, I was saying to her the other day how much everything's changed. We've watched it happen, but it must be a real surprise to someone who's been away as long as you."

It wasn't so much that he remembered Leslie as that she

reminded him of her mother. Plump and warm-natured, Emma Barber had loved to chatter whenever someone was in the store, the same way Leslie was doing now.

Suddenly, she stopped, then said, "I'm real sorry about your wife. And your pa. I lost both my parents. I know how it feels."

"Your ma's gone, too?"

Her voice lowered to a whisper. "Yes."

"I'm sorry to hear it. I remember her well. She was a kind woman."

The door joining the living quarters to the mercantile opened, drawing both their gazes.

"George, come here," Leslie called, her smile returning, although not as bright. "There's someone I'd like you to meet." As soon as the man was close enough, she reached out and took hold of his hand, then faced Jeremiah again. "This is my husband, George Blake. George, this is Jeremiah West, Warren's older brother."

George shook Jeremiah's hand. "Good to meet you."

He nodded his own greeting.

"Are you back to stay?" Leslie asked.

"Don't know for sure. I think so."

"Well, then. Tell us what you've been doing all these years."

What had he been doing? Running. Trying to forget. Staying alone so he wouldn't feel the loss—or the guilt. Living but not living.

He couldn't say any of that, but he might as well tell her what he could. Leslie wouldn't be the last person to ask the question. He'd better get used to it. "After Marta died, I moved around a lot. I worked cattle, did some bartending, even spent time with the railroad before going to work in a factory in New York City. Last couple of years, I was in the army."

"The army? Were you in the war?"

Scenes of the battlefield flashed in his head. "Yes. I was in the war."

"Were you hurt bad?" She glanced at his leg.

Hard as he tried to hide it, people noticed his limp. But he didn't want anyone's pity. Especially not in Boulder Creek. "No. Not bad." He put his hat on. "I'd better get over to the livery and see about renting a rig. Warren's not expecting me, and I need to get to the farm before dark."

Leslie shook her head. "You won't find your brother at the farm. He's got rooms above his carpentry shop, right down the street."

"A carpentry shop?"

"He makes furniture. Real good at it, too." She frowned. "He never mentioned you were coming home."

"He didn't know. We haven't been in touch."

He saw surprise flicker across her face, and he turned to leave the mercantile before she could ask more questions.

CHAPTER TWO

Jeremiah read the sign above the shop: WEST CARPENTRY. So this was his kid brother's place. It hadn't occurred to him that Warren would do something besides work the farm. But he supposed it was no more odd than their father leaving the place to Jeremiah, the wayward son.

He opened the door to the shop and stepped inside. In the dim light, he saw a man run a hand over the surface of a table in the back of the long, narrow room.

"Be with you in a minute." His brother's voice had deepened. Not unexpected after fourteen years. He'd been a skinny youth back then. He was taller now, too. Probably as tall as Jeremiah. Even bent over the table, his height was obvious. This was not the boy of Jeremiah's memory.

He cleared his throat as he took a step deeper into the shop.

Warren turned and squinted.

Jeremiah supposed he was nothing but a dark silhouette with the light from the windows at his back. "Hello, Warren."

The squint turned to a frown.

"Have I changed that much?"

The silence stretched into what felt like an eternity before Warren said, "Jeremiah?"

"Yeah. It's me. You've changed too."

"I didn't expect to ever see you again."

Jeremiah's gaze traveled around the shop, his eyes now adjusted to the dim light. "A business of your own. Dad must have been proud of you."

"I didn't have the shop until after he died." His brother took a step forward. "What brought you back to Boulder Creek?"

"It was time. I heard you're staying in town. Is there room for me at the farm?"

"The house is empty." A muscle flexed in his jaw. "I put the farm up for sale."

Jeremiah heard the challenge in Warren's voice and chose not to respond at once. Instead, he set his carpetbags on the floor and walked around the shop, stopping to run his fingers over the tables, bedsteads, and chairs that filled the room. When he'd come full circle, he faced his brother. "You can't sell the farm. It's legally mine. Dad left it to me."

"So what if he did? You weren't here. You never came

back, never wrote. For all I knew, you were dead. That made it mine."

"I'm not dead."

"I need the money. I'm getting married in a few weeks."

"Married?"

"Yes." Warren spun around and walked to the table at the back of the shop. "Why'd you return?"

"Sorry it's inconvenienced you."

His brother didn't look at him.

Jeremiah drew a deep breath. "Tell you what. I'll pay you half what the property's worth. That should help set you up with your bride."

"You'd do that?"

"Yeah. I'd do that. Half the farm should have gone to you anyway."

"I guess that's fair. As fair as it could ever be."

ABOUT THE AUTHOR

Robin Lee Hatcher is the best-selling author of over 85 books with over five million copies in print. Her well-drawn characters and heartwarming stories of faith, courage, and love have earned her both critical acclaim and the devotion of readers. Her numerous awards include the Christy Award for Excellence in Christian Fiction, the RITA® Award for Best Inspirational Romance, Romantic Times Career Achievement Awards for Americana Romance and for Inspirational Fiction, the Carol Award, the 2011 Idahope Writer of the Year, and Lifetime Achievement Awards from both Romance Writers of America® (2001) and American Christian Fiction Writers (2014). *Catching Katie* was named one of the Best Books of 2004 by the Library Journal.

When not writing, Robin enjoys being with her family, spending time in the beautiful Idaho outdoors, Bible art journaling, reading books that make her cry, watching romantic movies, and decorative planning. A mother and grandmother, Robin makes her home on the outskirts of Boise, sharing it with a demanding Papillon dog and a persnickety tuxedo cat.

Learn more about Robin and her books by visiting her website at https://robinleehatcher.com

You can also find out more by joining her in the following ways:

Goodreads | Bookbub | Newsletter sign-up

ALSO BY ROBIN LEE HATCHER

Stand Alone Titles

Like the Wind

I'll Be Seeing You

Make You Feel My Love

An Idaho Christmas

Here in Hart's Crossing

The Victory Club

Beyond the Shadows

Catching Katie

Whispers From Yesterday

The Shepherd's Voice

Ribbon of Years

Firstborn

The Forgiving Hour

Heart Rings

A Wish and a Prayer

When Love Blooms

A Carol for Christmas

Return to Me

Loving Libby

Wagered Heart

The Perfect Life

Speak to Me of Love

Trouble in Paradise

Another Chance to Love You

Bundle of Joy

The Coming to America Series

Dear Lady

Patterns of Love

In His Arms

Promised to Me

Where the Heart Lives Series

Belonging

Betrayal

Beloved

Books set in Kings Meadow

A Promise Kept

Love Without End

Whenever You Come Around

I Hope You Dance

Keeper of the Stars

Books set in Thunder Creek

You'll Think of Me

You're Gonna Love Me

The Sisters of Bethlehem Springs Series

For a full list of books, visit www.robinleehatcher.com

Made in United States
Orlando, FL
24 January 2023

29000539R00166